*I'm so happy Ada reconciling. I watched them have lunch together the other day. I knew that when Adam flipped through the family heirloom photo album, he would see that he was following too closely in his father's footsteps. Though Adam always resented that Jake worked a lot and was away from his family, Adam was doing the same thing with his children. But now, at last, they both realize the importance of family.*

*I wish that I could come out of hiding. But I still haven't figured out who tried to kill me and who is out to destroy the Fortunes. I hope some clue is discovered soon and this mess is resolved so we can all get back to our lives.*

## A LETTER FROM THE AUTHOR

Dear Reader,

It is my privilege to bring you Book Six of the Fortune family saga. This project has been a joy for several reasons, chief among them the fact that it is truly a *family* exercise. The Fortune family, with its variety of interesting characters, has proven to be an exciting but comfortable group with which to spend many an enjoyable hour for author and reader alike. However, another family is involved: the family of writers and editors at Silhouette.

Writing is usually a solitary enterprise. That's why it has been such fun talking to and working with other FORTUNE'S CHILDREN authors as we coordinated details, descriptions and new ideas, enriching the basic plot of the series.

In the same vein, I must compliment all the editors involved with this project. Organizing and editing a twelve-book series is a complicated, detailed endeavor requiring much patience, latitude and a firm, shared vision.

The heart of it all is a common purpose: to provide you with the finest reading entertainment possible. My sincere hope and expectation are that we've done our jobs well. If we have, the Fortune family will become as dear to you as it has to me. Family, after all, is everything in this life.

If you're a new reader, allow me to welcome you to the Silhouette family. If you're a faithful fan, allow me to express my gratitude for your support. *You* are what it's all about for the rest of us.

God bless.

*Arlene James*

# Single
## with
# Children

## ARLENE JAMES

*Silhouette Books*

**Published by Silhouette Books**
**America's Publisher of Contemporary Romance**

For Jim,
in honor of twenty good years
with a singularly good man.
I love you still...

D.A.R.

 SILHOUETTE BOOKS

SINGLE WITH CHILDREN

Copyright © 1996 by Harlequin Books S.A.

ISBN 0-373-50182-X

Special thanks and acknowledgment to Arlene James
for her contribution to the Fortune's Children series.

**Printed in U.S.A.**

## ARLENE JAMES

Growing up on a small ranch in Oklahoma made adjusting to the suburban life-style of Dallas, Texas, rather difficult, but once the move was made, she couldn't seem to stop. Her oldest son was born in Florida. In Oklahoma she met and married the wonderful man who has been her partner and joy for the past twenty years. They've spent almost all of that time in the Dallas area, where they produced a second son and helped raise a dear niece.

Her children have been her focus in her life, and as she sends her youngest off to college, she says, "The rewards of motherhood have indeed been extraordinary for me. Yet I've looked forward to this new stage of my life." Her need to write is greater than ever, a fact that frankly amazes her as she's been at it since eighth grade! She also expects to indulge her favorite hobbies of cooking, sewing and amateur theater, as well as her husband's love of travel and the nurturing of their many friendships.

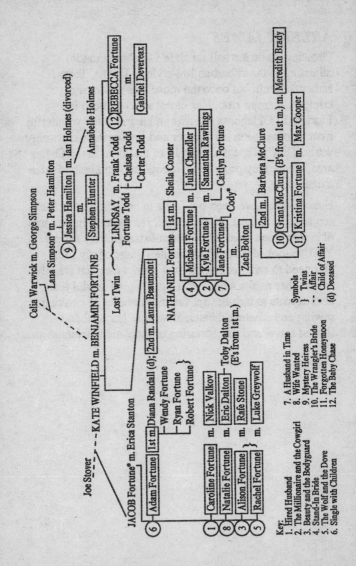

Celia Warwick m. George Simpson

Lana Simpson* m. Peter Hamilton

⑨ Jessica Hamilton  m. Ian Holmes (divorced)
m.
Stephen Hunter
Annabelle Holmes

⑫ REBECCA Fortune
m.
Gabriel Devereax

LINDSAY  m. Frank Todd
Fortune Todd ─ Chelsea Todd
└ Carter Todd

Sheila Conner

Michael Fortune ─┬ Julia Chandler
④          m.
Kyle Fortune    m. Samantha Rawlings
②          └ Caitlyn Fortune
Jane Fortune
⑦     m.
Zach Bolton

Joe Stover - - KATE WINFIELD m. BENJAMIN FORTUNE

Lost Twin

NATHANIEL Fortune  1st m.

2nd m. Barbara McClure

⑩ Grant McClure (B's from 1st m.) m. Meredith Brady

⑪ Kristina Fortune  m. Max Cooper

JACOB Fortune* m. Erica Stanton

⑥ Adam Fortune  1st m. Diana Randall (d); 2nd m. Laura Beaumont
─ Wendy Fortune
─ Ryan Fortune  }
─ Robert Fortune

Toby Dalton
(E's from 1st m.)

Caroline Fortune    m. Nick Valkov
①
Natalie Fortune     m. Eric Dalton
⑧
Alison Fortune   }  m. Rafe Stone
③
Rachel Fortune      m. Luke Greywolf
⑤

**Symbols**
} Twins
- - Affair
* Child of Affair
(d) Deceased

**Key:**
1. Hired Husband
2. The Millionaire and the Cowgirl
3. Beauty and the Bodyguard
4. Stand-In Bride
5. The Wolf and the Dove
6. Single with Children
7. A Husband in Time
8. Wife Wanted
9. Mystery Heiress
10. The Wrangler's Bride
11. Forgotten Honeymoon
12. The Baby Chase

# FORTUNE'S Children

*Meet the Fortunes—three generations of a family with a legacy of wealth, influence and power. As they unite to face an unknown enemy, shocking family secrets are revealed...and passionate new romances are ignited.*

**ADAM FORTUNE:** The ex-army officer is a clueless single father raising three small, rowdy children. Finding a nanny hasn't been easy...until a pretty young waitress offers to lend a hand.

**LAURA BEAUMONT:** Her dreams of having a family to love come true when she becomes the nanny of Adam's kids. But her happiness is threatened by the past she is running from....

**TRACEY DUCET:** She is the heart-stopping image of Lindsay Fortune. Is it possible that the missing Fortune twin has been found? Or is this a clever deception?

**JANE FORTUNE:** Single mother. Would an old clapboard New England home inherited from her grandmother give Jane the chance to build a new life for herself and her son?

# LIZ JONES— CELEBRITY GOSSIP

As I predicted, a big bombshell has dropped on the Fortune family!

The long-lost heiress has been found. Over thirty years ago, Lindsay Fortune's twin was kidnapped. Now, the twin, Tracey Ducet, has come home to claim her rightful place in the family. Everyone seems to be overjoyed by her unexpected arrival.

I'll bet she's a gold digger! After all, who wouldn't want a piece of the Fortune pie? I wonder if there are any other long-lost relatives that *I* could masquerade as? But I must admit, she does know her facts about the family, and maybe I'm just being cynical.

Whatever the truth is, it's bound to come out sooner or later. The family is having Ms. Ducet thoroughly investigated. And if she's got any skeletons in her closet, they'll find them....

# One

Adam swiped his hand over the flat, bristly top of hair the color of mahogany. It was a classic gesture of frustration for a retired military man used to sweeping a service cap off his head. He pushed his shoulders back and took a deep breath, trying to keep his voice carefully reasonable. Mrs. Godiva took offense at the tone of command, and pride would not allow him to succumb to the desperation of pleading.

"Now let's just talk this out calmly," he said. "I'm sure the snow in your slippers was just a little prank. They wouldn't understand the...the depth of your shock. They're only three, after all."

"And wouldn't have dreamed this up all by themselves!" the woman retorted, drawing herself up to her full rawboned height. "That Wendy is behind this! She had those scamps put snow in my slippers because I put her in the corner this morning for refusing to eat her prunes."

"Wendy doesn't like prunes, Mrs. Godiva," Adam pointed out tersely. "I've asked you time and time again not to—"

"Prunes are good for them!" the middle-aged widow insisted. "If you'd just let me guide you, we'd have both fared better, but like your daughter, you just won't listen to reason! Well, I've had it. Not only did she put her little brothers up to filling my brand-new house slippers with snow, she then cried out for me in the night, knowing my feet had only just warmed and that I'd thrust them trustingly into... into..." Her upper lip trembled in outrage.

Adam bowed his head, a dull ache setting in behind his eyes. She was undoubtedly correct. Everyone knew that cold feet were the bane of Godiva's existence, but the twins would not have dreamed up this particular act of vengeance—and it *was* vengeance, Wendy-style. Still, the blasted woman knew that Wendy loathed cooked prunes. Adam sighed.

"Couldn't we just forget about this?"

"We could not!"

"I'll make certain that it never happens again."

"Ha! You have no more control over that child than you have over the weather! It's beyond me how a man with your experience of command could allow that trio of miscreants to rule this . . . this house of chaos!"

"Mrs. Godiva, they lost their mother only eighteen months ago—"

"And you've lost seven nannies in that time!"

"Six," he corrected offhandedly.

"Seven!" she snapped, dipping low to grasp the handles of her bags. "You may forward my pay to my sister's in Minneapolis. I believe you have the address!" With that, she turned, struggled furiously with the handles of her luggage and the doorknob, and marched out into the night.

"Mrs. Godiva!" Adam called after her. "At least wait until the morning!"

His plea fell on her ears with no more effect than the fat flakes of snow that melted into the garish scarf tied about her head or the icy crust that crunched beneath her sturdy feet, presumably warm inside her clunky fur-lined boots. Within seconds, he heard the muted sounds of her car doors opening and closing, then the engine being gunned as headlights swung in an angry arc over the drifts of snow banking the drive.

Adam closed the door quietly, resisting the urge to lay his head against it and moan, but only just. Behind him, he heard the bumps and rustles of little bodies moving, encased in flannel pajamas. His spine seemed to straighten of its own accord, and his shoulders to level themselves and draw back. He executed a turn with all the precision of a soldier on review and scowled down at the three little faces that peeked around the corner of the foyer and the front hall.

"Is she gone?" Wendy whispered. Her freckled nose wrinkled in ill-disguised hope as her chubby fingers pulled at a thin reddish brown braid.

"She is."

"For good?" Robbie asked, his voice all little-boy innocence, the illusion abetted by the tousle of curly blond hair around his plump, squarish face.

"Afraid so—no thanks to you three."

Ryan, a slightly smaller version of his minutes-older brother, flashed a triumphant smile at Wendy before breaking out in whoops of sheer delight. Instantly the other two joined him, all attempts at feigning regret abandoned. Adam rolled his eyes, and in that short space of time, they bolted down the hall and erupted into the living room, where he found them, seconds later, gleefully jumping on the furniture.

"Gone! Gone! The witch is gone!"

Adam took a militant posture in the middle of the room. It was a cold, colorless room, one he particularly disliked, but in all the months since his wife's death, he had made no effort to change it. Nor did he intend to. "That's enough!" he barked in his best commander's voice.

Robbie turned an awkward cartwheel on the couch and tumbled to the floor with a thunk, howls of glee instantly becoming cries of pain and shock. Ryan crawled down to join him, giggling, and Robbie abruptly switched to laughter, one hand rubbing the back of his head as he sat up. Wendy ignored them all, dancing in place on the seat of an armchair. "Gone! Gone! The old prune's gone!"

The boys laughed all the harder at that, while Adam's face turned red and his temper frayed. "Stop that this instant, and go to bed!" What his bark had not accomplished, his roar did, as all three children went still and silent, their attention at last on their father. Not that they actually obeyed. The boys merely lay down on the floor and regarded him curiously, while Wendy slid down into a sitting position on the chair, her face set mutinously.

"I hated her. She was mean and ugly and—"

"You did everything in your power to drive her away!" he accused. "You know we need the help, but still you—"

"We don't need no help!" Wendy cried in a thin voice. "Mommy always took care of us with just Cook."

"Cook is part-time!" Adam exclaimed. "And I am *not* Mommy! I have to make a living for us, I can't stay home all day long to take care of you!"

"Mommy did!"

"Because *I* was off making us a living!"

"In the army," Ryan said accusingly, and something in his tone robbed Adam of all his anger.

"That's right," he muttered, swamped by the odd confusion that always came with that hint of resentment. Diana had never seemed to mind his career with the military. She had, in fact, on occasion during a long leave, seemed anxious to send him on his way. Maybe that was why he had always felt relieved to go. Maybe the kids had sensed his relief and felt it had to do with them, and that was at the root of their resentment. And maybe Diana had complained from time to time that he wasn't around. He would have been ashamed to admit that he hadn't really known his late wife well enough to say with any uncertainty what she might have said or done concerning his absences. He was depressingly irritated to know that the same was true of his children, and in the eighteen months since a traffic accident had taken Diana's life, that somehow had not changed. Adam sighed, too tired and too deflated to wrangle with his unruly children. How much easier it had been to deal with tough adult men! He made a sweeping gesture with one hand. "Get on to bed, all of you. It's late."

Robbie and Ryan sat up and folded their legs, watching their sister to see how she was going to respond to their father's order. Wendy stuck out her plump pink bottom lip and glared at Adam with his own light golden-brown eyes. "Who's gonna tuck us in, with Nanny Godiva gone?"

"You should have thought of that before you filled her shoes with snow, little Miss Ringleader. Now get to bed before I start smacking bottoms."

Wendy folded her arms stubbornly, but just as Adam felt his temper go, she suddenly bounced up off the chair and tore out of the room, her little arms swinging stiffly at her sides. The boys scrambled up and ran after her, singing, "Hey! Gone, the witch's gone. Hey, hey, witchy's gone…"

Adam put a hand to the back of his neck. What on earth was he going to do now? He had an important meeting tomorrow afternoon, with an auto lube franchiser from Minneapolis, and another on Friday, with a real estate agent. Surely Rebecca or Natalie could watch the kids for a few hours tomorrow. He'd worry about Friday later. He supposed he could always cancel, but only as a last resort. He was tired of living in limbo. He had to find something to do now that his retirement from the military was official. He needed a career, a business, a focus of some sort, but how could he concentrate on that, when the kids had just managed to drive off yet another nanny? Sometimes he wondered if those little rascals were actually trying to trap him here in the house—an unlikely scenario, since they seemed to actively dislike him much of the time.

He shook his head as he walked barefoot toward his bedroom, hitting light switches along the way. He groaned when the thought occurred to him that Godiva was likely to crack up her car on the snowy, icy roads and sue the pants off him. Wouldn't *that* just cap the New Year! He ignored the whispers coming from behind Wendy's door and trudged into the cold confines of his bedroom. Not even the blaze flickering in the fireplace could warm up the place, decorated as it was in shades of white and ice blue, but he crawled gratefully beneath the dark red coverlet—the one change he'd taken the initiative to make—and settled down to a happily blank sleep.

A little thumb pulled his eyelid up and back, nearly gouging out his eye in the process.

"Ow!"

Adam yanked away and surveyed his son with dismay and exhaustion. How many times could one little boy wake up in the space of a single night?

"God, Robbie, don't you ever sleep?"

"Ryan," corrected a petulant voice.

"Oh." The boys were alike enough to confuse, if one didn't look too closely, but Wendy claimed that their mother had *never* gotten them mixed up, and Adam could not quite squelch a spurt of guilt that he had, however seldom, done so. Sighing, he rolled onto his back and laid an arm across his eyes. "What is it now?"

"Ah hun-wy," said Ryan, his slight speech impediment exaggerated by the three fingers he had thrust into his mouth. Adam's aunt Lindsay, the family pediatrician, had told him that there was no reason for concern, but he worried anyway—when he had the energy, which he didn't at the moment.

"Ryan," Adam groaned, "it's the middle of the night."

"Na-a-aw. Id maw-ning!"

Surely not. It couldn't possibly be morning. He hadn't slept two full hours yet. *Oh, God, don't let it be morning,* he thought, carefully lifting his arm and slitting open his eyes. Oh, God, it *was* morning. Adam made a whimpering sound in the back of his throat and resigned himself to the inevitable, even as he rolled onto his side and craned his neck to read the time on the digital alarm clock beside the bed. Seven-forty. The alarm would screech in five more minutes. Five minutes was not worth fighting for.

"All right," he said, sitting up and yawning. "What's for breakfast?"

Ryan shrugged and popped his fingers out of his mouth. "I don't know."

Adam swung his legs over the side of the bed and reached for the T-shirt he'd left lying on the floor the night before. "Well, go see what Nanny's making, and come tell—"

"*Nanny's* gone," Ryan reminded him.

Adam closed his eyes. *Gone, gone, witchy's gone.* Godiva had left them the night before, and Cook didn't come in until just before lunch. Heaven help them. Well, surely there was something he could dish up...cold cereal, perhaps, doughnuts... He'd have given a thousand bucks to put on his fatigues and jog down to the mess hall just once more. But things were bound to look better after he'd gotten down a cup of coffee. Coffee. He groaned again, realizing that there wouldn't be any coffee, not this morning. The civilian world was hell.

Ryan scrambled off the bed and attached himself to Adam's leg, tugging with all the might in his little limbs. Adam laughed at the senselessness of it and got awkwardly to his feet, reaching for the bathrobe that hung over the bedpost. He threw it on and belted it over the fleece pants he'd worn to bed and the T-shirt he'd just donned. His shoes were around here somewhere, if he could just see around the bunched body of his son.

"Okay, okay, Ryan," he said, patting the boy's back. "I'm on my way."

Ryan let go and ran to the door, where he paused and called back. "Better huwwy." He shook his finger at Adam in a perfect parody of his older sister. "Wendy say if you don't come, she gonna make breakfast herself."

Adam's eyes widened in alarm. Forgetting his shoes, he pelted toward the kitchen, bawling, "Wen-dy!"

He burst through the louvered swinging doors in time to see his daughter standing on a chair that she had pulled up to the counter and dumping flour into a glass bowl from a sack. The flour hit with a *whump* and rose in clouds around the bowl, which wobbled ominously near the edge of the counter. Adam threw himself across the cooktop island and snatched Wendy off the chair, just as the bowl shattered into a thousand pieces on the floor. Flour and glass sprayed the narrow aisle between the counter and the island. Wendy immediately burst into loud wails. Adam pulled her up onto the island, expecting to see blood running down her legs. He sagged with relief when all he saw was flour dusting her legs. At that moment, the boys pushed through the door, Robbie first, then Ryan, his hand in his mouth.

"Out!" Adam barked. Neither of them moved a muscle. "There's glass all over the floor! Get out of here!"

Eyes wide, they backed through the swinging door, but then Robbie pushed them open again and stuck his head inside. "Wendy, you hurt?"

Wendy's wails had subsided to sobs now, but she made no effort to answer. Adam answered for her, still miffed—pained, if he was to be honest—that his children always seemed to need a reason to obey him. "She's not hurt, she's just scared," he said gruffly, pulling her to him and beginning to inch his way across the floor toward the door, on the lookout for the telltale sparkle of glass splinters.

Once safely on the carpet of the dining room, he set Wendy on her feet, went down on one knee and grasped her by her solid little shoulders. "What on earth did you think you were doing?" He hadn't meant to shout, and he hadn't meant to shake her, but the thought of glass embedding itself in her plump child's body both horrified and angered him. She went off into screeching wails again, her face scrunched up and her braids shuddering, but Adam noted that her eyes were dry. He guessed she was more embarrassed than frightened. Truth to tell, he was somewhat shaken himself. He let her go and wiped a hand across his brow. "All right," he muttered. "It's all right, but don't you *ever* do anything like that again. Do you hear me?" She nodded her head, sniffing phonily. Adam ignored the sham and schooled his tone to patience. "What were you doing anyway?"

"Making pancakes," she said challengingly, sticking out that lower lip.

"Pancakes!" Robbie echoed, jumping up and down. "Yeah, yeah, pancakes!"

Ryan immediately picked up the chant, clapping his hands together.

Adam winced. They would settle on something as difficult as pancakes for breakfast. Even if he could find a recipe, he couldn't begin to put together an edible batch of pancakes. Who was he kidding? He'd be lucky to get the milk in the bowl with the cereal—*if* he could find any. He wasn't about to go looking in his bare feet, not now. He made a sudden decision. He was good at decisions. In fact, deciding was what he often did best, and this decision let him off the hook in several ways. For one thing, they'd actually get to eat, and for another, he wouldn't have to face cleaning up the mess in the kitchen on an empty stomach. He pushed up to his full height. "All right, let's get you dressed. We're going out for pancakes."

That elicited paroxysms of delight. Robbie danced around, whooping in circles, knees knocked together, lower legs flying out at odd angles. Ryan took a look at his brother's improbable dance and settled for stomping up and down and hoo-hooing like a train. Wendy merely looked up at her father in that solemn way of hers, nodded sharply and spun away to drag her noisy brothers from the room. Adam smiled to himself. He might actually have scored some points with this one.

An hour later, Adam asked himself how a good idea could have gone so bad as he grabbed for the syrup pitcher yet again. He snatched it out of the way just as Robbie fell, chest forward, into his plate, his arms stretching out to knock salt and pepper shakers into ashtrays and ashtrays into toast baskets. Wendy snickered, one hand over her mouth, the other waving a fork bearing a speared piece of dripping pancake. Robbie giggled, looking down at the sticky mess on his shirt, and Ryan immediately went up on his knees, preparing to duplicate his brother's antics. "Oh, no, you don't!" Adam jumped up, trying to balance the syrup pitcher with one hand and grab Ryan's shoulder with the other. His hip hit the table, and coffee sloshed out of the cup, over the rim of the saucer and onto his khakis. "Damn!"

The children descended into loud laughter. Adam felt the syrup pitcher lifted out of his hand. An instant later, it was replaced by a damp white towel. "Allow me," said a soft voice. Adam caught a flash of pale blue uniform and brown hairnet as he bent to wipe at the stain on his thigh. He looked up in time to see a slender young woman tugging Wendy's leg down into place and sliding her chair farther under the table, situating the hand with the fork over her plate. She smiled down at the girl, then moved on around the table, putting Ryan back into his booster seat and pushing his milk glass away from the edge of the table. She leaned down and whispered something to him before moving on to Robbie, and Ryan instantly picked up his fork and began to eat. Robbie required a bit more attention.

"Well, now, handsome, you've made quite a mess of yourself, haven't you?" she said, going down beside his chair and ruffling his hair. "The food's supposed to go *in* your tummy, not on it." She dipped a paper napkin in his water glass and began carefully dabbing the worst of the syrup off his shirt. "What beautiful eyes you have," she said, smiling into moss-green eyes mottled with yellow and tiny spikes of blue. Robbie grinned, clearly besotted, and when she turned her smile on Adam, he understood the sentiment completely.

She was really quite astonishingly lovely, with an oval face built of high, delicate cheekbones, a broad smooth forehead and a slightly blunted chin. The straight, thick bangs that brushed the peaks of naturally arched brows were the palest gold, and fine as corn silk. Her lips were wide and rather spare, but perfectly shaped and rosy pink beneath a small, patrician nose with two small depressions high up on the narrow bridge, indicating that she wore, or used to wear, glasses. But her eyes were her dominant feature. Large ovals, widest at the inner edge, they were a clear, brilliant green spiked and veined with rich blue and thickly fringed with tawny lashes. Heavy lids gave them a sultry look, and Adam suspected that she was somewhat nearsighted. Perhaps she wouldn't notice that his mouth was hanging open. He snapped it shut and formed it into a smile.

"I think you've just averted a major disaster," he said, bowing himself down into his chair. "Thank you."

She turned the napkin in her hand, dipped it in the water once more and continued cleaning Robbie's shirt. "No problem." Her mouth quirked up at one corner. "You looked like you had your hands full."

Adam amazed himself with a warm chuckle. "You could say that, yes. Our nanny quit last night, and I'm sorry to say

I haven't quite gotten the hang of this single-father thing yet." Had he really said *single?*

She shot him a look that was part disdain and part curiosity. "What happened to your wife?"

"She dead!" Ryan announced at the top of his lungs.

Mortified, Adam felt the weight of gazes turning his way as colored heat climbed his neck and face. He shot his son a quelling glare and quickly looked back to the pretty blonde. "My, um, wife was killed in an auto accident eighteen months ago," he said softly. "The boys were only about a year and a half old, and you know how kids are. They don't always grasp the significance of—"

"You poor darlings," she said, standing to loop an arm around each of the twins' necks. "You're so sweet, I could just eat you up!" She bent to kiss first Ryan and then Robbie. They soaked it up as if it were sunshine, gazing up adoringly and laying their heads back against her arms. She rubbed noses with each of them in turn, making them giggle, before gazing across the table at a thoughtfully watching Wendy. "You probably remember everything, don't you, sweetheart?" Wendy nodded, round-eyed, but Adam would have bet a small fortune that she had only the scarcest notion what the waitress meant. "I bet you miss her awfully, too," the woman whispered, and Wendy's lower lip trembled, more in empathy with the woman's tone than from anything else. The blonde glided with a dancer's grace around the table to loop her arms around Wendy's shoulders. "What an angel! You must have loved her very much." Wendy nodded solemnly as the young woman hugged her to her bosom—a firm and bountiful bosom, Adam noted.

The woman went down on her knees, her full attention focused on Wendy. "I remember something Sister Agnes used to say about a mother's love. Do you want to know what it was?" Wendy nodded again, and the woman went on. "Sister Agnes said that a mother's love never dies. It lives on and on in the hearts of her children, and if you close your eyes and stay very still, you can feel it beating there, strong and happy and comforting."

Wendy said, "Who's Sister Agnes?"

"The nurse at the place where I went to live after my mommy went to heaven. She was a nun—Sister Agnes, I mean. It was a Catholic place, you see."

"How come you had to go to a Catholic place?" Wendy wanted to know.

"Because, you see, my daddy went to heaven even before my mommy did."

Wendy looked at her father with wide, surprised eyes. "My daddy went to 'Rabia," she said, "but he came home."

The blonde smiled at Adam. "Well, you're very lucky then, aren't you?"

"He did the army," Robbie said, tired of being left out.

A blond brow lifted at that. "Did he now?"

Adam cleared his throat. "I was in Saudi Arabia when my wife...had the accident. I hurried home to find my children with my aunt."

"My grandma died, too," Robbie announced.

The blonde gasped, a hand going to her chest. "Oh, my!" She looked to Adam for confirmation.

A shaft of pain speared through him. He resolutely pushed it aside. "Great-grandmother, actually," he said tersely. "Plane crash."

The waitress pulled in a deep breath, tears sparkling in her astonishing eyes. "Gosh, I'm sorry."

*Adam, you're a scoundrel,* he told himself, even as he bowed his head and swallowed noisily, wringing every possible ounce of compassion out of her.

"My heart just goes out to you all," she said, adding briskly, "Stop that right now, young man. We don't allow our food to be thrown."

Adam looked up in time to see Robbie drop a handful of soggy pancake onto the table. He rolled his eyes, leaning forward. "That's it, Robbie Fortune. You are going to get it just as soon as we get home!"

The waitress chuckled, getting to her feet. "You really don't know anything about children, do you?"

Just then a bald, portly man appeared at her elbow. "Laura, you have customers waiting."

"Oh. Sorry, Mr. Murphy, I was just trying to help this gentleman—"

"I told you when I hired you," the man said sternly, interrupting her, "no flirting with the customers!"

"But I wasn't—"

Adam cut in. "She wasn't flirting! She was trying to clean up after my son when he—"

The man pointed a finger at Adam. "I'll thank you to stay out of this. We have rules here, and as manager, it's up to me to enforce them. You don't see the other girls ignoring their own customers to bat their eyelashes at married men."

"I'm not married!"

"He's not married!" she cried at the same time.

The manager smirked. "Not flirting, huh? You've already determined his marital status, but you weren't flirting. I'm disappointed in you, Laura, very disappointed."

Laura's mouth fell open. "He was just telling me how his wife—his *late* wife—was in an accident while he was in Saudi Arabia."

The manager glared at her. "I don't like argumentative employees. You have five seconds to get back to your station or you're fired. Five. Four."

Adam got to his feet. "This is absurd! She hasn't done anything to warrant this kind of heavy-handed bullying."

"Three. Two."

"Don't bother!" Laura ripped off her hairnet, freeing a sleek cascade of hip-length blond silk. Adam's breath caught. She threw the net on the floor. "I quit!"

The manager sneered. "I knew you wouldn't last the day!"

"You're just mad because the owner made you hire me!"

"It obviously wasn't for your waitressing skills," he returned snidely.

Adam threw his napkin on the table. "Mister, you're asking for a broken nose!"

Laura gasped and threw up a protective hand. "No, don't! I don't want the job, honestly, and I can't stand fighting. *Please.*"

Adam looked at the mixed desperation and hope on her face and felt his heart lurch inside his chest. He swallowed down the anger and glanced around the table. "Get your coats on, kids," he ordered brusquely, digging into his pocket. "We're getting out of here. And we won't be back," he added for the manager's benefit.

The odious man snorted. "Now that's a real tragedy."

Adam fixed him with a narrow glance. "Tell your boss that he'll be hearing from Adam Fortune."

At the mention of the Fortune name, the man went pale. Adam nodded with satisfaction and helped Robbie down from his chair, while the woman named Laura hurriedly did the same for Ryan. Adam stepped to her side, reached out and grasped her by the arm. "Where's your coat?"

Her eyelids lifted with surprise. "I-in the back, but—"

"Get it," he said flatly, leaving no room for argument. "You're going with us."

"B-but I can't just—"

"Look, you were just trying to help out an inept father when this jerk came storming over and fired you."

"He didn't fire me, I quit," she pointed out, lifting her chin.

Adam smiled. Oh, he liked this woman, a lot. "Fine, you quit, but you wouldn't have had to quit if it hadn't been for us. So, in my book, that means I owe you. Now get your coat." He turned her toward the back of the little café, then counted money out onto the table. "That should do it." He looked up at her. "Go on!"

"I—I'll have to change out of the uniform," she told him over her shoulder, hurriedly threading her way through tables full of gaping diners.

"We'll warm up the car," he said, grabbing Ryan by the hand as he reached for a milk glass. He snagged the collar of Robbie's coat as he dropped toward his knees, intending to crawl under the table.

"Uh, n-no need for this," the manager stuttered nervously, scooping up the money and shoving it into Adam's coat pocket. "Breakfast is on the house...sir. S-sorry for the, um, misunderstanding."

"Nice try," Adam said through perfect white teeth, "but I still think I'll speak to the owner."

The man gulped and mopped his brow with a shaking hand. "M-Mr. Fortune, c-couldn't we, ah, discuss this?"

"No." Adam hauled Robbie to his feet and moved him bodily toward the door, dragging Ryan behind him.

Wendy stuck her tongue out at the man and ran before them to hold open the door. It hadn't even closed behind them when she launched into speech. "I like her, Daddy! Don't you? Wouldn't she be a good nanny? Wouldn't she?"

Adam grinned down at his astute young daughter. Maybe she understood more about everything than he realized. Her happy, expectant doll's face sent a surge of love through him. "Yeah," he said, "I think she might at that, but she has to agree, hon, so don't get your hopes up just yet."

"Oh, but she needs the job!" Wendy assured him sagely.

Adam cocked his head. "Maybe so, but she might not want it. We'll see. Now get in the car. It's cold out here."

He opened the driver's door, and Wendy scrambled inside. "Back seat," he said, flashing her a grin, "just in case."

Nodding, she crawled over and squeezed in between the twins' car seats. Adam went through the laborious routine of getting the boys into their seats and buckling them in. Robbie hated being restrained in any way, but he stopped fighting when Adam told him that he had to check on *her*. Adam glanced at the front of the café, but he had learned a few things in the past eighteen months. Before he stepped away from the car, he fixed each one of the little heathens with a stern glare. "Don't touch a thing!" Three little heads nodded eagerly. He closed the door and trotted over to the front of the café, flailing his arms against the brutal cold.

Just as he suspected, the manager had waylaid her to plead for clemency. Fat lot of good that would do him.

Adam pushed the heavy glass door open and leaned inside. "Laura?"

She looked up in surprise at the mention of her name. "Coming."

She threw on her coat and left the manager massaging his temples. Adam watched her graceful, long-legged glide with a dry mouth. She looked taller in those skinny blue jeans than she had in that dumpy uniform. And that hair! His fingers itched to get into it. His heart whammed in his chest as she slipped through the door and by him.

"It's Laura Beaumont," she said huskily, her smile suddenly shy.

"Laura Beaumont," he repeated dumbly.

"And you are Adam, I think you said?"

He realized abruptly that he was staring and stuck out his hand. "Adam Fortune."

The name didn't seem to mean a thing to her. "Nice to meet you, Mr. Fortune."

Her hand felt delicate and weightless and utterly feminine in his. "Call me Adam."

"Yes, of course, if you'll stick with Laura."

"Oh, I will," he mumbled absently, warmed by the bright golden droplets of laughter that filled the cold February air. "Indeed I will."

It suddenly seemed no burden at all to be single with children.

# Two

"I'll make a deal with you," he was saying. "I won't call the owner of the diner if you'll come to work for me. You see, we need a nanny."

Laura pulled her gaze in and tamped down her excitement. He was entirely too good to look at, and if she had learned anything, it was to be leery of good-looking men. And yet... She shook her head. "I don't have any experience or training in that area."

He looked at her, momentarily taking his eyes off the road. "No? Well, maybe that's a good thing. You sure seem to have a way with them, and maybe that's more important."

She sucked in her bottom lip, wavering. Something good could happen once in a while, couldn't it? Her luck didn't have to be all bad. What did she have to lose, anyway? She tried to think. "I, um, don't have a car."

"Oh? Well, that doesn't matter, really. It's, um, a live-in position. Room, meals, salary." He shot her a grin. "And I think we can do better by you than that pancake house back there."

Laura caught her breath. Room, meals, *and* a salary? He went on talking.

"Breakfast is the sticking point. Trained nannies don't like to cook. However, our cook doesn't like to live in. She's married, you see, and by the time she can feed her husband and get him off to work, straighten her house and get out to ours, it's time to fix *lunch*. And since I'm about as useful in a kitchen as a coat hanger, the nanny has to fix breakfast. Think you can handle that?"

Laura had to smile. As if making breakfast were a problem. She'd once thought that she'd gladly do without just to escape kitchen duty at the group home where she spent the majority of her childhood. Once again, however, the home had proved its value, *home* being the operative word. It would be nice to have a home again. She frowned. If she did this thing, she mustn't let herself fall into the trap of considering Adam Fortune's home to be her home. Still... Room, meals, and a salary—it was just too good to pass up. She took a deep breath. "You have to understand, it would only be temporary."

His brow wrinkled at that. "How temporary?"

"Well..." She thought quickly, looking for a fair way to protect herself. It was February. March, April, May, June... School would be out, summer would come, traveling would be easy... School. Yes, that could work. She winced inwardly at how easily the lie came to her. "The thing is, I promised, um, Sister Agnes that I would finish my college degree. I had help the first year, sort of a scholarship, but the rest is up to me, so I've been working and saving my money, and now I almost have enough to go back to school."

He nodded. "Okay. Can't argue with that. So what you're saying is that you'd be leaving us in the fall."

"Well, maybe sooner. It—it all depends."

He sent her a quizzical look, and for a moment she thought he'd demand a firm date of departure, but he only inclined his head, shifted in his seat and said, "About your salary, shall we say..."

He named a dollar amount that made her mouth drop open. When she recovered, she very nearly told him that it was too much, but then she thought about how far she could go on such an amount, how well she could hide. She could save almost every penny of it, since she wouldn't have to pay rent or buy groceries. She closed her eyes and silently gave thanks. Perhaps God had not abandoned her after all. Perhaps she had finally atoned for the past, and the long nightmare was over. Her eyes popped open. No, that was dangerous thinking. She dared not let down her guard, especially now. She was responsible for the care and safety of three precious children now, and she would protect them, as God was her witness, with her very life.

Adam supposed that he should be pleased with himself. He hadn't had to cancel his appointment or call on his sister or his aunt. Granted, all he had accomplished with his meeting was to cross another prospect off his list. Auto lube was definitely not his thing. The problem was that he was no closer to finding his *thing* than before. He would have to draft a letter for his secretary to type informing the franchise people that he wasn't interested in lubing cars. He shook his head. He had an office. He had a secretary. He just didn't have anything to *do*. Well, at least he'd solved the problem of the nanny—hopefully. He was feeling a little less sure of that decision now.

It had seemed so right at the time, but what did he know about Laura Beaumont, really, besides the fact that she was beautiful? He supposed that was part of it. What had a woman like her been doing living week to week in a seedy motel on a poorly traveled road and slinging hash in a pancake house? She might be just what she seemed, a rootless young woman without family or friends, trying to make her way in the world alone, saving up tuition for college, but it seemed preposterous that she wasn't attached to someone by now. She wasn't the sort men passed by without a second look. It just didn't add up. *She* didn't add up.

He opened his front door with more than a little trepidation, uncertain what he was going to find. The place was silent, almost ominously so, given that *his* children were in residence. Had she gagged and bound them? Locked them in closets? Tied them to their beds? He hung up his coat, the hair standing on the back of his neck as he silently surveyed the area. He stepped across the hall and into the living room.

"Wendy? Rob? Ryan? I'm home."

Nothing. He stepped back into the hall and moved swiftly toward the bedrooms. He turned the knob on Wendy's door and thrust it open, stepping aside, as he'd been taught to do in the army. The room was empty—and neat. The bed was made, the clothing was put away, the toys were stashed out of sight. What was going on here?

He crossed the hall to the boys' room. The place was neat as a pin, and Robbie was lying on his bed, looking at a book. A book! Adam walked over and slipped his hands in his slacks pockets, noting that an egg timer from the kitchen was ticking away on the dresser.

"What're you doing, Rob?"

The boy dropped the book. "I'm it," he announced.

It. "Uh-huh. How come?"

He looked not in the least repentant as he confessed, "'Cause I spitted on Ryan."

Nothing surprising in that. Adam sat down on the edge of the bed. "You shouldn't spit, Robbie. It's not nice."

"I know. Laura told me."

Adam glanced at the timer on the dresser. "Is this your punishment for spitting on Ryan?"

Robbie nodded. "I got to lay on the bed and read this book till it dings, then I'm it."

It again. Adam nodded as if he actually understood what the boy was saying and stood, unbuttoning his collar and stripping off his tie. Obviously he was talking to the wrong person, if he wanted to know just what was going on here. "Where's Miss Laura?" he asked nonchalantly.

Robbie shrugged. "I dunno."

"You don't know?"

He shook his head, all innocent eyes. Adam frowned. "Where are the other kids?"

"She hided them."

"Hided? *Hid* them?" Oh, God!

Robbie nodded, smiling when the timer dinged. He tossed the book aside, threw his chubby legs over the edge of the bed and scooted over to drop down onto the floor. "I'm it!" he called, running out of the room. "Look out! I coming!"

It. They were playing hide-and-seek. Glory be. He hung his head, silently laughing at himself. In the distance he heard a sudden burst of laughter, followed by squeals and cries of dispute. He walked down the hall, back the way he'd come, past the bath and Wendy's room on the right, the storage closets and the foyer on the left, then on past the living room and, finally, the formal dining room. The hall turned right, coming to an end at the expansive den. It was his favorite room, big and warm, with brick walls and a rock fireplace, comfortable, slightly worn furniture, a TV, bookcases, framed photos on the walls. This room had been a gift from Kate. Diana had assured him that his grandmother had been insistent on decorating it herself when they first built the house. Dear Kate. How he missed her! More, even, than his very proper, very patient, very aloof wife. The house had been nearly a year old, this room included, before he first saw it, but he'd never walked into this room without feeling his grandmother's hand. Had he ever adequately thanked her for it? He couldn't remember.

He caught movement from the corner of his eye and turned his head in time to see Laura crawl out from behind the big green suede couch, all three kids hanging on to her. They were giggling and wiggling and having a ball. Laura flipped her hair out of the way, then, with a dramatic groan, collapsed on her belly.

"I give! You win!"

Wendy, whose fine hair had pulled free of her pigtails to fall into her face, laid her head next to Laura's and sprawled on the floor close at her side. The twins began clapping their hands and chanting as they piled all over Laura Beaumont. "We win! We win! We win!"

Suddenly Laura surged up into a sitting position, tossing her hair back and steadying wiggling boys with her hands. "All right, all right! Do your worst!"

To Adam's intense amazement, his children began attacking Laura Beaumont with smacking kisses all over her lovely face, shoulders and arms, giggling as she made disdainful sounds. "Uck! Pooh! Yuck! Ick! Phooey! Oh, it's awful! Torture! Torture!" Ryan wrapped his arms around Laura's neck and gave her a larynx-crushing hug. She gagged appropriately, and the other two promptly followed suit. She collapsed back against the side of the couch, overcome by the sheer weight of their affection. Adam could not remember ever receiving more than a quick, dry peck from any of his children. He didn't know who he envied more, Laura or the kids.

He knew the instant Laura realized he was in the room. Her smile faded, and she stiffened, communicating silently that the fun was over. The giggles died away. Little arms loosened. Small feet found purchase on the thick, sand-colored rug. Four pairs of eyes looked upon him with all the welcome of condemned prisoners awaiting the hangman.

"Hi," Laura said, getting to her feet amid small bodies. She smoothed a hand over her hair, sweater and jeans. "We were playing."

Adam allowed himself a tiny smile. "I noticed that."

She seemed uncertain. Afraid, perhaps? He looked closely then, and saw it in all their faces—the fear of his disapproval. He made himself relax, picked up the newspaper from a table and dropped down onto his favorite chair. "How was your day?"

"Fine." Laura sat on the couch. Wendy climbed up to sit next to her, her head leaning against Laura's arm, while each of the twins picked a leg and wrapped himself around it. "Wendy's kindergarten teacher called to ask why she wasn't in school this afternoon. I didn't know what to tell her."

School. How could he have forgotten that? Adam forced a smile. "I'll, um, call and explain tomorrow."

Laura nodded and folded her hands.

He opened the newspaper and tried to read, but he couldn't seem to find a single word on the whole page. His mind was reeling. Already they loved her. He didn't know anything about this woman, but already his children loved her. And school. What was he going to do about that? Could she even drive? He put down the newspaper. "Do you drive?"

She seemed momentarily stunned. "Yes."

He nodded. "It's just that I prefer that Wendy be driven in to school rather than ride the bus. It's so dangerous to wait out in this cold."

Laura nodded, her brow creased. "That's fine, except..."

He waved away the obvious concern, remembering that she had no car. "Oh, that's no problem. You can take the station wagon. I prefer the truck, anyway."

She almost visibly relaxed. "Well, that's settled, then."

He smiled and opened the newspaper again, but his mind just wasn't on local news. "When's dinner?"

"Any time now, I imagine. Beverly—uh, that is, Cook—said about six."

Beverly, was it? Even the cook was on a first-name basis with the new nanny. He couldn't remember that ever happening before. "Fine," he said from behind his paper, uncertain why this was so difficult. He needed to draw her out, get to know her. He was getting nowhere fast this way, and yet he couldn't seem to put that paper down. What would he say? What could he ask her without making her feel that he was interrogating her? To his relief, she took the matter out of his hands momentarily.

"Well," she said, getting to her feet, "time to wash up. We can't go to the dinner table with dirty hands and faces, now can we?"

Adam hummed noncommittally behind his paper as they exited the room. He heard one of the boys whine something about not getting soap in his eyes, and heard Laura's low assurance that it wouldn't happen. Adam shook his head and put the paper aside. What was wrong with him? The woman was wonderful, just as he'd instinctively known she would be. He had nothing to fear, nothing at all, and yet...

"Dinner in ten minutes, Mr. Adam."

He looked up at the quiet, efficient middle-aged woman who had been cooking his meals for the past eighteen months. "Thank you...Beverly."

Her eyebrows flew up, and she paused in the act of drying her hands on her apron, and then she smiled, tentatively at first, and then with a blinding show of white dentures. "I'll be leaving a little early this evening, sir, if that's all right. My husband, he wants to see a movie, and

Laura, she said she'd put the plates and flatware in the dishwasher for me. I'll wash up everything else before I go... if I may."

Adam nodded. "Certainly. Ah, tell me, what do you think of our Miss Laura?"

Beverly the Cook beamed. "Oh, she's a treasure, that one! Took things right in hand, and do you know, I think she actually likes children? Why is it, do you suppose, that so many nannies don't like children? You'd think they'd do something else, wouldn't you?"

A very astute observation. Adam smiled. "Enjoy your movie."

"Thank you. I will, and, um, Mr. Adam, sir, if I may say so, I think she's just what those young ones need."

Her eyes said something more, but he wasn't very good at reading unspoken messages, and he wasn't sure he wanted to know what she was thinking, anyway. Man, planning war-game strategies and mass mobilizations had been a walk in the park, compared to this life he led now. But maybe it was going to change for the better now, temporarily, anyway. He frowned. Temporary just wasn't good enough. He couldn't be hiring a new nanny every two or three months. The children's lives were continually overset by such changes, and one day—soon, please!—he was going to have a new career to dedicate himself to, not that his search for a compatible business had yielded much so far. He was feeling a new sense of pressure about that, too. His military retirement wouldn't put children through college or allow the kind of upkeep on a home that winters in Minnesota required, especially as that home grew older. And he couldn't just sit, day in and day out, perusing the newspaper. He put that aside for good just as Laura returned to the room.

"It's ready," she told him, crossing to the sofa.

He nodded and got up out of his chair at the very moment Laura sat down. "Aren't you coming?"

She sent him a sheepish look. "I wasn't sure what was... proper in my situation."

"Well, it's proper to eat," he said blandly.

She stood, smoothing her hands over her bottom and the backs of her thighs, as if straightening a skirt. "I just wasn't certain if I ought to be eating at the table with you and the children."

In truth, several of the nannies had preferred to take their meals alone. Often, mealtime had been the only time they could get away from the children. He made a sudden decision not to tell Laura that, though. Maybe if they treated her like family she would stay longer. On the other hand, maybe he needed to find out more about her before he pushed her to stay. That, too, could be accomplished at the dinner table. He lifted an arm in invitation. "We're pretty informal around here. Come on."

She nodded and bit at her lower lip, and her head was bowed almost shyly as she stepped up next to him. His arm just seemed to sort of naturally curve around her, of its own volition. He didn't remove it until they reached the dining room.

The kids were giggling when they came in—not a good sign. Sure enough, Robbie had reached into a bowl of mashed potatoes with his hand and was squishing the pulp between his fingers. Adam opened his mouth to snap an angry order, but something in Laura's demeanor gave him second thoughts. He glanced sideways at her. She had drawn herself up tall and folded her long, slender arms. Her face was impassive, not censuring, not smiling, her gaze as steady as time. Robbie slowly pulled his hand back. Laura moved to the chair opposite him, pulled it out and sank down upon it gracefully, her gaze now studiously averted. Adam sensed a method behind her behavior and calmly copied her. Once carefully ensconced in the chair at the head of the table, he looked around, mentally noted the uncomfortable expression on Robbie's face as he eyed his potato-encrusted hand and smiled at Laura.

"Would you serve the children, please?"

She sent him a look of approval, nodded and reached for the bowl of potatoes. "Wendy, would you care for potatoes?"

"Yes, please," Wendy replied in a small voice, and Laura duly dispensed them.

"Ryan?"

Ryan crossed his eyes and waggled his tongue. "Yes, pwease!"

Laura smiled ever so slightly at his antics and spooned creamy potatoes onto his plate. She then turned to Robbie.

"Robbie, would you care for potatoes?"

Robbie nodded and bowed his head, frowning. Adam hid a grin, knowing that his scapegrace son was wondering how such a brilliant prank had turned into a embarrassment. Laura doled out the serving and set down the bowl. Utter silence followed, and then Adam heard the sound of sniffles. He looked at Robbie, whose head was practically in his plate now, then at Laura. Her expression of compassion for Robbie put a sudden lump in his throat. He had to look away.

"Adam," Laura said quietly, "would you clean Robbie's hand for him so he can eat?"

Brilliant. She was brilliant. Adam slipped out of his chair and knelt at Robbie's side, using his napkin to clean Robbie's little fist. "You know, Rob," he said gently, "there are reasons for rules. Dining wouldn't be a very pleasant exercise if everyone helped themselves with their hands, would it?"

Robbie shook his head. Adam followed instinct and patted the boy's shoulder before moving back to his chair. Laura beamed as she reached for the dish of baked pork chops.

"Robbie, would you care for a pork chop, dear?"

Robbie wiped his nose on his wrist and nodded. Tacitly agreeing to overlook that little faux pas, Laura shared a tiny smile with Adam as she forked a chop onto Robbie's plate.

Before long, the table was alive with the muted sounds of a pleasant family dinner, the most pleasant in memory, in fact. The giggles that erupted on occasion were not of the mischievous sort, but rather a happy sound. Adam marveled. It was only with effort that he remembered he had reason to question Laura, and only with effort that he found the means to do it.

"So tell me, Laura," he began with costly aloofness, "what were you studying?"

"Studying?" she echoed blankly, and Adam thought, *A-ha*. His thoughts must have shown in his face, for she blanched, then recovered swiftly. "Oh, you mean what was I studying in college."

"Yes. In college."

She smiled grimly, concentrating her attention on what remained of her food. "Early childhood development."

"Ah." Perfect answer, but he'd already determined that she was brilliant.

"Although," she went on hesitantly, "I hadn't declared a major yet."

"Um. When do you expect to return to school?"

She shrugged uncomfortably.

"In the fall?"

"Maybe," she said. "Then again, I might want to start with summer school, sort of ease back into it, you know."

Summer. He worked his frown into a smile. "Where were you thinking of going?"

She gulped. "I—I haven't decided yet."

He made an understanding sound, utterly convinced that she was lying to him. "Well, no rush," he said.

She smiled. "Right. No rush."

He steeled himself for the killing thrust. "Where did you go before?" She yanked her gaze up to meet his, and in the instant before she covered it, he saw what she hadn't wanted him to see: fear.

"No place you've ever heard of," she murmured.

"Out of state?" he asked pointedly.

She folded her napkin and laid it beside her plate. The gaze she leveled at him was implacable, unapologetic. "Yes," she said flatly, pushing back her chair to stand. She swept the table with a look. "Excuse me." Then she turned and left the room without another word.

Adam took a deep breath. She had lied to him, and she was afraid that he knew it, which he did. The question now was why, and what he was going to do about it.

"Bedtime, my lovelies."

Adam looked at the crew on the couch and chuckled to himself. Bedtime, indeed. Not one of them could keep his or her eyes open. Laura's change in the evening schedule had been a wise one. Instead of putting off baths until right before bedtime, she had played with the kids for a while after dinner, then bathed them early and cuddled them on the couch, reading. They had slipped, one by one, into a relaxed stupor. Bed undoubtedly seemed delicious right about now. Laura was urging first one and then another twin to his feet when the doorbell rang. Adam got up immediately to answer it, suspecting who would be stubborn enough to call at this time on a cold February night.

Sure enough, he opened the door to find his father flapping his arms on the stoop.

"Adam."

"Father."

It was the standard greeting.

Jake moved inside without waiting for an invitation and closed the door behind. "Frigid out there."

"Some might even be inclined to stay inside," Adam commented lightly.

"All right, all right, don't give me any of your attitude. I have a couple of important reasons to be here."

Adam knew very well what at least one of those reasons would be. He put his hands in the pockets of his pants. "What's up?"

Jake grimaced. "It's your sister."

"Caroline?"

"No. Caroline's fine."

Adam was glad to hear it. "Married life seems to agree with her."

Jake nodded and suddenly grinned. "Who'd have thought it? The career woman has definitely softened. I've never seen her so happy."

*At least you've finally noticed,* Adam thought uncharitably. He said, "Well, that leaves three. Natalie's the level-headed one, so it must be one of the twins."

Jake's grin abruptly turned to a grimace. "Can we sit down?"

Adam could tell that Jake was genuinely concerned about something, so he led him across the hall to the living room. Laura was herding the kids down the hall toward them, and they brightened predictably at the sight of their grandfather. Instantly they were pelting after them and swarming over Jake the moment he dropped onto the sofa.

Adam squelched a flash of irritation as Jake patted and hugged his children. He was actually relieved when Laura appeared.

"Sorry," she said.

"No, that's all right. Laura, I'd like you to meet my father, Jacob Fortune." Again Adam noted that the Fortune name meant nothing to Laura. Ever the gentleman, Jake stood. She stuck her hand out.

"Hello."

"Dad, this is Laura Beaumont, our new nanny."

Jake's eyebrows went up at that, but he smiled almost flirtatiously at Laura as his big hand swallowed her delicate one.

"My pleasure."

She smiled apologetically at Jake. "We were on our way to bed."

"Oh, well…" Jake kissed each child in turn and sent them back to Laura.

"Thank you."

She smiled at Adam as they exited the room. Jake watched with undisguised curiosity.

"She's worlds more attractive than that Godiva creature," he said, reclaiming his seat.

Adam had to laugh. "Yes, well, she's that much and more a better nanny, too."

"Truly?"

Adam nodded and wandered over and dropped onto a stiff chair. "She's accomplished more with those kids in one day than Godiva and all the rest of them put together."

Jake frowned. "You've never understood children."

Adam gaped. "*I've* never understood—? You're one to talk!"

"That isn't fair, Adam. At least I tried—"

"I believe," Adam said, interrupting firmly, "that you were going to tell me which of my sisters has done the unforgivable."

Jake's face turned red, but, to his credit, he gritted his teeth until his anger abated. "Rachel," he said flatly.

Adam rolled his eyes. He should have known. "Look, Rocky has a right to live her life her own way. I knew you might not approve of Luke Greywolf, but he seems like a decent fellow to me. He's a doctor, for pity's sake!"

"She's pregnant," Jake told him. "Did you know she's pregnant?"

Adam kept his face carefully impassive. "Good thing you're a better grandfather than you were a—" He stopped, feeling the color drain from his face. "I didn't mean that the way it sounded."

"Didn't you?" Jake curled his hands into fists.

Adam sighed. "I know you're worried about her," he said placatingly, "but honestly, I don't think you have to."

"You know how careless she is," Jake pointed out.

"Not careless," Adam replied. "Adventurous, maybe, independent, definitely, but not careless."

Jake made a face. "When I spoke with your mother she said that Rocky really loves him."

"I'm sure she does," Adam said, "or she wouldn't have agreed to marry him, baby or no baby."

"But what about him?" Jake's voice rumbled dangerously. "That's what I want to know."

"Well," Adam said, sliding his hands into his pockets once more, "I'd say you have to trust Rocky for that." But Jake Fortune had a hard time trusting any of his children. Adam lifted a hand to the back of his neck. "Look, as independent and stubborn as Rocky is, do you honestly believe she'd settle for anyone who wasn't absolutely wild for her?"

Jake looked up at him with something very near gratitude. "You're right. Yes, you're exactly right." He sat back and smiled. "I hadn't looked at it that way."

Adam smiled to himself, feeling inordinately proud. Maybe there was hope for them, after all.

"Your mother wants to give them a party, sort of a family reception."

Adam shook his head, grinning again. "Are we welcoming him or disemboweling him?"

Jake scowled. "Your mother means to welcome him, but frankly, I'm not sure it wouldn't be the other way around, given the current climate."

Adam folded his hands. "You're talking about the Monica Malone thing now."

Jake's face instantly closed up. "The less said on that subject, the better."

Adam shrugged. "Fine with me."

"I only wish my brother and his crew agreed with you."

"That'll be the day."

"I suppose so."

Adam fingered the crease in his pants silently, sure they weren't through. He didn't have to wait long.

Jake drew himself up and put on a stern face. "Now," he said, "when are you are going to give up this ridiculous search and come to work for the company?"

"Oops!" Adam shot up to his feet. "Time to go. Sorry you can't stay longer, but for once I'd like to part without daggers drawn."

"Damn it, Adam, I'm being serious!"

Adam swept a hand over his head. "Will you drop it? I don't want to have this conversation again."

Jake came to his feet. "Why can't you see that you belong with the family company?"

"No."

"Adam, please, I need you now. The cosmetics company is in dire need of leadership. You're a natural. You could—"

"No! Damnation! Why do you always do this to me? I won't step into the great maw of the Fortune companies!"

"Then just what *are* you going to do?" Jake demanded. "Sell cars? Install central heating?"

"No! I don't know! But I'll find something, something right for *me.*"

"But this job *is* right for you!"

"No!"

"Won't you even hear me out?"

"No."

Jake balled his hands into fists, obviously struggling with his temper. "I don't understand you."

"Tell me something I don't know."

"You've never understood what being part of this family means."

"It's not the family," Adam told him firmly. "It's the family business that I want no part of."

Jake looked to be gathering himself for a real explosion when Laura meekly interrupted.

"Can I get you gentlemen anything before I call it a night?"

Jake swallowed whatever he had been about to say and shook his head.

"My father was just leaving," Adam said, pointedly but quietly. "Thank you anyway."

"No problem. It was good to meet you, Mr. Fortune. Be careful out in that cold, won't you?"

Jake nodded and buttoned up his coat. "Good evening, Miss Beaumont." He started forward, then stopped and passed a look from Adam to Laura. "It is 'Miss,' isn't it?"

Laura blinked, then blushed. "Yes."

"I thought so," he murmured. "A pleasure to meet you." He sent a hard look at his son. "Adam."

"Father."

He stormed out of the room, muttering that he could see himself out.

Adam sighed. Would it never change? His gaze went almost involuntarily to Laura. Or had change already begun? She had certainly derailed a shouting match with her timely, gracious interruption. Had she meant to do just that? he wondered as she said good-night and slipped away. Yes, he believed she had. Now if only he could decide how he felt about that and just how important the truth about her was.

# Three

Adam used a piece of toast to wipe up the last of the egg on his plate, popped it into his mouth, chewed, swallowed, and followed it with a mouthful of coffee, his pleasure evident. He touched his mouth with his napkin, then laid it on the table in the large, welcoming kitchen, where he sat with Laura.

"Tell me again why these are low-cholesterol eggs?"

Laura balanced her chin on an upturned palm, smiling. "It's really very simple. Say you want to scramble a dozen eggs. You just whisk up nine egg whites and three whole eggs, add a drop or two of food coloring, heat a nonstick pan, put the eggs in and stir them around. It makes enough for us and the kids."

"You put something else in these," he accused teasingly.

She inclined her head. "You can add almost anything to them. I used some of the leftover mashed potatoes from last night—any are okay, as long as they're already cooked—and some fat-free cheese I found in the refrigerator. It's a real high-protein, low-fat, low-cholesterol breakfast, especially with toast and a little apple butter—which isn't butter at all, actually."

"So that's how you keep that marvelous figure," he said, eyes crinkling at the edges with his grin.

Laura felt heat sweep upward from her chest. For Pete's sake! What was wrong with her? She'd been told that she had a nice figure before—but not by him. Dismayed at her own reaction to a simple compliment, she quickly averted her gaze. "Th-thank you. Uh, now, if you would stop by the grocer's today and pick up some turkey bacon, we could have that, too."

He wiped his mouth with his napkin and tossed it on the table, then got to his feet, shaking his head and reaching into his back pocket. "Not today. Sorry. But the roads are clear, so you might as well go and take the kids." He opened his wallet and extracted a bill, which he thrust at her. "Get whatever you need."

"Oh, no, it's not..." Mechanically she glanced at that bill, and then she stared. "A hundred dollars! For turkey bacon?"

"For whatever you need," he said, laying the bill beside her plate.

She looked up at him with her mouth hanging open. "You can't go around handing out hundred-dollar bills like that!"

His mouth twitched and his eyebrows rose. "Oh? And why not?"

"It's too much money!"

He shrugged. "So you have some left over for the next time you need something."

She shook her head. "I don't need anything, and if I did, I wouldn't let you pay for it."

"No? Okay, then use it for things the family needs, like turkey bacon."

Laura gulped. "I don't know if I should."

He put his foot up on the seat of his chair and leaned over it, his arm crossed over his knee. "What's the matter, Laura?" he asked lightly. "Can't I trust you with cash? Is money some kind of great temptation for you?"

She knew then that it was a kind of test. He was willing to pay a hundred dollars to find out whether she was honest or not. In other words, he didn't trust her, and that hurt more than it should have.

"I'll give you an accounting," she said softly, picking up the bill and folding it until it fit snugly in her palm.

He neither moved nor spoke for a long moment, and Laura kept her gaze stubbornly averted, not wanting him to see the sheen of disappointment in her eyes. Well, what had she expected? This whole thing had been an impulsive move on his part, and he would understandably regret that, given time to think about it. She shouldn't be so bothered by it. She hadn't been trusted by very many people in her life—and she knew better than to trust anyone else, especially with the truth. If he knew about her...

He took his foot down from the chair and straightened. "Look, you have to go into town anyway. Wendy's school starts at nine, and I need to be in the office before then. Do you know where it is? The school, I mean."

"Yeah, I think so. Anyway, I can find it. St. Cloud's a pretty small town, after all."

"Right. You can use the station wagon. We keep the boys' car seats in it. I prefer to drive the truck, anyway. It's four-wheel-drive."

"Fine." Laura nodded without looking up.

"You can drive, can't you?" he asked, his voice teasingly light, and yet she knew he had reason for concern.

"Certainly. I had driver's training in high school, and I've never had an accident or ticket of any kind."

"How old are you, Laura?" he asked gently, surprising her into looking up and blurting the truth.

"Twenty-two."

He smiled apologetically. "I knew you were young."

She bit her lip, but she couldn't keep from asking, "How old are you?"

He laughed, his eyes sparkling fondly. "Thirty-one."

"That's not exactly ancient."

"No, it isn't. To hear my father tell it, I'm practically a teenager still."

She heard the faint tone of bitterness. There was definitely trouble there, and she hated fighting or discord of any kind, especially between family members. She remembered what she'd overheard the night before, and it occurred to her that she might owe Adam an apology. "Um, about last night... I wasn't eavesdropping on your argument with your father. I was just coming down the hall, and I couldn't help hearing."

"Yeah, well, as to that," he said lightly, withdrawing eye contact, "we always wind up shouting, and your timing was excellent. Thanks. You didn't have to step in."

"I didn't mean to, actually," she admitted. "I'm afraid I did it without thinking. I hate conflict, just hate it."

"Well, conflict's about all there is between me and Jake," he said.

That was so sad to hear that the awfulness of it nearly choked her. She closed her eyes and whispered, "I never knew my father."

"Oh, say, I'm sorry." He sat down again. "It's not that we don't care about each other, Jake and I," he said after a pause. "It's just... I don't know, maybe we're too much alike. The big thing is, though, he got pushed into the family business, when what he really wanted to do was be a doctor. He was firstborn, and it was like this huge family-responsibility thing, you know? I don't think he even tried to fight it, and I've seen what it's done to him. Well, I made up my mind a long time ago that it wasn't going to happen to me, even if I am firstborn of the firstborn, and he just can't accept that."

"I see. It's just a shame that you can't avoid the issue or something."

Adam chuckled. "Avoid the issue with Jake Fortune? That'll be the day."

Laura bit her lip. "It's none of my business, anyway. I have this thing about family, that's all. You know how it is, when you don't have something that everyone else does, it seems like the most important thing in the world to have."

Adam nodded. "My grandmother was like that. She was raised in an orphanage back before the Second World War."

"They don't call them orphanages anymore," Laura said slowly. "They call them group homes or halfway houses, but they're still the last stop for a kid with no one and no place to go to."

Adam seemed to be choosing his words carefully. "Isn't there any family?"

She shook her head. "Nope. Both of my parents were only children. My grandparents were already gone when I was born. My dad died in some kind of farming accident when I was just a baby, and my mother..." She was surprised how difficult it was to broach the subject. "Well, we never knew if she took too many pills by accident or on purpose. Anyway, I was five then.''

"Wendy's age," Adam mused solemnly.

"Just about."

"And you went to one of those group homes?" he asked.

"Not at first." She sighed. "I was shuttled around from one foster home to another for so long I've forgotten how many there were. I lived in a group home during my early teens, then I applied at this Catholic boarding school for state wards, and I was accepted, because my grades were pretty good, and that's where I actually met Sister Agnes."

"She was special to you," Adam surmised.

"Yes, she was."

"So do you still keep in touch?" he asked.

Pain clouded her eyes. "Sister Agnes died when I was a senior. She was very old, and—" She broke off, then said, too briskly, "Well, I'd better check on the kids."

"Oh. Yeah, and I better get going." He got up again, saying, "I've got research to do."

She wanted to ask what kind of research, but she didn't. They'd talked long enough, and she'd already told him more than she intended to. She couldn't remember the last time she'd mentioned her mother's death to anyone. She didn't like to think about it, because the truth was that, despite all the counseling and the self-help books and Sister Agnes's thoughtful instruction, she still couldn't shake the feeling that she had mattered so little that her own mother had checked out without a second thought. She got up and followed Adam into the den to find the kids lolling in front of the morning cartoons in their pajamas.

"I'm going, kids," Adam announced, reaching for the briefcase he'd left on the coffee table earlier. "Be good for Laura. See you later." They didn't so much as glance in his direction, but he seemed to find nothing amiss as he turned away. "There's a card with my office number pinned next to the telephone in the kitchen," he told Laura, "and my mobile phone number's written on the back of it in case of emergencies."

"We'll be fine," Laura assured him.

He nodded briskly. "Be careful on the roads."

"I promise."

"See you for dinner." He walked away with a wave of his hand.

Laura watched him move into the hallway, then studied the kids sprawled on the floor in front of the television. Shouldn't there be goodbye kisses and words of affection between a parent and children taking their leave of one another? If she was lucky enough to have children of her own someday, she'd never leave them without hugs and kisses and reassuring words, not even for a single day. It bothered her that this family seemed to take one another so much for granted. Something wasn't right about it. She walked over to the sofa and sat down, close to where Wendy lay against it. "Dad's gone," she said lightly.

Wendy shrugged. "He's always gone." Something in the way she said it made a chill of unease sweep over Laura. Well, it wasn't any of her business. And yet . . . She shook her head, got up again and walked into the kitchen, calling over her shoulder, "I'm going to clean up after breakfast, kids, then we have to get dressed and take Wendy to school. That means the TV has to be shut off."

There were whines and grumbles about that, but they ceased as soon as she left the room. Laura smiled to herself. The Fortune children weren't ones to waste their energy complaining when no one was around to pay attention. The thought that followed, however, was one to give even the most formidable nanny pause. No, the Fortune kids wouldn't waste energy complaining; they'd much rather be dreaming up mischief.

Laura sighed. Ten minutes late already, and she didn't even have them in the car yet! As if reading her thoughts, Ryan wiggled out of her grasp at the last instant, bounced off the edge of the bench seat, shoved her aside, kicking her shin in the process, and ran shouting gleefully down the drive. Two pairs of nylon stockings, the thick black leggings that she wore over them, a pair of wool socks and the tops of her tall insulated boots cushioned the blow, but

Laura groaned and laid her forehead against the edge of the car door anyway. Robbie giggled inside the car, alerting Laura to his own escape from his car seat, but it was Wendy at whom she leveled her gaze after he shoved by her and ran to join his brother. Sitting backward in the front seat, her hand clapped over her own grinning mouth, she was the picture of innocence, but Laura knew better.

"I'll have to write you a note for being late, Wendy," she said apologetically. "Do you want to know what it's going to say? It's going to say that you and your brothers misbehaved so badly that I couldn't do my job. I guess I'm not a very good nanny, after all."

Wendy blinked, putting all that together. "Well, when I'm very late, Godiva just always says I might as well not even go, and she lets me stay home...to help with the boys."

Laura seemed to consider that. "Hmm...well, I did promise your father that I'd do some shopping this morning. If—if I could just get the boys into the car..." It was pretty sneaky, but she figured a dose of her own medicine was just what Miss Wendy needed at this point.

Convinced that she'd won, Wendy opened her car door and awkwardly climbed down to the garage floor. She walked to the edge of the drive, put her chubby fists to her hips, stomped a foot and bawled, "Cut it out, you guys, and get back in the car!"

The little miscreants actually stopped in their tracks and looked at their sister, their faces a study in puzzled surprise. Wendy smiled the smile of the supremely victorious. "Get in the car," she said again. "Laura's taking us shopping."

The boys looked at each other, then at Wendy, before breaking out in whoops that froze on the cold morning air. Making sounds like screeching tires, they tore up the drive and practically knocked Laura down getting inside. With a wealth of other sound effects, they both climbed into their seats and waited to be buckled in. Laura obliged, her lips pursed against a secretive smile.

Fifteen minutes later, they pulled up in front of Wendy's school. Wendy turned a mutinous face on Laura, but Laura shook her head. "I never said you didn't have to go to school," she pointed out.

Wendy's bottom lip poked out. "You t-tricked me," she accused.

"Yes, I did," Laura admitted smoothly. "It feels bad when somebody you trust, somebody you care about, tricks you, doesn't it?"

Wendy merely narrowed her eyes.

"I know you put the boys up to misbehaving this morning," Laura told her softly, "so you'd be late for school, so late you wouldn't even have to go, but that won't work with me, Wendy. All it does is make my heart hurt because it's so disappointed that you would try to trick me and make my job so difficult."

Wendy abruptly burst into sobs. "I just wanted to stay home with you and the boys!"

Laura nodded in understanding. "Yes, I know, but it's not good for you to miss school, Wendy. My job is to take care of you and your brothers. How can I look your father in the eye and tell him that he can trust me to take care of you if I don't see to it that you do what is best for you? How can I even call myself your friend if I let you do things that are going to hurt you in the long run?"

"I don't knooow!" Wendy wailed.

"Well, I do know," Laura said evenly. "That's what makes me the adult here, Wendy. That's why *I* make the decisions. Well, some of them. Your father makes most of them. The point is, school is important, and even if you aren't big enough to know that, you still have to go. I wouldn't be doing my job if I let you stay home any time you felt like it, and if I can't do this job the way I should, well, then I'll just have to find something else to do. Now I'm going to make you a promise."

"A promise?" Wendy echoed, wiping her eyes. "What kind of promise?"

"We'll do something fun this afternoon when you get home," Laura said. "Something special."

"Something special?" Wendy repeated. "Like what?"

"Well ... How about if we make a snowman in the front yard? No, wait! A snow castle! We'll build a snow castle in the front yard! How would that be?"

"A castle? Really?"

"Sure, why not? As long as it's dry out and we bundle up real warm, we can build anything we want in the snow!"

"Okay!" Wendy said, smiling. "Oh, boy! Godiva wouldn't ever let us play in the snow! She said we'd catch new money and die!"

Laura laughed. "We won't let anybody catch pneumonia, I promise. Now, you'd better go inside. Can you find your room by yourself?"

Wendy nodded eagerly. "Uh-huh." She opened her door. Laura leaned over and released her belt. "Bye!" Wendy said, swiveling in her seat to get her feet outside.

Laura suddenly thought of that sterile leave-taking between Adam and his children earlier that morning, and she found that she couldn't let Wendy go without some gesture of affection. "Wait!" Wendy turned back, and Laura wrapped her arms around the girl's small body. She gave Wendy a brief hug and kissed her silky temple. "Bye, sweetheart. See you later."

Wendy's golden eyes glowed happily. "Don't do no other job, Laura," she whispered. "Stay with us."

Hot tears pricked Laura's eyes. She wanted to promise this little girl forever, but she knew that it wasn't in her power to do so. Sooner or later, she'd have to go. If Doyal should find her here ... She shuddered at the thought of what he could do to this already troubled family. She couldn't let that happen, and going away before he found her was the only way she could protect them. But she couldn't tell this little girl that. She couldn't tell anyone. She smiled and brushed the rusty brown hair from Wendy's eyes. "We'll see. Go on now."

Wendy wiggled out of the car, grabbed her backpack from the floorboards, then slammed the door. Without looking back, she ran up the walk and into the building. A pleasant-looking woman in a heavy skirt and sweater stepped outside to wave Laura on. Laura eased the car away from the curb. How long? she wondered. How long before she had to leave them all?

Laura crawled on her hands and knees through the narrow opening, scrunched her body into the tiny space left over by the other three occupying the small chamber and smiled broadly.

"It's warmer than I'd have thought."

Wendy giggled. "Snow isn't warm!"

"No, of course it isn't, but a snow castle is... sort of."

"Oh, I love my snow castle!" Wendy sighed.

Robbie punched her in the arm. "It isn't yours! It's *all* of us's. Isn't it, Laura?"

"Yes, but you mustn't hit your sister. Hitting isn't acceptable behavior. Make apology please."

Robbie had "made apology" several times already that day, and he screwed up his face at the effort it took to make another. "Sor-ry."

Wendy patted him companionably on the head. "That's all right, Robbie. It didn't hurt, anyway. Tomorrow," she said to Laura, "can we play knights and princess in our castle?"

Laura laughed. "If the weather's clear, but we'll have to be very well bundled up knights and princess. Okay?"

"Okay."

They sat hunched together on a piece of cardboard on the cold ground. Laura had drawn planks on it to represent a wooden floor. She shivered, knowing they would have to go into the house soon, but wanting to give them as long as possible. With luck, Adam would be home before they had to go in and would be able to look over their handiwork and make appropriate noises of praise. At least she hoped he would. She decided to gauge the likelihood. "Won't Daddy be impressed with our snow castle?" she asked no one in particular.

Robbie and Ryan looked at Wendy, who shrugged. "Dunno. He might not notice."

"Well, sure he'll notice." How could he not notice an eight-foot-tall snow sculpture in his front yard? "I bet he'll be sorry that he wasn't here to help us."

Wendy shook her head. "No, he won't."

"No, he won't," Ryan echoed.

Laura swallowed a lump in her throat and put on a smile. "Why, sure he will. Um, h-hasn't he ever . . . played in the snow with you?"

Wendy dropped her gaze. "Daddies don't play," she said. "'Sides, he wasn't never here for snow before."

"Never here for snow?" Laura mumbled. "I don't understand."

"He didn't never live with us," Wendy said, "until Mommy went away."

"No?" Laura tried to bite back the question, but it tumbled out before she could. "Were they divorced?"

They were clearly confused by the question, looking to one another for clarification. Finally Robbie threw up his arms and said, "No! Daddy, he lived with the army!"

"The army? You mean, he was a soldier?"

"Yes, with the awmy!" Ryan said, clearly exasperated with her lack of understanding.

Well, that explained the haircut and his superb physical condition. But it didn't explain why he'd never spent a winter with his own children. She looked to Wendy for answers. "Why didn't you all go with him?" Wendy merely shrugged. Laura tried again. "Well, I'm certain he came home often. I mean, he wouldn't have missed your birthdays or the holidays . . . would he?"

"Daddy was home Chwistmas!" Ryan said, adding with relish, "he and Gwandpa Jake got in a fight!"

A fight. At Christmastime. Laura gulped. "That's too bad," she murmured, "but it was just one Christmas in many." She looked at Wendy. "Wasn't it?"

That shrug again. "I don't know."

She didn't know. She didn't remember whether her father had spent other Christmases with her. What was wrong with that man? Laura blinked to cool hot eyes, and tried to put the best face on the situation. "Well, he's here now, and

I'm sure that he spends every minute with you that he can." Wendy made no reply, but her little face was simmering with suppressed anger. *Oh, Adam,* Laura thought, *what are you doing to your children?*

Ryan said, "I'm cold!"

Laura snapped out of her reverie. "I bet a cup of cocoa would warm you up, wouldn't it?"

"Yeah! Cocoa! Cocoa! Cocoa!"

Laura flipped over and led the way out of the snow structure. The temperature had dropped in direct proportion with the descent of the sun, which had now dipped beneath the horizon. Adam's four-wheel-drive was nowhere to be seen. Laura swung a shivering Ryan up onto her hip, then took Robbie and Wendy each by a hand. Together they went into the house, stopping in the entry to let tingling body parts adjust to the sudden warmth and divest themselves of a whole closetful of outer garments. The next stop was the big bathroom, where everyone washed up. Then it was on to the den for the kids, while Laura went into the kitchen.

"Hi," she said to Beverly, who was stirring a pot at the stove and flashed her a smile over her shoulder. "Is that cocoa ready?"

"It is, but so is dinner."

"Smells great. What is it?"

"Stew. Should I serve it up now?"

Laura shook her head. "We'll wait on Mr. Fortune."

Beverly shot her an odd look. "Oh, I forgot. He called a little while ago. He said not to wait for him. Something came up."

Laura's spirits plummeted, but it wouldn't do to let the children see that she was upset. She closed her eyes and made herself think. "We'll have the cocoa first, anyway," she decided. "Why don't you put the stew pot in the oven to keep warm, and go on home? We'll serve ourselves when we're ready."

Beverly was untying her apron strings before Laura finished speaking. "Well, if you're certain."

Laura nodded. "Absolutely." The cook was gone before Laura got the cocoa poured into cups.

Laura put the cups on a tray, sprinkled them with small marshmallows and carried them to the door, where she put a determined smile on her face. No one should know that inside she was grieving, grieving for the father she'd never known, grieving for what Adam's children should but did not have, grieving and beginning to get angry.

Adam walked tiredly down the hall and into the kitchen. Beverly had promised to leave him some dinner in the oven. Not that he was hungry, really. He'd eaten earlier, with an old friend from high school and his wife, but it was politic not to offend the household help, especially when one depended upon that help for survival. He swallowed a few bites of the stew at the kitchen sink, then put the rest down the garbage disposal and rinsed out the bowl. It was good stew, but he just wasn't hungry. He went to the cabinet, took down a bottle of brandy and poured a measure into a small snifter, which he warmed with his hands as he walked into the den.

Laura was sitting on the sofa, her legs folded beneath her, poring over the family photo albums. Adam felt a quickening that he could only have called interest. "Hello," he said, stopping in the middle of the floor to sip his brandy. She was amazingly attractive, her long blond hair swept onto a shoulder bared by the droop of the wide collar of her pale yellow nubbly-knit sweater. The slender length of her legs was not diminished either by her position or by the thick black leggings she wore. Likewise, heavy wool socks in no way disguised the delicate turn of her ankles or the petite perfection of her feet. Her graceful hands abandoned the book to her lap. She sat upright and folded long arms beneath breasts almost too ample for her slender frame. When she turned her face up to him, his first thought was that not even anger could make her seem less than pretty. Anger. The realization was secondary, but correct nonetheless.

She dropped her gaze once more to the pair of photo albums overlapping on her thighs. "You aren't in any of the pictures," she said. Her oddly husky voice took on a hint of challenge. "Have you noticed that you aren't in any of the pictures?"

He didn't know what she was talking about, or why it affected him as it did. He only knew that something clutched at his heart, sending rills of panic surging through him. Instinctively he stepped into the firm, indifferent role that had served him so well in the military. "I don't recall giving you permission to go through my family keepsakes."

The gaze she jerked up at him was first wide with shock, then lax with contrition, and finally narrow with hurt. She closed the books gently, the glossy gold-embossed navy blue one first, then the ragged hemp-colored one. "My apologies," she muttered softly, sliding the books onto the coffee table. "I didn't think you'd mind." She got swiftly to her feet and weaved her way past the table, a displaced footstool and him. He couldn't help noticing that, though her grace rivaled that of a ballet dancer, she managed to stub her toe twice.

His indifference fled, and he didn't have time to question why. He only knew that he didn't want her to go, and his body reacted to that desire. Stepping back and to the side and throwing out an arm, he managed to block her path and catch her against him at the same time.

"I, um, I'm sorry. I didn't mean to bark. It . . . it's been a long day."

She bowed her head, standing very still in the curve of his arm. "Yes, I know." The gaze she lifted to him this time glittered with accusation. "They waited until after nine o'clock."

They? His children, of course, though why they would bother to wait up for him, of all people, was pure mystery. Most of the time, they ignored everything about him, including his commands. He dropped his arm, put his head back and swallowed his brandy in one hard gulp that burned all the way down and hit his belly with the force of a fist. He inhaled cooling air through his mouth, bit down on the fiery aftertaste and sighed with satisfaction. He immediately felt better. "Suppose you tell me what they wanted," he said smoothly, loosening his tie with one hand. Suddenly her anger was back. It leaped like bolts of clear blue lightning in bright green eyes.

"They wanted their father!" she told him sharply. "We built a snow castle in the front yard today, and they wanted to be told what an amazing structure they'd made, what brilliant children they are."

"A snow castle," he repeated dully. He hadn't noticed. He stepped over to his chair and sank down upon it, all at once weary beyond bearing. "I'll tell them in the morning," he said, pressing the brandy snifter to the ache beginning between his eyes.

Laura shook her head slowly from side to side, but he was too tried to ask what it was all about. This time, when she muttered, "Good night," and stalked away, he let her go.

After a while, the pounding in his head seemed to lessen, and he sat forward, trying to work up the energy to get up and go to bed. His gaze fell on the photo albums on the table. Leaning far forward, he could just reach them. He pulled them into his lap, stacking one on top of the other. He ran a hand over the ragged cover of the first and wondered again why his grandmother had left him this shabby piece of memorabilia in her will. You could never tell about Kate. Her mind had seemed to work in several arenas at once, weighing seemingly unrelated matters and reaching often amazing conclusions. He missed her. He was surprised at how much he could miss her after all those years away in the military.

*What were you doing, Kate, flying off to the Amazon alone, leaving your family to fend for themselves?* He had the lowering feeling that he wasn't doing too well on that score himself. After eighteen months, his children seemed hardly to know him, and he was still drifting, still looking for an anchor.

Slowly he opened the cover of the photo album and looked once more upon his parents' wedding picture. They had been the perfect couple, the heir apparent and the unspoiled beauty. It was difficult to think of them apart now, despite the reality of their separation, and yet, when he thought of home and his youth, he thought of his mother and her apologetic explanations for his father's continual absence.

"He has the whole weight of the family business on his shoulders," she would tell him. "So many are dependent on him. He's doing the best he can."

He thumbed through the photos, watching himself grow from infant to toddler to mischief-maker to rebel to man. Here were the hallmarks of his life—first steps, birthday parties, eighth-grade graduation, the football championship, hockey play-offs, proms. In these pictures the family grew, too, from first and only son, to Caroline, then Natalie, and finally the twins, in precise two-year intervals.

Laura was wrong. He was in nearly every one of these pictures. The only person missing here was, as always, his father. Who did that woman think she was, *scolding* him for not coming home in time to compliment his kids on a silly snow castle? He came home, didn't he? When they needed him, he was here, wasn't he? He was doing his level best, and that ought to count for something. Shouldn't it? He pushed the photo albums back onto the table and set the brandy snifter on top of them. Then he got to his feet and dragged himself to his bed. He never even opened the second album, the pictorial journal—navy blue, leather-bound, embossed in gold—so painstakingly put together by his late wife, the one that chronicled the years of his own young family's lives—the one from which he *was* missing.

# Four

She expected him to shout at her, or at least to tell her to mind her own business. Instead, he came in to breakfast all smiles. His only reference to the evening before was a pointed glance in her direction before he heaped lavish praise on the snow castle on his front lawn. To Laura's dismay, his children merely traded looks among themselves before the twins followed Wendy's lead and hunched over their cereal bowls in damning silence. An obviously crestfallen Adam sat at the table and erected the dreaded newspaper barrier before him. Laura got up and poured him a cup of coffee, then pulled a toasted English muffin and a bowl of creamed wheat from the oven to set before him. He smiled distractedly, murmured his thanks, and went back to his paper. The children finished their breakfast and were herded from the room by Laura. She cast a last wistful look at Adam, shook her head in frustration and followed her charges through the door. He left before she could get the children's clothing laid out and return to him.

That became the pattern for mornings in the Fortune household. Adam was always last to the table. He and the children paid only nominal attention to one another, and despite Laura's best efforts, he always left without saying goodbye. His saving grace was that he regularly came home early to share dinner with his children, and with Laura's calm direction, the family had begun to evolve their own good-night ritual.

It wasn't much to brag about initially. She merely marched the children past him, one by one, for a solemn good-night. Before long, however, he was leaning forward to give clumsy pats on the shoulder, and the children,

Wendy first, were tentatively reaching out to him for more, and now they were actually hugging. Laura eagerly awaited the evening when one or the other of them would pucker up and the kissing would begin. It would only be a small step on a long road to wellness and normalcy for this family, but Laura felt that it would be a very important step.

Sometimes she told herself that if she could only stay until she saw that first good-night kiss between father and child, she would be content, but the truth was that she was more content at the moment than she had been in a very, very long time—except for those instances of sheer terror when she thought about what would happen if Doyal found her here. She never intended to actually contemplate such hideous thoughts, but on occasion they took her unawares.

Late at night, while she lay in her bed and pondered the day to come, plotting games and treats and subtle teachings, Doyal would flash into her head, his ruggedly handsome face smiling, then sneering, and finally bearing down on her with rage distorting every feature. She would feel his hands around her throat and know that she was going to die, and then, in her mind's eye, she would see Wendy or one of the boys charge at him, tiny fists flailing. She would sit up straight and shake herself out of it before she could form that last grotesque picture, but it was always there in the back of her mind, the specter of a small body collapsed in trauma. She couldn't let that happen. She wouldn't let that happen. She couldn't just walk out and leave Adam and the children in the lurch, but she had to leave before Doyal found her. She *would* leave before Doyal found her. She comforted herself with that thought. It became her litany, her mantra. She would go before it was too late—just not yet.

The terror was never far below the surface, however. She would wake in the black hours of morning, drenched in sweat and trembling with fear and disgust, having witnessed again the daming scene that had confirmed Doyal's guilt. She could almost laugh, had she not feared that hysteria would overwhelm bitterness as she thought of how she'd followed Doyal that day over seven months ago in a jealous pique, believing that he was seeing another woman, only to find that his destination was a run-down house on the rough side of town. She had watched in horror, concealed by a Dumpster and a tree, as a wide spectrum of humanity breezed in and stumbled out of that old house. Some of them hadn't come out for hours. Some of them had come out right away, the house barely behind them before they were gobbling their pills, snorting their powders or jabbing needles into their veins. Most of them had been so desperate that they ignored the gun brandished by Doyal's "friend" Calvin, whom Laura now realized was nothing more than an armed goon. She had stumbled away from that scene to vomit, knowing now that the money showered so generously on her by her first serious boyfriend was not the result of his enigmatic investments in the stock market, but of the drug trade that crippled whole neighborhoods and shattered so many lives.

Her mistake had been in confronting him. When she demanded to know how he could live with himself, he had laughed at her naiveté. Still, she had not understood her situation until she proceeded with the grand exit she had planned. He had grabbed her and vowed that she was going nowhere. He was not through with her, he had said, and when he was, he would make sure that she could never tell what she knew about him and his "business." Angry and outraged, she had demanded her release, and he had beaten her senseless. Afterward, he had sworn that she would never be free of him. No one, not even the police, could protect her, for if she dared implicate him, he vowed that both he and Calvin would swear that she, too, was involved.

Going to the police seemed impossible; yet she had known that the worse thing she could do was to stay. Fleeing might result in instant death at any unguarded moment, but staying would have meant dying by inches. She had chosen the former. It had taken three weeks of hell, and another, even worse beating, before she was able to slip away. He had assumed that she was too badly injured to run and briefly left her unattended. She had literally crawled out the window and down the ivy lattice of their second-story apartment with nothing more than the clothes on her back and a wallet with less than a hundred dollars in it.

She had been running ever since, from city to city, town to town, state to state, for more than six months. Twice he'd nearly caught her—the last time over five months ago—but in all her dreaming, asleep and awake, she had never dared to entertain the fantasy that he might have given up, that he wouldn't come for her. The guarantee that he would come, the certainty that she must go before that could happen, was all that gave her hope of seeing tomorrow. But beyond the next day she dared not look with more than longing.

That was exactly what she was doing, looking at the future and longing for a place in it, when Adam's voice took her completely unawares.

"Penny for your thoughts."

She nearly leaped up onto the kitchen counter. Her heart was beating wildly, even as she placed the voice and turned to face him. It was late. The children were in bed. The evening news was over, and she had delayed turning in herself only long enough to make a hot cup of cocoa to sip on her way. Adam had disappeared into other parts of the house as soon as the children went to their beds, saying that he had some material to read before an appointment the next day. That was the first thing that came to mind.

"You finished your reading," she said lightly, ashamed of her reaction, her fear, of even having known a man like Doyal Moody.

Adam rubbed his hand over his head. "Not really. I just got incredibly bored with it. I don't think insurance is for me."

"No? Well, you'll find something," she told him offhandedly.

He shook his head, his golden eyes dull with worry. "I don't know. I..."

She could tell he wanted to talk, and the idea that he had sought her out to do so was flattering in a way she hadn't expected. She took another cup from the cabinet and reached for the cocoa mix. "Sit down. I'll make you a cup."

He nodded with poorly disguised relief and pulled out a chair at the kitchen table. She joined him a minute later, and they sat in companionable silence for a bit, sipping and stirring cocoa. Finally she thought to ask, "What is it you want to do, Adam? Have you given it any thought?"

It was as if she'd struck at the root of his frustration. He pushed his cup away and ran his hands over his hair, sighing deeply. "I don't know. I feel like I'm stumbling around in the dark, trying one door after another, but none will open for me! I've never known anything but the military. Without that, I don't quite know who I am."

Laura understood how he felt. She said, "It must have been difficult to give up your career."

He folded his arms and perched his chin on them. "It's so blessedly simple in the army. Here is the day's objective. Here are the rules. You've had your training. You know your role. Now go and do it." He turned his face down, sucked in a deep breath and straightened, leaning back in his chair. "These days, I know my objective, but that's where it ends. There are no rules, and no training can prepare you for a role without definition. I'm lost! I'm trapped in the dark, where the only door I know will open for me is the one that I came through, but I can't go back."

Laura trailed a finger around the rim of her cup, choosing her words carefully. "It's not the children's fault that they need you, Adam."

He closed his eyes, but not quickly enough to hide the flash of anger in them. "I know that. Don't you think I know that? It's just— If only Diana hadn't been in that awful accident!"

Laura clamped a hand over his wrist, ignoring the intense awareness that she seemed always to feel in his presence. "Adam, don't you see that your children have always needed you? That didn't change when Diana died. You just couldn't ignore it any longer."

"It wasn't all me, you know!" he lashed out. "That was the way Diana wanted it." He pulled free and laid his hands palms up on the tabletop, beseeching her for understanding. "At first, she went wherever I was sent, but she never liked that life-style. She hated military housing. Then, when Wendy was about a year old, I was called into action, so I brought Diana and the baby here to my family, and she *liked* being a Fortune." He laughed mirthlessly. "I know the name means nothing to you, but you're a minority of one in that regard."

"I'm not dense," Laura told him defensively. "I know now who the Fortunes are. I just don't see what that had to do with it."

His smile was cold and self-deprecating. "To Diana," he said softly, "being a Fortune became more important than being my wife. When my tour was over, she informed me that she was staying here. I'd drawn another overseas assignment, and I knew how she hated that, so I agreed, thinking that if I got the overseas duty out of the way, she and Wendy would join me when I came stateside. But she wasn't interested in any place but here. She said that this was where Fortunes belonged, and this was where she meant to be. Then the boys came along, and she built this house, and every time I mentioned taking them with me, she would say that their home was here, with the family. I finally realized that she had no intention of *ever* living anywhere else." He shrugged. "I considered divorce, actually, but by that time our lives were so separate that there didn't seem any point in it. So I came when I could, and if Diana was ever unhappy with the arrangement, she never let on. In fact, I think the distance was all that kept the marriage intact. If you want to know the truth, by the end of every leave we were always carping and snapping at one another over every little thing." He rubbed his hands over his face. "I don't know...maybe if I'd given it up sooner...but she never asked that of me. Not once."

Laura wasn't aware of having reached out to him again, but somehow her hand wound up in his, and they were both looking at it, staring as if neither of them had ever seen two hands clasped together on a tabletop before. She had to search for her voice, and when she found it, it was nothing more than a husky shadow of itself. "Adam, I didn't know.

B-but however it happened, your children have missed you terribly."

He chuckled. It was not a happy sound. "They miss their mother, Laura. Quite frankly, I think you fill that need a lot better than I do. Undoubtedly they're more fond of *you* than they are of me."

"It's not the same thing at all!"

"Isn't it?" he asked softly. "Laura, I love my children, but I'm not very good with them."

"You can be!"

He was shaking his head before the words were out. "Not like you. I know, I've tried." Then: "If I thought you would stay with them..."

"No!" She pushed back, yanked free and came to her feet. Didn't he understand that she could not stay? No, of course he didn't. How could he? And she couldn't make him understand without telling him the truth and endangering him and the children more than she already had. She had no choice but to lie. "I—I told you, I want to go back to school. I've waited so long for my chance, and... Well, if you want to know the t-truth, I've been feeling a bit...itchy-footed." She had to turn away to say the rest of it. "I'm used to going from pillar to post as the mood moves me. I've—I've hardly spent two weeks in the same place in...so long." She couldn't go on without risking that her voice would break.

"Well," he said bitterly, "far be it from me to point out that three innocent little children are—" He stopped abruptly. "No." The chair scraped as he got to his feet, and then he was there at her back, his hands hovering over her shoulders. "That wasn't fair," he said in a near whisper. "They're my children, my responsibility, and I'm the one who has... I *want* to take care of them, but I don't know how, and you're so very good with them." He sighed. "Maybe it's just that I'm frustrated because I can't seem to find anything to *do*. I need a job, damn it, a business, a career!"

She turned slowly, careful to step back and keep a safe distance between them. "You'll find something," she assured him, "and the kids will come to trust you. It'll all be worth it. You'll see. They're great kids."

"They're scamps," he said bluntly, grinning. "But they're my scamps."

She nodded. He was exactly right. He was their father, and she couldn't stay, no matter how much she might want to. "You'll do fine together," she said, putting on a bright face. "They just have to see that you aren't going to leave them again, and they need to know that you love them. They need to be reassured about that as often as you can."

He backed away, lifting a hand to the back of his neck. "I'm not very good at that sort of thing," he said, "but I'll do my best."

She chanced one look into those golden eyes. "I'm sure you'll do fine."

He nodded briskly and looked away. "You, ah, will stay until I can find a replacement, won't you?"

"Oh." A replacement. Somehow she hadn't expected that. She swallowed down a lump in her throat. "Of—of course." She tried to sound light and teasing. "I didn't mean that I was ready to walk out the door, you know."

He nodded and slipped his hands into his pockets. "Sure. Good. I'll...start to look. It's, um, liable to take some time, though."

"Right. Well ... whatever."

He backed away. "I'm tired. I think I'll go on to bed."

"Me too."

Yet neither of them moved for a very long moment. Then he slowly leaned forward and kissed her lightly on the cheek. It felt right and friendly and comforting—until she looked up into those golden brown eyes.

She looked away again as quickly as possible, but she had already seen enough to wonder whether there might be another reason he didn't want her to go, a personal reason. She had seen enough tangled emotion to begin thinking that maybe there was another reason to want to stay, which meant that she had seen ... too much.

* * *

She jerked awake, her pounding heart and a sense of terror telling her that something was very wrong. She lay in the dark, warm beneath the comforters piled on her bed, but still able to feel the intense cold lurking beyond the dark confines of her room. Was it the storm? The evening news had warned of the possibility of a late, intense blizzard in the next few days. It was hard to imagine a cold more intense than what she had already experienced, but she'd heard talk of subarctic temperatures and raging snowstorms since coming to Minnesota. She lay in the stillness, trying to hear winds whistling beyond her heavily insulated window. She heard only the swish of fabric and the nearly imperceptible slide of footsteps over carpet. Her soft bed felt suddenly chilled. She threw back the covers and leaped out of the bed. Ignoring her cheap quilted bathrobe, she hurried across the room in nothing more than a big, loose T-shirt that skimmed her thighs and the heavy wool socks she'd worn to keep her feet warm in bed.

Quietly she cracked open the door of her room and peered down the hall. Across and down the hall a bit, the door to Adam's room was tightly shut, and no thread of light showed beneath it. Was it one of the children, then? She slipped out into the hallway. A tiny orange light burned low on one wall. It illuminated a space perhaps three feet across to about the height of her knees, enough for one of the children to make his or her way to Adam's room, not enough to let her see who or what waited beyond it. Laura gulped and began moving slowly and silently forward, the fingertips of her right hand trailing along the wall at shoulder height. The door to the boys' room swung silently inward when her fingers gently pressed. In the faint glow of another night-light, Laura saw that their small beds were empty. Had they awakened her, or had they, too, been awakened?

She moved swiftly past the remaining rooms at that end of the hall, pausing only when she reached the foyer and felt a wave of intense, unusual cold, as if someone had recently opened the front door. Someone from the outside? Doyal!

The thought engendered terror that was not at all abated by the furtive sounds of movement farther down the hall. Oh, God, where were the boys?

She ran on eerily silent feet. As she passed the dining room, she snatched up the heavy crystal wine decanter that sat empty on the end of the buffet, its etched facets glowing dully in the murky light emanating from the den. Raising the decanter high over her head with both hands, she rounded the corner and slid to a teetering halt. A ghostly light flowed from the den, its gray-blue haze cut by a partial shadow upon the floor, a shadow cast by a figure standing to one side of the open doorway *inside* the room. Across the huge, dim expanse of the den, Laura saw two little boys lying in front of the television on their bellies, their legs bent at the knees, bootied feet waving in the air, chins propped on plump hands suspended above elbows dug into the plush carpet. They whispered and giggled, obviously enjoying this illicit moment of forbidden TV, while the silent figure by the door watched and waited.

Laura rushed forward. The distance was but steps, and yet in the brief flash of time that it took to cross it she wondered frantically what she would tell Adam when he found Doyal Moody with his head bashed in on his den floor. Worse, what if she failed? What if Doyal, in all his evil, heard or saw her coming and escaped? What would he do to those precious little boys then? She had no doubt about what he would do to her.

It was with crushing dismay, then, that she felt her quarry step sideways, twist slightly and throw out both arms just as she swung the decanter down. The decanter thumped uselessly to the floor and a hand slapped over her mouth. Suddenly she was being propelled backward and shoved up against the wall, a firm, hard body pinning her in place. She stared, wild-eyed, up into the face of Adam Fortune.

This was an Adam she did not know, fierce, menacing, silently expert at quelling her senseless attack. This was the soldier Adam had trained to be. This was an efficient killer. And yet the fear that had clutched at her since the moment she had awakened abruptly drained away. Limp with relief, she sagged against the wall, confident that he would hold her up.

"Thank God!" she whispered, tears welling in her eyes.

Some of the fierceness left Adam's face, and he looked to the boys, twisting his neck and canting his head backward. Laura followed his lead, and found the boys relatively undisturbed. Ryan had rolled up into a sitting position and was casting a glance at the door, but he obviously could not see into the hallway, and the lure of late-night television was just too delicious to be ignored. Within heartbeats, his whole attention was focused once more on the screen.

Adam backed away slightly, his gaze once more trained on her face. He quirked an eyebrow upward in silent interrogation, grasped her by both shoulders and propelled her around the corner and down the hallway. Just short of the foyer, he shoved her up against the wall again and held her there with a hand splayed flat against her breastbone.

"You damned near cracked open my skull!" The steel beneath the words belied the softness of his tone.

"I—I thought you were an intruder!"

His finely honed senses zeroed in on that word. "Intruder?"

She quickly corrected herself. "A—a burglar! I was afraid if the boys saw you...*him,* I mean...h-he might hurt them."

Adam shook his head in disbelief. His hand left her chest to skim over his hair. Even as she babbled her explanation, Laura noted in some perverse part of her mind that he wore soft gray sweat pants and a white short-sleeved T-shirt that molded almost lovingly to the firm contours of his muscled chest and upper arms. "Something woke me up—a sound in the hallway. Your door was closed. The light was off. B-but the boys weren't in their beds, and—and someone had opened the front door!"

"That was me, checking to be sure they hadn't slipped out to play in the snow. It wouldn't have been the first time."

"Well, how was I to know that?"

"You might have asked."

"I didn't think of that, and when I saw your shadow...
The boys were just laying there, and I thought, if they see
him, he'll h-hurt them!"

"So you grabbed the wine decanter and tried to bash in
my skull," he said wryly. He shook his head again, a slow
grin curving his mouth. "This is St. Cloud, Minnesota,
Laura." He leaned a forearm against the wall, his body
swaying close to hers. "We don't have 'intruders' much in
these parts, you know."

She was intensely aware of her own body, of the silk
panties she wore beneath her oversize T-shirt, the hugging
knit of her socks. She should have been cold, but she was
not, and her lungs clamored for oxygen that she couldn't
seem to provide them. "Th-that never occurred to me," she
gasped. "Burglars are all too common where I come from."

"And where," he said, fingering a strand of her hair, "is
that, exactly?"

It wasn't the first time he'd asked, but it was the first time
she wasn't able to dissemble. She simply couldn't think
quickly enough to keep the truth from tumbling out.
"Denver."

"Ah." He curled a finger beneath her chin and lifted,
tilting her head back and bringing her face close. "You
know, Laura, I'm very pleased that you're so protective of
my children that you'd take on a burglar with nothing more
than a wine decanter, but next time, you might just knock
on my door first. Better yet, you could just open it and come
on in. If I should be there but I'm not, you can safely assume that I have the matter under control. If I'm there...
Well, either way, I have a lot more experience at subduing
dangerous 'intruders' than you do. Agreed?"

She nodded, but when she dropped her gaze, he lifted her
chin again, and this time his hand stayed to caress the curve
of her throat. For some reason, all she could see was his
mouth, and she swallowed, trying desperately to shift her
gaze. "We..." She had to close her eyes to think logically.
"We should get the boys back into bed."

He brushed his thumb across her mouth. "Yes." Then his
mouth covered hers, gently at first, his lips parting and

moving subtly, drawing her into the kiss with aching sweetness. She found herself leaning into him, her head sliding to one side. His mouth slanted across hers, and he pulled her away from the wall, wrapping his strong arms around her, holding her against his body. She felt softness, softness in his lips, in the cotton and fleece of his clothing, and beneath that softness the hardness of muscle and desire, strong male desire. Suddenly her woman's body was aware of every hard inch of him. Her arms convulsed, pulling tighter, breasts swelling against his chest, pelvis rocking forward. If she hadn't been standing on them, her legs would have wrapped themselves around him. She welcomed his tongue into her mouth. Something opened in the pit of her belly, and secret female muscles tightened in response. She could feel herself growing damp, feel the world spinning away, reducing itself to this tiny space in a darkened hall where two bodies pressed together, mouths melded, limbs entwined, desire blossoming.

She forgot everything—the children, Doyal, that she was leaving, that he was her employer, the terrible folly of her own judgment. He pressed her back against the wall, his hands sliding down to lift the hem of her oversize T-shirt and cup her buttocks, pulling her up and against him. With one hand, he held her there; with the other, he journeyed upward and around to capture her breast, the nipple lifting and hardening against his palm. One of them moaned, Laura was uncertain which. She didn't know what she was doing anymore. She only knew that he was pressing between her legs, and that she wanted, needed, more. She tried to pull it from his mouth, tried to catch it with her hands, hold it with her arms.

Suddenly he was tearing himself away, his hands at her waist, pushing her from him, holding her against the wall. He was panting, gulping, trying to force out words. "Damn! I . . . never . . ." He jerked his hands away and stepped back, swallowing and licking his lips. "I—I'm sorry. I didn't mean . . ." He turned away, as if unable to look at her. "The boys . . . Someone better—"

"I'll do it!" But she couldn't seem to peel herself off the wall.

He nodded, pushed a hand over his face, then shook his head. "No. I'll go. You'd better get to b—get some sleep."

He was dismissing her. Still, she couldn't move. Her body seemed unable to shift gears. She felt a stab of resentment that he could turn away so easily. It was some consolation when he reached out a hand to her, but then he fisted it and pulled it back, turning to move purposefully down the hall in the direction from which they'd come.

Laura bit her lip, slumping with dejection and misery, as if suddenly freed from whatever bonds had held her to the wall. God, what was wrong with her? It had only been a kiss. She should be glad that it had stopped at that, glad that she was safe, whole. She turned and made her way slowly to her room, where she leaned against the closed door and blinked away her tears, telling herself it was relief that produced the need to cry them. After all, it had only been a kiss shared in the dark of night after a moment of fear. It meant nothing. Nothing. And that was precisely why she cried.

Adam tucked the covers beneath the chins of his small sons, hoping the lecture he had just given them would curtail their late-night activities, and shut off the overhead light before slipping out the door. He walked to his own room and closed himself inside. He was tired. He went to the bed and lay down, lifting the covers to slide his feet beneath them, but he had hardly settled down when the first memory flashed across his mind's eye.

Laura, in that big T-shirt that covered little and revealed all, her feet encased in bulky wool socks. He closed his eyes and felt his arm wrapping her firm, slender waist. He sat up and passed an arm across his eyes, as if that would sweep away the memories.

Laura, turning her head, her mouth trembling beneath his, her breasts heaving beneath their thin covering.

His breath quickened. Blood rushed to his groin. He groaned and fell back upon his pillow.

Laura, her small, sleek buttocks in his hands, her fingers clutching at his shirt, her nails scraping his flesh through the soft cotton.

He had meant to drag her in here, rip off what little clothing she wore, put her back to the bed and make love to her. He hadn't thought about his children or the fact that she was leaving or how little of herself she had revealed. It had only been when he pulled away that the doubts slid in. They had come weighted with one word: Denver.

Three or four times he had asked where she was from, but only tonight had she answered him, and that after she'd nearly bashed his head open, after he nearly broke her neck. He gulped, remembering that moment when the hairs had stood on the back of his neck, remembered grabbing her, feeling the weight of that wine decanter in her hand. Had he followed protocol, he'd have twisted her arm behind her back, wrenching it from the socket in the process, cupped her chin, braced the back of her head with his shoulder and twisted. It had been the blond hair that swept his face, the soft feminine curves that melted against him, the *perfume of Laura,* that stopped him.

She had her own unique smell, clean, fresh, wholesome. He had inhaled it as he tasted her mouth. It had wafted through him, turning on desires he'd long ago shut off. It had felt so good to think and act like a sexual being again, but then he had moved away from her, and he had thought, *Denver. What else don't I know about her? How will I feel when she goes back there?*

And she was going. She had made that plain. He didn't want to live separate from the woman in his life again. He had almost conquered that feeling of loss, that emptiness. Loving Laura, making love to Laura, would only bring it back again. Only this time it would be worse, somehow he knew it would be worse.

He sighed into the darkness, feeling cold seep into his bones. Maybe it would be best, after all, if she didn't stay. Maybe it would be easiest for everyone if she went on her way as quickly as possible.

*I'll call the agency tomorrow,* he told himself. The children would be sad and disappointed, but he'd find someone else for them, someone who would do just as well. He knew what to look for now, he assured himself. There had to be someone who could make them laugh and behave with the same look, someone who would love them unconditionally and yet let them go when the time came, someone who would protect them with her life, who would make him face his responsibilities as a father, who could teach him to love and be loved by his own children. Laura. Only Laura.

But Laura was leaving them, and it would be better if she did so while they, he, could still let her go. He closed his eyes and clenched his teeth against the memories of a kiss that never should have happened, and he promised himself that he would start looking for a replacement first thing tomorrow. He promised himself. He swore it.

Tomorrow.

# Five

First thing the next morning, Adam got up and put on silk liners, then his insulated underwear, two pairs of socks, his jeans, a turtleneck and a wool sweater. He donned his military-grade arctic boots, dug his best gloves from a drawer, pulled on a knit toboggan hat and draped a wool scarf over his shoulder. He gathered up a second pair of silks from the corner where he'd tossed them and went out to face Laura.

"These are for you."

She stopped lifting plates onto a rack in an overhead cabinet and turned from the kitchen counter, shivering inside her quilted robe. She had dreaded this moment all night long, but now that it was here, she was surprised at the ease—no, the eagerness—with which she met him.

"Good morning."

He draped a pair of long silk liners over the back of a chair at the breakfast table and picked up a piece of toast, which he began slathering with margarine and strawberry jam. "In case you haven't noticed, the temperature dropped to a deadly low during the night. I want you and the kids dressed in at least three layers of warm clothing, hats, scarves, best gloves and parkas. Wendy is *not* to wear those mittens she's so fond of. They won't keep her safely warm on a day like this."

"All right."

"Storm's coming in, this evening, they say, but I'm not taking any chances. You can go ahead and drop Wendy off at school, then I want you and the boys to meet me at the discount store. I'll haul in a supply of firewood and be sure the generator's gassed up, in case the utilities are knocked out. I have the feeling we're in for a long haul with this one."

Laura moved across the floor, nodding, and poured him a cup of coffee. He took it gingerly, lest his fingers come close to hers, it seemed, and sipped without ever actually looking at her. He didn't sit down. She prepared him another piece of toast and placed it on a saucer, offering it warily. "You'll need this, if you're going out in that cold."

He slipped the jam-smeared toast from the plate and devoured it without a word. Laura set the plate on the counter and hurried from the room. He wouldn't touch her, wouldn't even look at her, and it hurt more than she wanted to admit.

The children were half dressed by the time she got to them, but she quickly pulled out the necessary underclothes and convinced them to start over, making a grand new game of it. Wendy put up a fight about the mittens, but acquiesced when Laura threatened to call her father in to deal with her. She hated to make Adam the bad guy, but after the night she'd had, she was at her wit's end.

She hustled the kids into the station wagon, glad to see that Adam had hooked up the electric ignition heater. Even at that, it took some time to crank up the car. Then she had to get out and manhandle the garage door. Its metal parts had frozen during the night. The skin on her face felt blistered by the time she got back into the car.

The road crunched beneath her tires as she drove toward town. Loud cracks came from the forest around them as the breeze shattered frozen tree limbs. She let Wendy out at the curb and watched as she ran awkwardly into the building, then drove to the discount store on the edge of town.

They bought new cold-weather underwear for the boys, who had outgrown those bought at the beginning of the winter. Then Adam insisted that she let him buy her better gloves, house shoes and a pair of heavy flannel pajamas before moving on to choose several sizes of household batteries, motor-oil additives and gallons of bottled water.

From the discount store, they went to the grocery, where Adam seemed to throw at least two of everything into their

cart. It was as they were leaving there, the groceries loaded
in the back of the wagon, that he paused to survey the sky.
The clouds had built to an amazing height, seeming to grow
darker as they grew taller. The sunlight was watery and
weak, and the air utterly still, though the clouds churned
above them.

"I don't like the looks of this. I want you to take the boys
on home. I'm going after Wendy at the school. Call Beverly as soon as you get there and tell her not to come in." He
really looked at her for the first time. "I hope you can cook
something other than breakfast."

His eyes said that he was depending on her. She nodded,
smiling slightly. "I can manage."

He chucked her under the chin, smiling down into her
eyes. It was the most warming thing she'd encountered all
morning, that look. She thought, *I can't let myself fall in
love with him.* Dear God, it was going to be so hard to leave
as it was, much harder than she'd realized. She got into the
car and headed home, her heart every bit as heavy as the
skies.

Flurries of fat, puffy flakes were swirling in front of the
car's windshield long before she reached the house. By the
time Adam and Wendy got home, the wind had picked up
considerably and the sun had completely disappeared, leaving only a watery duskiness as evidence of daylight.

It snowed and blew—*howled*—all that afternoon and into
the night. By midmorning the next day, it had begun again,
and it blew off and on for days afterward. When it was over,
there were snowdrifts as high as the house, and the temperature stayed low enough to freeze skin on contact. There
were limbs down, sometimes whole trees, and the little
toolshed out back had collapsed early on. A slamming door
brought *whump*s from the forest as standing trees shed their
white burdens. It was the kind of storm that made every
household its own small world, and to Laura it felt oddly
safe.

Adam tried to keep himself apart from Laura, but he
couldn't help wanting to join in when she got down on the

floor of the den and started rolling around with the kids, helping them burn off some energy. All three flopped down on top of her and started trying to tickle her, but she bucked them off like a horse, arching her back and twisting her hips and shoulders. Ryan was the first to bite the dust. He reeled across the room and bounced off Adam's knee, giggling and wrapping his arms around Adam's leg to steady himself. When he gave a tug and said, "Come on, Daddy! Come on, let's get her!" Adam found he simply couldn't resist.

It was great fun. It was also a mistake, for it wound up, inevitably, with Laura pinned on the floor beneath him, her arms held captive above her head, breasts thrusting upward pronouncedly beneath the layers of her clothing, her pretty eyes trained on his mouth. He momentarily forgot that Robbie was trying to walk up his back, that Wendy and Ryan were yanking at the arms he used to hold himself above Laura. Right there, right then, he almost lowered his head and kissed her. Only Ryan's shrieking in his ear averted a very embarrassing scene. Even at that, it was damned difficult to get up and walk away.

Afterward, he made sure he stayed out of temptation's way. He stoked the fire and went to work at the desk in his bedroom, emerging only for meals and a glimpse of the weather report on the evening news. The fourth day after the storm began, Adam ventured out, but the entire countryside was frozen in. Only those desperate for supplies and those charged with providing them were out and moving around. He filled up the truck with gasoline, invaded his freezing office for more reading material and returned to his bedroom.

It was another two days before the din drove him out into the house proper again. The screams had him running into the den, where Laura was trying to separate Wendy and Robbie. The two were going at each other like windmills, fists flailing. Ryan launched himself into the fray on Robbie's behalf just as Adam entered the room.

"Ow!" Laura grabbed her shin, where Ryan had accidentally kicked her, and hobbled away to sit on the end of the coffee table. Suddenly the hostilities ended, as all three kids ran to her side.

"Waura! Waura! You hurt bad?" Ryan dropped to his knees beside her.

Laura didn't answer him, her cry of dismay aimed at the small scrape welling beneath Robbie's left eye. Wendy's bottom lip jutted out, but then she dissolved into tears of contrition, flinging herself around Laura's neck as Laura tried to dab the beads of blood from Robbie's face.

Adam waded in where he thought he could do most good, hauling Wendy off her feet and into his arms. "Here now. Somebody tell me what's going on."

Everyone started talking at once. He did it. She did it. They did it. "All right! All right!" Adam barked. "That's enough!" He sat down on the coffee table next to an obviously exhausted Laura, Wendy on his lap. Suddenly he felt like a heel, leaving her to deal with the children on her own all this time. He covered her hand with his. "Suppose you clue in the idiot father."

She laughed at that, but he noticed that she was dabbing at her eyes, too. "Cabin fever," she said succinctly. "Everyone's short-tempered and edgy."

"Ah." He should have known that he wasn't the only one feeling trapped. Would he never learn how to be a caring, responsible father? He remembered the phone call from his mother that morning. "Tell you what, you guys get bundled up, and we'll go see your grandmother Erica."

Robbie threw his arms over his head and hooted, knowing he was bound to garner the lion's share of attention with his wound. Wendy was already scrambling off her father's knee, and Ryan was clapping his hands. Only Laura bit her lip and gave her head a truncated shake. Adam's disappointment was severe. He tried not to acknowledge it. "Don't you want to get out?"

She smiled wanly. "To tell you the truth, I'd enjoy some time to myself more." She lowered her voice. "Besides, I don't belong at a family visit."

Adam had to bite his tongue to keep from arguing with her. What was he doing? After locking himself away from her for days, was he going to beg her to come along? It seemed he didn't have to—the kids were doing it for him. But Laura was firm. She stood and looked down at them, her hands on her hips.

"Listen, I'm dreaming of a long, uninterrupted soak in a hot tub of bubbles. Besides, you won't even notice I'm not there. Wendy, you've told me how much you all enjoy visiting your grandmother. You go on and have a good time. I'll be perfectly happy right here on my own."

Adam gulped mentally at the thought of Laura reclining in a bubble bath. He was up off the coffee table before she finished speaking, a little hand in each fist. "Come on, let's get bundled up. I'll call Mother and let her know we're coming."

"Laura, please!" Wendy wheedled.

The boys added their voices to hers. "Pleeease, please!"

She remained adamant, however, as she helped Adam get them ready to go out. They finally accepted her decision, but Adam watched with something close to dismay as his children pulled her down to their level and covered her in kisses before trudging out into the cold with him. He didn't know what was worse, his own disappointment or his children's. Was it wise of him to allow them to become so attached to her? No more, he was sure, than the attachment that he himself was forming. Yet he didn't have the heart or the will to put a stop to it. Later, when he sat talking with his mother in the warm, stately home he'd grown up in, he was almost grateful for the distraction that her problems provided.

The children had exhausted themselves showing off for their doting grandmother and the house staff. Erica had given them lunch and tucked them into her own bed for naps, an old and treasured routine. Adam joked that she was going to be doing that when they were in their twenties and that they would probably let her.

"I hope so," she said, leading him back to the sitting room. "It will be nice if just one thing stays the same."

He hadn't missed the lines of strain marring her still-lovely face. He took her hand as she lowered herself into her chair, then sat down beside her. "What's wrong, Mom?"

She made a watery sound meant to pass as laughter. "You mean, besides my leaving your father?"

"It's only temporary," he assured her. "Whatever Dad's faults, I can't see him giving you up."

She lowered her gaze, shaking her head. "I don't know, Adam. He's not himself anymore, and it's not just his selling the stock. He's holed up in Kate's house and there are rumours that he's drinking."

Adam sat back, sighing. He'd tried not to think about this. He didn't like to get involved in Fortune business, but even he knew that it was uncharacteristic for Jake to sell stock to anyone outside the family, especially Monica Malone. "Have you asked him why he did it?"

She nodded, eyes blinking rapidly. "He just says, 'Trust me,' and turns away, but how can I, when he won't trust me with the truth?"

Adam shook his head. "I'm not the one to be asking about Jake. I've never understood him."

Erica sniffed and straightened her already elegant posture. "We won't go into that now. That's an old problem, not likely to be solved at this late date. The real concern just now is Nathaniel."

Adam groaned. "What's Uncle Nathaniel up to now?"

"Just what you'd expect. He's trying to push Jake out, take over the company himself. You know he's always felt that he ought to be at the helm of the business. I'm afraid Jake's given him the ammunition he needs with this stock sale to Monica. I just don't know what's going to happen."

Adam squeezed her hand, but he couldn't find much comfort to offer her. "There's more going on here than Dad's admitting, isn't there?"

"Dad's not admitting anything," Erica commented bitterly. Then she shook her head. "I just don't know what to do, Adam. I want to pull the family together for a reception in honor of Rachel and Luke, but I just don't know if it's wise at this time."

"Poor Rocky," Adam said. "What a time to be bringing a new sheep into the fold."

"Sounds more like a wolf to me," Erica snapped.

But Adam was on solid ground here, having met the "wolf" in question. He chuckled. "Hey, Greywolf's a tough cookie, but he loves my little sister. What's more, she loves him. Bank on it."

Erica squeezed his hand. "I don't mean to be judgmental. It's just that she's my baby."

Adam laughed outright. "Yeah, right, a baby with nerves of steel and a backbone of titanium! Give the kid a break, Mom. She's known her own mind for as long as I can remember. She's with the man she wants to be with. Trust me on this."

Erica smiled affectionately. "I wonder if you know how much like your father you sound at times."

Adam's less-than-gracious reply was canceled by the sound of the door of the hall crashing open. Sheila, his uncle's ex-wife, swept in with a flurry of foxtails and mink. She had worn slacks in deference to the weather, but the heels on her shoes were at least three inches tall. She slung a fur muff and a five-hundred-dollar purse onto a chair as she passed, the mink sliding from her shoulders.

"We've got to do something!" she told Erica. "No wonder you threw him out! He's gone too far this time!"

Erica snapped her mouth shut and rolled her eyes at Adam. "Good afternoon, Sheila, and whom might we be discussing?"

"Why, Jake, of course! What the hell does he think he's doing, selling off family stock to that faded actress?"

Erica instantly bristled. "I'll thank you not to speak of my husband in such terms."

Adam disciplined a grin and got to his feet. "Hello, Aunt Sheila. How are you?"

She passed an arm over her forehead, careful not to disturb her carefully drawn eyebrows or her brassy blond hair. "How do you think I am? Down to my last penny, and Nate refuses to part with a cent, now that the business is in crisis."

"The business is not in crisis," Erica insisted hotly. "How dare you imply—"

Adam stepped forward and took Sheila's arm, which was heavy with gold. "I suppose you could always hock the family jewels," he teased, "or find some attractive gentleman to support you. Why, with your looks, I'm sure you could find a much younger man."

Sheila extricated herself with a pout, but it was obvious that she was pleased by the flattery. She preened a moment, smoothing her expertly coiffed hair with ringed fingers. "I wouldn't give Nathaniel the satisfaction," she said through her teeth, "but with Jake undermining the family finances like this, I may not have a choice! What does that man think he's doing?"

"That's quite enough!" Erica said, coming to her feet rigidly.

Sheila sneered. "One would think you'd be ready to listen to reason, but you're as besotted as ever! Did he leave you for her, then? Is that what it's all about? Is he panting after that aging actress?"

Adam stepped between them, his smile stiff with distaste. "You really shouldn't have come, Sheila. Be a good girl and go sink your fangs into someone else."

She narrowed heavily made-up eyes at him. "You're the last one I expected to defend him," she said craftily. "Everyone knows you despise him."

"That's not so."

"Then go and talk to him. Make him see what he's doing to the rest of us. If you're so close to your dear father, talk some sense into him, for pity's sake!"

Adam forced himself to relax, and shook his head. He was the last one to talk sense to his father, the very last one to make Jake listen, but he resented this expensively turned-out hussy making an issue of that fact. What was between him and his father was personal, and he knew better than anyone to what lengths his father would go to protect and guide the family business. "I don't involve myself in Fortune business, and frankly, you'd do well to follow my example, since you're no longer even a member of the family."

Sheila flinched when he pointed out that she was technically no longer part of the family, but she merely lifted her cosmetically sculpted chin a little higher and looked down her nose at him. "I have my children to think of."

"Michael, Kyle and Jane have done quite well all on their own," he told her, "despite your interference."

She gasped and drew herself up so rigidly he feared that she might fall off her impossibly high shoes. But Sheila was a master of hauteur. She swung around and made for the door, snatching up her treasures as she went. "I should have known it was useless. You're closing ranks around him from sheer habit, it seems. Well, let me tell you something— you're on your own this time. The rest of the family will not flock to Jake's defense after this, and Nate knows it! I just hope to God that he gets control of the company before it's too late, before Jake drives us all into the poorhouse!"

She stormed out even more forcefully than she'd blown in, but Adam's concern was not for the door hinges. It wasn't even for his mother. This time, for once, his concern was all for his father.

Laura watched Adam push his food around his plate. The children had finished their dinners long ago and been excused, but Adam seemed hardly to have noticed. Laura sat quietly for some time, but then she couldn't keep silent any longer. "Not hungry?"

Adam looked up, as if surprised to find her there. "Oh, uh, sure. I mean, uh, no. Sorry." He sighed and pushed away his plate. "It's not the food. I guess we just had too big a lunch at Mother's today."

As she rose to begin clearing the table, she refrained from pointing out that the kids had eaten like lumberjacks, despite "Grandmommy's" lavish luncheon. Instead she said, "Well, Beverly insists on coming in tomorrow to cook her famous rack of lamb. Save your appetite for that. I think she believes I've been feeding you bean sprouts and tofu."

He nodded distractedly, as if he hadn't heard a thing she'd said. She left the room in silence, genuinely concerned. Something was bothering him, something that must have happened this afternoon, at his mother's. She shook her head. These Fortunes were a hard lot to figure. Their family relationships seemed unusually complicated. But it was really none of her business. Still, he seemed awfully concerned about something.

She loaded the dishes in the washer, straightened up the kitchen, laid out tomorrow's breakfast things and played a rousing game of dominoes with the boys. There were no rules, it seemed—other than the one about having to perform a silly little dance after every play—and therefore no winner, but it was fun anyway. Adam stared right through them, seemingly oblivious. The only time he seemed to come out of it was when Wendy crawled up in his lap to say good night.

"Thank you, Daddy, for taking us to see Grandmommy today."

"Hm? Oh, you're welcome."

"Can we go again tomorrow, Daddy?"

"What? Tomorrow? No, I don't think so, but Grand mommy said something about luncheon on Sunday."

"Will Granddad be there?"

A spasm of something very nearly like pain flashed across Adam's face. "Um, I don't know, honey. Maybe. We'll see okay?"

"'Kay. Night, Daddy."

"Good night, Wendy."

He gave her a shoulder-crunching hug, and she started to slide off his lap, but just as she got to his knees, she stopped and leaned far back, her legs thrust out straight and her hands grasping the arms of his chair in order to balance herself. Without a word, she looked up at him and puckered up, smacking her lips. There was no mistaking what she wanted. Adam looked faintly shocked, but then he lowered his head and kissed his daughter loudly on the mouth. Wendy swung up and hopped down, running to the doorway, where she waited shyly for her brothers to take their turns. *She knows,* Laura thought. *She knows he's upset.*

Robbie looked as if he'd gag if his father did more than pat him affectionately on the shoulder. Adam leaned for ward and did just that, then got a fierce hug as his reward. One arm hooked around his father's neck, Robbie squeezed so hard that his feet left the ground. Adam laughed, making a gurgling sound that prompted Laura to pry Robbie off him before he passed out. Ryan played the clown, wagging his tongue and crossing his eyes as he launched himself onto Adam's lap, both arms thrown around Adam's solid torso. Almost before Adam could hug him back, Ryan was gone, zigzagging toward the door, but then he stopped and turned back. Looking perplexed by the idea that had just seized him, he ran to Adam and fired a kiss at his chin. Adam caught him up and squeezed him hard. He wiggled free and ran out of the room, Robbie hot on his heels. Wendy waited for Laura, her eyes large and soft. Laura took her hand and led her away, telling her with a smile how proud she was of her.

The children were unusually subdued after that, and Laura suspected it had as much to do with the growing bond with their father as with their day at their grandmother's house. She followed their example, keeping her voice low and soft, her movements gentle and soothing, as she prepared them for bed. They looked settled in for a long night of heavy sleep when she left them.

She hesitated for a moment at the door of her own room. Sometimes she chose to spend these final hours of the day in her room, with a good book, but not tonight. Instead, she walked back to the den, finding Adam standing over a silent television, staring at a blank screen. She took a seat on the couch, slipping off her shoes and drawing up her legs beneath her. "Want to talk about it?"

He hunched his shoulders, his smile self-deprecating. "It's a funny thing," he said, walking back to his chair. "No matter how... *inadequate* a father may be, his kid can't seem to help... I don't know." He shook his head, dropping down into his chair.

"They love you, Adam," she told him softly, and he smiled, nodding his head.

"Yeah, I know. I love them, too, more than I realized."

"But you're not just a father, are you?" she said intuitively. "You're also a son."

He leaned forward and clasped his hands together, his elbows braced against his thighs. "Something's wrong," he said in a near whisper. "Something's not right." He shook his head. "I don't know. I don't *know*! I've never understood anything about Jake Fortune in my whole life, but..."

She copied his position and said, "Why don't you tell me about it?" And he did, beginning with his father's dedication to the family business, despite his personal ambitions, and about his own refusal to fall into the same trap. He talked about feeling abandoned as a boy, about his father's preoccupation with what he perceived as his duty to the family at large. He even spoke about his uncle Nathaniel's envy of his older brother, about his parents' marriage and Jake's expertise in handling the constant crises that came with running an international conglomerate. He talked about Kate and Ben, and the problems, as he saw them, with the cosmetic company. And he told her, too, about Monica Malone, and about Jake selling her family stock. "So the family want answers," he finally summed up, "and if he doesn't tell them what they want to hear, Nathaniel's poised to take over, encouraged, no doubt, by the queen of greed, dear old Auntie Sheila."

"And you're afraid that he won't give them the answers they want?" she queried gently.

Adam spread his hands. "He hasn't so far, and for the life of me, I can't imagine why. For that matter, I can't imagine what he could say. It just doesn't make any sense, selling stock to Monica Malone, of all people, with the company hanging in the balance like this." He shook his head. "All he does is avoid the issue, and that's what's at the root of this separation. I mean, he's always told Mom everything. Whatever his shortcomings as a father, that marriage seemed rock-solid—until now. And now... I just don't know."

"You could always ask him," Laura suggested lightly. "Or... you could just try to trust him."

"I'm the last person he would confide in," Adam admitted, passing a hand over his face. "And I don't think my trust matters to him one way or another."

Oh, that was a sad, sad thought. Laura cocked her head. "So what's left then, Adam?"

"I don't know. Just being thankful I'm not like him, I guess."

"Aren't you?" she asked gently.

He frowned. "What do you mean? I've stayed out of the family business expressly to avoid the mistakes he's made."

Laura bit her lip. Should she risk pointing out again that he, too, had let career and other considerations keep him apart from his own children, that there were other ways to abandon a child than simply not coming home for dinner? On the other hand, what did she have to lose? She glanced at the photo albums stacked on the top of the coffee table, then slid off the couch onto her knees, in front of them. "I want to show you something."

She separated the two albums and flipped them open. "You told me that your wife put together one of these, didn't you?"

"The newer one."

"And the other was left to you by your grandmother?"

"Yeah, so?"

"Haven't you ever wondered why? I mean, have you thought that the two might be connected in some way?"

He got up and walked around the table to take a seat on the sofa next to her. He leaned forward, scanning the two albums. She knew the moment he realized what those two photo albums had in common. "Oh, my God," he said, his hands flipping through the pages.

Laura knew exactly what he was seeing. The mundane family moments, the outings, the little celebrations, and in every one the father was missing, his father and then him. They might have been identical sets, but for the old-fashioned clothing and hairstyles and the faded coloring of the older photos. They were eerily similar, he and his sisters together with their mother, Diana and Wendy and the boys, but no Jake, and no adult Adam, at least not pictured together with his family. And the reason was very simple—he hadn't been there. Just as Jake hadn't been there, neither had Adam, at least not before Diana's death forced him to be.

She saw that his hands were trembling, and she gathered them into her own. "Don't you see, Adam?" she said softly. "Like you, he didn't mean to be preoccupied. He was only trying to do what he felt he must."

"I never saw it before," he whispered. "I always blamed Diana. I didn't feel that I had any choice. I was only...trying to do what I felt I must." He pulled his hands from hers and covered his face.

"There's more, Adam, if you'll just think of it, another way to understand your father through your own experience."

He sighed and cleared his throat. His eyes were suspiciously fluid when he lowered his hands, blinking. "What would that be, Laura?"

"You love your children, Adam," she pointed out, smiling. "You've always loved them."

"Yes," he said, and then the harsh lines of his face softened and smoothed as he carried the parallel thesis to its logical conclusion. "Oh. Yes." The thought obviously pleased him.

"Whether they know it or not, you'll always try to do what's best for them, won't you?"

He nodded, smiling gratefully, and his large, strong hand skimmed her jaw and curled around her chin before his arm came around her in a friendly, affectionate hug. "How'd you get so smart, little Miss Laura?"

She shook her head, pulling away to sit back on her heels. "Oh, no, it's not that," she said. "I've done some awfull stupid things, Adam. I'd be ashamed to tell you.... I'm just that kid with her nose pressed up against the window, looking in. It's just easier to see the whole room from where I'm sitting."

He tapped the end of her nose. "I'm glad you picked my window, then."

She smiled wistfully and said no more. He'd never know how badly she wanted to come inside, just once, to blend into that room full of family, to see it from his side for a change. But that would never be, not as long as Doyal was out there looking for her. She knew in her heart of hearts that it could end only one way. She couldn't run forever. Doyal Moody would catch her sooner or later, but she would run again before she let him catch her here, and she would take with her the memory of something special, even if it was only a look shared through a cold glass window with a man she could never call her own.

# Six

Adam smiled down at his children, finding delight in their expectant faces, the result of his latest attempt to prove that he loved them and wanted to spend time with them.

"Well," he said, drawing out the anticipation, "how about a matinee?" The whoops he'd expected did not gush forth. He looked to Laura for help. Her mouth quirked in a quickly hidden smile.

"Your father wants to take you to a movie this afternoon," she explained.

Still no whoops, just gasps and young eyes rounded in surprise. He gulped, no longer certain of the path he'd chosen. "It—it's an animated feature." Three pairs of big eyes merely blinked.

Laura's aid came uninvited this time, but it was no less appreciated. She simply said the title of the movie, one that had been advertised repeatedly on national television for some weeks, and Adam got his whoops at last. Robbie was so impressed that he scrambled up on the couch and started jumping up and down. Adam thought of scolding him, but then he reminded himself that celebration was just what he'd wanted. He opted for saving the furniture by simply scooping the exuberant little body into his arms. Robbie immediately wrapped his arms around Adam's neck and tried to strangle him with glee. Ryan threw himself at Adam's legs and promptly began to jump up and down on his feet, nearly crippling him. Laura lifted him away, her hands beneath his arms, and pointed him toward the door before peeling Robbie off and sending him in the same direction, with a firm admonition to them both to use the potty, wash up and comb their hair. They sped away with all the appropriate sound effects, squealing tires, revving engines and so forth, Laura calling out that she would be along shortly to assist.

It was only then that Adam realized his daughter was standing at his side, wringing her little hands, her big golden eyes brimming with tears, that fat bottom lip trembling wrenchingly. He laid a hand on her shoulder. "Wendy?"

The little wretch burst into sobs, big *hoo-hoo-hoo*s that shook her sturdy body pitifully. Adam went down on his knees and pulled her against his chest, casting beseeching looks at Laura, only to find tears spilling from her eyes, too. He flattened his lips in confusion and disgust. Laura laughed and wiped at her cheeks, then bent forward and whispered in his ear, "She's female, Adam, and we are known to cry when happy."

Happy. Adam closed his eyes and held his daughter close. When he opened them again, Laura was gone. He lifted and backed himself into a chair, pulling Wendy onto his lap. With an awkward pat, he tried his best to calm her. "Here now, Princess. It's only a movie."

She sniffed and wiped her nose on his shoulder. "I know, Daddy, but I wanted to go so much, and Laura only said, 'We'll see.'" She lifted her face and instructed him solemnly, "That means no."

He chuckled and rubbed her back. "Sometimes it does, and sometimes it means 'I don't know yet.'"

"Oh." She rubbed her eyes with both fists, and then she stopped and looked up expectantly. "Then why don't you say, 'I don't know yet'?"

Adam's brows shot up in surprise. "Jeepers, Wendy, I don't know!"

She fell against him, laughing brightly. "You're so funny, Daddy!" Then she grew still and turned her small face up to his and whispered, "I love you, Daddy."

Adam's heart swelled so that it nearly choked him. He swallowed it down and tucked his daughter's silky head into the crook of his shoulder. "I love you, too, honey." He was glad that Laura had left the room. He'd have hated to give away a closely held secret of his sex, namely that men, too, sometimes cried when very, very happy.

That tentative, brand-new happiness gave way to personal disappointment a little while later, when Laura stubbornly refused to join them in attending the movie.

"This should be your afternoon with the children," she told him, "and I much prefer having some time to myself. Go on now. No one's going to miss me."

*I will,* he thought, surprising himself. He wanted to bite his tongue when he heard himself saying, "I want you to come."

For a moment, pleasure blossomed in her eyes, but then wariness replaced it, and she literally stepped back. "Not this time."

He felt an overwhelming urge to shake her. "You know you want to."

She shook her head, dropping her gaze. "I can't."

"Why not?"

"I just can't. *Please,* Adam."

"For Pete's sake, Laura," he snapped, "what are you afraid of?" But he knew what she feared. Him. She knew that she was driving him crazy, and she was putting distance between them because of it. He couldn't blame her, but he couldn't like it, either. What did she think he was going to do, force himself on her? He was hurt. She ought to know better than that by now. No matter how beautiful she was, no matter how much he wanted to touch her, he would never force himself on a woman who didn't want him. And he could only conclude that she didn't want him. From the panicked look on her face, he could only conclude that she obviously didn't want anything to do with him. Fine. So her only concern was for his children. That was, after all, what he paid her for. He zipped his coat and followed his children out into the garage, as angry with himself as with her.

He was angry with her. Laura told herself that it shouldn't matter. He had tried so hard lately to be attentive to the children, and that was what mattered. The movie had evidently been a great success. She had never seen such closeness and interaction between him and the children. The twins had practically reenacted the whole movie for her, looking to their father for confirmation at every step along the way, and Wendy was doting on him, hanging on the arm of his chair and giggling flirtatiously as he coached the boys in their antics. Laura was thrilled—and worried. Did he suspect that she was hiding out here? Why else would he have demanded to know what she was afraid of? Would he send her packing the moment the children were safely out of hearing? She couldn't keep her hands from shaking while she waited through dinner, the usual evening activities, baths and bedtime rituals for a moment alone with him.

She didn't know whether to be relieved or hurt when he virtually ignored her after she got the kids down for the night. It took all her courage to join him in the den, but then he just sat there staring morosely at the television, pretending she wasn't even in the room. She told herself that was a good sign. Surely, if he meant to get rid of her, he'd have taken advantage of this time to do so. Maybe, if she could just smooth things over, they could go back to being... what? Friends? Were they friends?

She took a deep breath and chose the only safe subject available. "You made them so happy today, Adam."

He shifted in his chair, eyes glued to the screen. "It was actually a pretty good movie," he said dryly. "You would have enjoyed it."

She didn't miss the dig. "I know I would've, but the children needed that time alone with you."

His gaze switched to her for the first time. "You make it sound like they'd have resented your being there, and you know that's not so."

"I know," Laura conceded, avoiding his eyes, "but you're their father, Adam, and I'm just the nanny."

"Just the nanny!" he muttered deprecatingly.

"You know what I mean," she insisted patiently. "You're the one they need to depend on, Adam. You're the one constant in their lives."

He lifted a brow and shifted again, leaning one elbow on the arm of his chair as he raked a flat gaze over her. "Maybe you're right," he said deliberately. "Maybe they're too dependent on you. Maybe we're *all* too dependent on you. But don't let it worry you. We've no intention of letting ourselves become *burdens.*"

"Oh, Adam, it's not that!" she said, coming to her feet. "It's just the opposite. *I'm* becoming too dependent on *you.* Don't you see that I can't let that happen?"

He looked at her, his expression unguarded for the first time. "Since when is mutual dependency such a bad thing?" he asked. "We need you, Laura. You're the best thing that's ever happened to us, and if we can—"

"No!" She shook her head, blinking back tears. "I'm not even a trained nanny. You could do so much better than me! You just don't realize it, because you're only now beginning to relate to one another, and you're crediting me with that, I think."

He came up out of his chair, his hands seizing her upper arms. "Of course I am!" he was saying. "We're finally getting where we ought to be as a family, thanks to you. Don't you realize that? Can't you see how much we—*I*— owe you? You've opened my eyes, Laura. You've shown me that I was repeating behavior learned from my father, behavior I hated as a kid. My mother was great with us, but somehow I didn't learn to be a parent like her. Somehow, it just didn't translate, until I began watching you with my children. You're a natural mother, so easily affectionate, so calm and patient and levelheaded."

"Oh, Adam, I'm not at all what you think I am!"

"Then what are you, Laura?" he demanded roughly, shaking her so that her head fell back and she was forced to look up into his face. "If you're not the beautiful, loving, generous woman you seem to be, then just what are you?"

"I'm a fool," she whispered, her eyes swimming with tears. "I'm the world's biggest fool!"

She knew even before he bent his head that he was going to kiss her—and that she ought not to let him. She should turn her head or, better yet, turn around and walk away. She should move to his chest the hand that had somehow found its way to his shoulder and push until he understood that this could not happen. But she did none of those things. Instead, she leaned closer, her arm sliding around his neck, and laid her head far back, granting him access to her mouth. Her eyes closed as his mouth settled over hers, and she swayed into the heady sensation of being wanted, of being appreciated.

His arms dropped around her, coaxing her to align her body to his and pressing her against him. His mouth parted hers, and his tongue slipped inside, to curl and nudge and seduce her own into an erotic duel of slow, deep thrusts that lit fires within the depths of her body and sensitized her skin. She felt everything acutely, the silky fabric of her underclothes, the slight rasp of knit outerwear, the hard soles of her shoes, the weight of her wristwatch, the cool metal of the tiny studs in her earlobes, the swing of her hair against her shoulders and back. Most of all, however, she felt the heat and the strength of him, the overwhelming masculinity that was part and parcel of Adam Fortune, father, ex-soldier, grown son, her friend, her... The word *lover* rang through her mind, but the fearful, careful voice inside her head replaced it with the word *employer,* and that was what galvanized her, gave her the strength to turn her head away from his kiss.

He did not at first perceive that she was no longer an enthusiastic participant. When she turned her head away, he merely moved his mouth to the smooth column of her throat, kissing, licking, nipping with his teeth, sending shudders of desire through her, prickling her flesh. He loosened his embrace, his hands roaming her body, one coming to rest splayed in the small of her back, the other slipping between them to cover her breast. She gave a small cry, arching against him even as she attempted to push away, wedging her forearms into the hollows of his shoulders.

His hands slid up her back to press between her shoulder blades, his mouth working its way down to her collarbone, his tongue flicking along its delicate ridge. She was gasping for breath, attempting to fight off the sensations that swamped her, even as she succumbed to them. It was only when he returned to her mouth that she began in earnest to repel him, knowing that if she allowed another kiss she would be truly lost. She began to squirm and push away, her head thrashing from side to side. Obviously confused, he lightened his hold, his hands sliding to her waist. But even that was too much contact, too compelling, too tempting.

She wrenched away, at once feeling bereft, but determined, too. Adam Fortune was not a man she could love and leave, and she mustn't forget that the time was coming when she would have to go, for to stay would endanger not only Adam but his children. Loving Adam, making love with Adam, would bind her too tightly, make it much too difficult to go. Perhaps she should go now, she thought wildly. Why stay, when staying would only make it more difficult to go when the time came? But it was already too late. The very thought of leaving here, of leaving him, brought pain so sharp and so deep that it immediately reduced her to tears.

"Laura?" He reached out to bring her to him once more, but she skittered out of his way, shaking her head.

"No! I..." But what could she tell him? That she wanted above all things to be held close by him, to be treasured and loved and never let go? That such desires could never be fulfilled? That the woman he thought so giving and caring would in reality bring danger to him and his children if she allowed her selfish heart to bid her stay? She did the only thing that she could at the moment—she turned and fled the greatest temptation she had ever know. She heard him calling her, heard him following, but when she reached her room, closed the door and locked it, she knew that he had not followed beyond those first few steps. She knew, with great relief and equal sadness, that there would be no tearful explanations and no warm assurances. It was for the best, she told herself, and intellectually she had no doubt that this was so, but convincing her heart was another matter entirely.

* * *

She was doing it again. Adam shifted in his chair and rubbed a hand over his chin and jaw. Once more, the moment the children were in bed, she'd disappeared without a word. Well, tonight she wasn't going to get away with it. The past three days had been miserable with tension. She wouldn't look him in the eye, wouldn't speak to him unless asked a question, wouldn't spend a single moment alone in his company. How in heaven's name were they to get through this? He couldn't apologize to a phantom, and the children were already confused enough, without him trying to fashion oblique references to an episode better kept private. But how the hell did he get her alone? He'd tried knocking on her door last night, but she had ignored him, her silence as cold a rebuff as a knife in the ribs.

There was a way, of course, but he'd avoided it thus far, for fear that she would misunderstand. He couldn't see that he had any other choice, however. Reluctantly he got up from his chair and switched off the television he hadn't been watching anyway. Slowly he closed up the house and switched off the lights, then made his way to his room, where he opened a drawer in a bureau and located a long, thin spike with a small knob on the end. He'd faced covert missions with less trepidation, but none had ever elicited such determination. Somehow he had to inject normalcy into a situation that had become ludicrously tangled—again. His mouth compressed grimly, he crossed the hall, the spike in his hand.

Taking a deep breath, he tapped lightly on the door. "Laura? Laura, please come to the door."

The silence that greeted him was disappointing, even though it was exactly what he'd expected. He tamped down the feeling and squared his shoulders, one hand trying the doorknob. Locked, just as he'd expected. No matter.

He laid his head against the door. "Laura, we need to talk. I'm coming in." With that, he inserted the spike into the small hole common to all the interior doorknobs in the house and pressed. The lock released. He turned the knob and swung the door inward. She caught the edge with both hands and tried to force it shut again.

"How dare you!"

"Stop it!" he hissed, giving the door a shove hard enough to let her know that she couldn't win a physical contest with him. She abruptly backed off, her arms folded across her middle, pulling her ugly quilted robe tight protectively. He cast a look down the hall, toward the rooms of his children, detected no disturbance and stepped inside Laura's room, quietly closing the door behind him. She backed away another few steps, her gaze downcast, her expression sullen. He pocketed the spike and spread his hands. "I didn't know what else to do. You won't talk to me, and—"

"Can't you just leave me alone?" she snapped.

He blanched, more hurt than he could have imagined. "Yes. I—I've every intention of leaving you alone. That's one of the things I've come to tell you."

She flashed an enigmatic glance at him. "Oh."

He told himself that was not disappointment he heard. He wanted to hear it far too much to trust his ears to detect it. No, it was surprise or confusion... or distrust. He pushed back a sweep of shame. He had forced himself on her that night, and he had been too caught up in his own passion to even notice until she'd fought her way free. He had to make amends, or she would be gone before he could prepare himself or the children for it. He felt a trembling in the hollow of his throat and tried to swallowed it away.

"Laura, I owe you an apology," he began. She looked up and seemed to relax a little. He pushed on. "I—I don't know what came over me the other night. I don't usually... force myself on unwilling women. I can't explain it, really, except to say..." But he didn't dare say what he was thinking, what he was feeling. He couldn't tell her that he wanted her so badly it was all he could do to keep his hands to himself at times, that he dreamed about slipping into her bed at night, about stripping her bare and laving all that pale, creamy skin with his tongue, about... He forced away the erotic thoughts, swallowing again and searching for some logical explanation for his behavior. "Uh, the thing is... I, uh..." It struck him that if one truth wouldn't do, then perhaps another would. Inspired, he rushed on. "I haven't enjoyed the, ah, companionship of a woman since Diana's accident. Well, actually, it was before that, *months* before that. I, um, hadn't been home in quite some time, and, well..." He pinched the bridge of his nose. "I've just been so preoccupied with the kids and the search for a means to support them that I haven't... well, I haven't..." The look on her face stopped him. He wasn't mistaken this time. Wishful thinking wouldn't have put *anger* on that lovely face.

"Oh, it's quite all right," she said smoothly, sarcasm dripping from every word. "I understand. I see now that I just happened to be in the wrong place at the wrong time. Nothing personal. *Any* female would have done at the moment."

His mouth dropped open. "No! I didn't say that! I didn't mean—"

"Didn't you?" She swept back her hair with one hand. "Tell me something—do I have the word *easy* stamped across my forehead? Or is it the way I walk, the way I talk?"

Cold, hard rage sluiced through him. How could she speak of herself so? How could she even think it? "Stop it," he said deliberately. "You know better than that. I never said—"

"Let's just lay it on the line, Adam! You want me to sleep with you."

The accusation slapped him squarely in the face. Yet he couldn't deny it. He swept a hand over his head. "You're a very beautiful woman, Laura. Naturally I think about... I can't help thinking that we..." He closed his eyes. "We would be very good together, you know." When he opened his eyes again, she had turned her back on him. He walked forward and lifted a hand to her shoulder. "Laura—"

She jerked away, rounding on him. "Don't touch me!"

"I only wanted..." He wanted her to melt and throw herself into his arms. He backed up, putting distance between them. "I'm sorry. I didn't mean to offend. And you're wrong about any woman.... You're very special, Laura. I'd venture to say that no one else could possibly take your place. That's why I feel so badly about what happened, why I want very much to wipe it all out and begin again, for the children's sakes, if nothing else."

"Oh, that's big of you," she retorted, wiping her eyes with short, jerky movements. "Rather liberal, don't you think, trusting the care of your children to the very woman you've targeted for sex?"

He cocked his head. "Not really. I once felt very much the same way about their mother, and *targeted* is definitely the wrong word."

She dropped her gaze. "I am not their mother."

He sighed. "Yes, I...seem to have forgotten that."

"What's that supposed to mean?"

He licked his lips, searching desperately for the right words. "What I'm saying is that I trust you to care for them every bit as much as I trusted Diana, so much so that I've evidently...placed you in that role. That, combined with my obvious attraction to you, confused me. Instinctively I approached you as I would my...*wife*." He gulped on that word, as shocked as she was by it, and no more pleased.

"I'll thank you not to make that mistake again," she said crisply.

He nodded his head. "Fine. Now could we please get back to normal around here?"

She lifted her chin. "If by that you mean anything sexual..."

He didn't even hear the rest of it. Anger roared in his ears. How could she say that, after all he'd just said and all he felt he was giving up by keeping his hands to himself? "Stop treating me like a convicted rapist!" he snapped.

She gasped. "I have not!"

"Well, what the hell do you call it? You haven't spoken to me in a civil tone for days. You won't be in the same room alone with me if you can help it. You won't answer the door. You sulk around like a kid who's lost her candy."

"I do not!"

"I came here to apologize, and you're spoiling for a fight!"

"Oh, I'm supposed to be all sweetness and light after you break into my room?"

"I didn't break in! I knocked on the door, and when you wouldn't answer, I warned you I was coming in!"

"Whether I wanted you to or not!"

"Somebody had to do something!" he shouted, throwing up his hands. "You expect me to just accept being persona non grata in my own house?"

"Well, if you didn't expect me to fall into your bed—"

"It was a kiss, for God's sake. One simple kiss!"

"Two!" she yelled back. "And there was nothing simple about it either time!"

"Well, rest assured, there won't be a number three!"

"There darn well better not be!"

"Count on it! I won't make that mistake again!"

She drew herself up, hands on her hips, and leaned forward to rub his nose in it. "I'm beginning to think I'm the one who made the mistake when I came here. I had a perfectly good job before you came along and ruined it for me!"

He was so mad he was incoherent. "Ruined? Good? Y-you call that nothing of a— For Pete's sake, that moron fired you on the spot just because he though you were flirting with me!"

"I wasn't flirting with you!"

"I didn't say—" He broke off and rolled his eyes, smacking his hands to his temples. "What did I do to deserve this?" he asked the ceiling.

"You kissed me!" Laura retorted, and it was just too much for a man who'd been tormented day and night by the memory of that folly.

"Yes," he said, deadly calm in his rage, "God forgive me, I kissed you! I actually even thought you might enjoy it! Obviously, I must be punished. Will this wall do?" He asked, jabbing a finger. "Do you think we'll have enough room for the whip to snap? Maybe you'd prefer a public flogging in the town square?"

She had the grace to look slightly abashed. "Just leave me alone," she muttered.

"The hell I will! We live together—"

"We don't—"

"In the same house, and I'll be damned if I'll tiptoe around like an escaped convict in my own home!"

"Nobody asked you to."

"No, but that's just how you've treated me. Well, I've had enough! It's over. Do you hear me?"

"Oh, I hear you," she said, haughtily sticking her nose in the air, "and you seem to forget *again* that you're not my husband."

He wanted to shake her, and before he realized that the desire had translated itself into action, he was doing just that. "No, but I'm your employer," he reminded her gruffly, "and by God, you'll do just what I say, or so help me..."

"What?" she snapped, flipping her long hair with a jerk of her head. "Or you'll kiss me? And when I refuse to let it go beyond that, what then, Adam? Will you fire me, or will you make me—"

"Stop it!" He shook her again, roughly this time, sending her long hair flying, and then he abruptly released her. He swallowed, alarmed by the riot of emotions churning through him, and rubbed his hand over his mouth and chin. "Obviously," he said through clenched teeth, "you're in no mood to be reasonable."

"Reasonable?" she echoed, folding her arms and striking a belligerent pose. "Get out of my room, and then maybe I can be reasonable."

Stiffly, mockingly, he inclined his head, and then he strode out of the room, slamming the door behind him with all the force he could muster. He was across the hall, at his own door, before he heard the shuffling of little feet behind him. He looked down into his daughter's troubled face.

"Daddy? What's wrong, Daddy?"

He forced a smile and tugged a thin, messy braid. "Nothing important, sweetie. Don't worry about it."

"Are you mad at Laura?"

He started to shake his head, but then he thought better of it. "Yeah," he said, "and she's none to happy with me at the moment, either."

She cocked her head, brows drawn together. "How come?"

He grimaced. "It's... adult stuff, Wendy, which means that it doesn't make a lick of sense." She bit her lip, clearly worried, and his heart turned over in his chest. He bent and scooped her up into his arms. "It's all right, honey, I promise. Now, we better get you back into bed, or you won't be up in time for school in the morning." He drilled a finger into her belly button as he carried her to her room. She giggled and pushed his hand away, threading her arms around his neck.

He tucked her into bed, kissed her forehead and smiled down at her. "Sweet dreams, angel."

"Good night, Daddy."

He dimmed the light as she rolled onto her side, tucking her folded hands beneath her cheek. He looked at that chubby face, seeing something of Diana in her for the first time, the line of her jaw, the shape of her eyes. She was so very precious, his daughter. He wondered whether he was doing the best things for her, whether she needed something he couldn't see, something he hadn't done. *Oh, Diana*, he thought, *I'm only beginning to understand what I asked of you, what I expected of you, what you were to our children.*

He was all alone in this now. What, he wondered, if his best was not good enough? This was a whole new ball game to him, and now that he looked back at the mistakes he'd made, he wasn't at all sure that he could trust his own judgment. He should have been here more. He should have made them understand how much they meant to him. He should have taken more joy in these three little people for whom he bore responsibility. He shouldn't have entrusted them to hired help. He'd told Laura that he trusted her to care for his children as he had his own wife, and that was true, but should he have done so? Was he right to feel that she was overreacting, behaving irrationally? Maybe he was the irrational one. What father in his right mind picked up a total stranger in a restaurant and took her home to be a surrogate mother for his children? And yet, it was Laura

who had opened his eyes, who had moved him to release
pent-up emotions and allow himself to really love his children. It was Laura who was going to break Wendy's heart
when she left them—and not only Wendy's.

He closed his eyes, sighing, before tiptoeing silently from
the room. What could he do? What should he do? Should
he send her away, try to cope on his own? Or could he tamp
down his own feelings for her for the sake of his children?
What was the safest course? The right one?

He turned off the hall light and wandered toward his
room, pausing as he passed her door. A muffled sob drifted
through that barrier, and his hand was on the knob before
he realized what he was doing. He snatched his hand back
as if stung. He was the last person, the very last person,
she'd want comfort from now. Moreover, he didn't dare
chance it. He simply couldn't trust himself to keep his emotions in check—and his hands to himself. With nothing resolved, in her mind or his, he took himself off for a long,
miserable night of self-recrimination.

# Seven

Laura smiled at Ryan for wiping his mouth on his napkin, shook her head at Robbie for using his sleeve and pushed Wendy's spoon away from the jelly jar for the third time.

"That's enough, Wendy," Adam said. "You have plenty of jelly on your toast already."

Wendy scowled, her mouth too full for her to protest. Laura sent Adam a resentful glance, put the lid on the jelly jar and leaned back in her seat to place it out of the way, on the counter behind her. Ryan mimicked her movements, leaning his chair back on two legs. The chair teetered precariously. With a cry, Laura bolted up and caught it before it tipped over backward.

"For Pete's sake, Ryan!" Adam snapped over the top of his paper. "Are you trying to hurt yourself?"

Ryan's eyes were big with shock and leftover fear, but they abruptly squinted together as his face crumpled and he doubled over in tears, wailing softly. Laura glared murderously at Adam, but kept silent, her arms comforting Ryan. Adam swallowed whatever else he might have said and ducked his head behind his paper again. Laura felt an unaccountable sense of defeat. Why must she glare at him every time he looked her way? Why couldn't she relax, tell him that she accepted his apology and get on with life? It wasn't as if she were even really mad at him anymore.

She knew that what had happened between them was every bit as much her fault as his, the kiss, as well as the fight, but she couldn't help raising her hackles every time he got close. It was as if giving up her anger would render her vulnerable to his every word and gesture, not to mention his touch. The situation was completely untenable, and if she had a lick of sense, she'd leave now before something really awful happened. And yet, she couldn't seem to quite do that, either.

She patted Ryan into silence, dried his tears with a napkin, settled him once more at the table and whispered that he should finish his breakfast quickly. Adam slapped his newspaper together, tossed it on the table and slammed his fist down on it, glaring at her.

"That's it! I'm sick and tired of this silent treatment! Speak in a normal voice, damn it!"

Laura felt her temper rise. She twisted her hands together in front of her and glared back at him over the top of Ryan's curly head. "All right, I will, provided you do the same and stop *shouting at everyone!*"

Adam's face turned red, and for a moment she thought he would explode, but then he sucked in a deep breath, turned his head away and got a grip on his own temper. He swallowed and looked at her. "Fine," he said in a very carefully controlled voice, lifting his coffee cup.

Laura felt a little deflated. She realized that she was primed for another battle. With her guns effectively spiked, there was nothing for her to do except sit down and resume eating her breakfast. She did so with little grace, plopping down in her chair, snatching up her toast and ripping into it with her teeth as if it were shoe leather. Adam stared at his cup, then abruptly switched his gaze to her and asked tersely, "What are your plans today?"

Laura realized that he was trying to make normal conversation, and that she would be extremely rude to rebuff him. "I'm doing the same thing I do every day," she snapped. "Taking Wendy to and from school, tending the boys, overseeing homework. I do have a little laundry to wash," she added glumly.

He waved a hand irritably. "I've told you that you can send your things out along with ours."

"And I've told you that I don't have enough *things* to send out. It takes too long to get them back."

"Buy some more," he practically ordered.

"I will not! I have other plans for my money."

"I didn't mean that you should pay for them," he told her. "I'll pay for them."

Laura sniffed, her nose in the air. "No, thank you. I'll accept nothing I don't earn . . . as a nanny."

Adam grimaced, his forearms on the table. "I don't pay you half what you're worth as a nanny," he said, switching his gaze up to meet hers, "and I never, ever, intended that you should *earn* anything in any other way, no matter what you think."

Laura softened, in spite of her better judgment. "I know. I didn't mean to imply—" She broke off, glancing nervously at the children, who were hanging on every word.

Adam sighed. "Neither did I. And about the other night, I was just trying to get things back on an even keel, honest."

Laura's hands fluttered around her head, smoothing hair as smooth as silk. "I—I realize that now, but at the time . . ." She bit her lip, all too aware that the children's eyes had moved from Adam's face to hers and were now swinging back again.

Adam's smile was beleaguered. "I guess we both kind of overreacted."

Laura bowed her head in shame. "I know I did."

"You weren't alone," Adam said softly.

Laura glanced up. Their gazes snagged and held. She saw the sincerity in his eyes, and something warm and soft unfurled inside her. She mouthed the words I'm sorry.

Adam's face melted into smooth, fond lines. He reached across the table and covered her hand with his. "That's what I've been trying to say to you for days."

Laura nodded in apology and understanding, and Adam squeezed her hand. Wendy giggled, and Laura snatched her hand back, while Adam straightened in his chair, cleared his throat and composed his features into a bland expression.

"Well, I'd better get going," he said briskly. "I have an appointment today with a fellow I've been trying to see for nearly two weeks. The weather's played havoc with us." He got up from his chair.

His gaze fell on Laura, and she felt unaccountably flustered. True to form, she turned her attention to the children. "Finish your breakfast, boys. Wendy, it's time to get ready for school. Say goodbye to your father."

Wendy gulped down a last bite of jellied toast, smeared jelly around her mouth with a sticky napkin and lifted her face for her father's kiss. She puckered up, but he wisely kissed her on the forehead, then repeated the procedure with each of the boys. He paused at Laura's side, and for an awful moment she thought he was going to kiss her, too! But he simply smiled and turned away. Laura smiled at herself and got up, her spirits lightened considerably, her pulse fluttering.

It didn't last. Wendy was slow as molasses that morning and late to school again. It took Laura twice as long as usual to get the boys belted into their car seats. To cap an already difficult morning, they released themselves just on the edge of town and began climbing out of their seats, laughing and thrashing about wildly. While looking for a safe place to pull over, Laura tried reasoning with them, pointing out that they were going to get hurt if they didn't get back into their seats. They ignored her and immediately began throwing themselves against one another in mock battle. Ryan ricocheted off his brother and onto the floorboards, howling in distress. Laura lifted up in her seat and glanced over her shoulder, trying to ascertain the extent of his injuries and causing the car to weave across the narrow traffic lane. Abruptly a siren punctuated the chaos. Laura's gaze flew to the rearview mirror. Colored lights flashed from the top of the light blue police cruiser behind her.

"Oh, no!"

Robbie jerked around and looked behind them. "Police!" he yelped, and instantly began climbing back into his car seat.

Ryan suddenly stopped wailing and crawled up off the floorboards to see for himself, voicing his skepticism. "Uh-uh, the powice not going to get us." But when he peeked up over the back of the seat, he yelped and stuck his fingers in his mouth, hunkering down in sudden fear.

On the verge of panic, Laura continued on a little way farther until she found a wide, level space on the shoulder of the road. Whipping over, she immediately wrenched open her small handbag, extracted her wallet and stuffed it under the seat. She didn't dare let that officer get a look at her Colorado license. It was routine practice in some localities to run every out-of-state driver's license through the system, and that could be disastrous if Doyal or anyone else had filed a missing-persons report on her. She'd known him to do it before, when a so-called "friend" of his had gone missing. She'd thought it admirable at the time, but then a policeman had called with the information that his "friend" was safe and well and at a certain address. Doyal had thanked him, then immediately dispatched Calvin to pay their "friend" a long-delayed visit. When Laura remarked that his demeanor was less than friendly, he had confessed that his "friend" owed him a great deal of money, which he would now collect, after having allowed the Denver PD to do his legwork for him. Laura had felt uneasy, as she had increasingly done for some time, and had filed the incident away in her mind.

Oblivious of Wendy's small, strident voice berating the boys, and not even cognizant that the five-year-old had twisted around and struggled to her knees, Laura tightened her fists on the steering wheel as she waited for the policeman to reach her window. She saw his clipboard first, balanced as it was against the top of his holstered pistol. Only when he bent, thrust his muffled face toward her and tapped a finger on the window did Laura reluctantly lower the glass. To her surprise, he pulled down the muffler wrapped around the bottom of his face, tugged off his mirrored sunglasses and stuck his head inside the car, bellowing for the children to calm down. Only then did Laura realize that utter chaos had erupted all around her.

She twisted away from the officer, turning her attention gladly to the children. "Turn around and sit down, Wendy. You know better than that."

"Ryan's gonna get us arrested!" she shot back, twisting around within the strangling confines of her safety belt.

"Am not!" Ryan roared from the back seat.

"Are too!" Robbie shouted from his car seat. "Godiva told us so!"

"Hush, all of you!" Laura ordered, releasing her belt so that she could more easily renegotiate her position and take in the situation. "Ryan, get back in your car seat, and don't get out of it again. Since you and Robbie are so good at releasing those safety belts, you can just fasten them for yourselves this time."

"Guess I know why you were weaving back there," said the officer through the window.

Laura bit her lip and slowly eased around to face him. She made herself smile, despite the fact that her heart was beating like a bass drum. "I'm sorry, Officer. It's been a difficult morning."

He was surprisingly young and good-looking, and the smile he flashed her was potent in the extreme. "Looks like you have your hands full."

Laura nodded, somewhat relieved. "You could say that."

He leaned his forearm on the car and let his gaze slip over her. "Are they, um, yours?"

Laura shook her head. "Ah, no."

The smile with which he gifted her this time was not only potent, it was downright sizzling. "Excellent," he said, and began tugging off his gloves, using his perfect white teeth. Laura felt a spurt of hope, which he dashed in the very next instant. "Could I see your license, please?"

Laura fought the urge to gulp, and reached for her purse. Her hands were trembling. Her whole body was trembling. She made herself dig through the bag, pretending to look for her wallet. Finally, when any idiot could have seen from a mile away that she wasn't going to find it, she turned back to the window.

"Oh, my goodness." It sounded flat and unconvincing to her own ears, but she was stuck with it. "I guess I left my wallet at home."

He straightened, tugged a ballpoint pen from the clasp of his clipboard and began clicking the button. Laura knew he was trying to decide what to do with her. Wendy hissed something at her, but Laura hushed her with a snap of her fingers, as the policeman was bending to speak to her again.

"And where is home, ma'am?" he asked lightly.

Laura began to relax. She had learned over the past few weeks that the Fortune name meant something in this small town, and for once she felt no compunctions about using it. "These are the children of Mr. Adam Fortune. I'm their live-in nanny."

The Fortune name worked its touted magic. Mr. Policeman lifted his brows, lips pursed for a whistle. "I see. I assume Mr. Adam Fortune will confirm that."

"Certainly."

"You'd better give me your name, then."

There was no way out of it. "Laura Beaumont."

He produced the clipboard and began scribbling. "That's *L-A-U-R-A B-E-A-U-M-O-N-T?*"

"Yes."

"And Mr. Fortune can be reached at..."

Laura supplied the telephone numbers at both the office and the house. The policeman stowed the pen and, to her surprise, offered his hand. "I'm Officer Raymond Cooper. Pleased to meet you, Miss Beaumont. It is Miss Beaumont, isn't it?"

Laura gulped and put her hand in his for a warm, brief shake. "Yes. Miss."

His teeth flashed white. "Excellent. Well, *Miss* Beaumont, try to watch your driving a little closer. I'd hate to think of you in an accident."

"Of course. Th-thank you."

He stuck his head inside the car again. "As for you three..." He divided a stern look between the children. "You stop giving this pretty lady a hard time. You're endangering your lives when you start fooling around like that inside a car. From now on, you stay in your places and keep those belts buckled. Hear?"

Three wide-eyed faces bobbed up and down. Officer Raymond Cooper nodded and withdrew, the full force of his smile trained on Laura.

"You have a nice day now," he said before straightening to his full and—Laura suddenly noticed—impressive height. Her smile was genuine and rife with relief as he took his leave of her. Only when he'd driven away did she began breathing normally again. She felt lucky beyond belief, and yet it never occurred to her as she got out to check the boys' safety belts that this might well be only a reprieve.

Robbie balanced on his knee on the chair seat, his tongue stuck out the corner of his mouth as he concentrated on placing the plate just so. His relief obvious in the simple clap of his hands, he sat back on his heels and smiled at Laura, who dutifully praised him.

"That's very good, Robbie. In fact, that's perfect. Now the napkin..." She handed over the folded linen rectangle and lifted a brow skeptically as he moved to place it on the left side of the plate. Catching her hint, he quickly switched it to the other side and stroked it proudly with his hand.

"My turn," Ryan declared, his fists clutching knife, fork and spoon. Robbie stuck out his tongue at his brother, but climbed down off the dining room chair. Laura relieved Ryan of his burden of flatware while he climbed up to take Robbie's place. First she handed him the case knife, instructing, "Blade toward the plate, sweetie. That's the curved part. That's right. Now the spoon..."

Laura paused in the act of passing Ryan the spoon, catching the muted sound of now familiar steps. Adam stepped into view and leaned a shoulder negligently against the casing of the wide doorway. He had loosened his necktie and removed his coat and was in the process of rolling up his sleeves.

"Hello, family," he said, his gaze flickering over Laura. She felt her skin heat with remembered sensation.

"Hewwo, Daddy," Ryan said. "Waura, gimme the 'poon!"

Laura snapped her attention back to the waiting child and abruptly thrust the spoon at him. He plunked it down on the wrong side of the plate and reached for the fork, which she mindlessly handed over.

"We're learning to set the table," Wendy announced proudly, a water tumbler clutched to her chest.

Laura heard the smile in Adam's voice. "So I see. You're doing it very well, too."

"I got the most important job," Wendy said.

"Uh-uh!" Robbie objected. "I put down the plates and the na'kins!"

"I do 'poons and forts and knives!" Ryan said importantly.

Adam laughed. It was a frightening sound, a happy sound. Laura extended a hand to Wendy. "We just need this one tumbler and . . . There! A perfect table."

Wendy slipped away and ran to her father. "See, Daddy! A perfect table for Beverly's perfect lamb chops. That's what Laura says."

Adam swung her up into his arms. "Lamb chops, yum!" He pretended to take a bite out of her cheek, much to her giggling delight, but even as she threw her chubby arms around his neck, his gaze strayed to Laura once more. She couldn't help feeling that there was a purpose behind those golden eyes. He hugged Wendy and sat her down, then strode across the room and around the table to gather up the boys. One riding the crook of each arm, he kissed their foreheads before looking straight into each set of eyes. "So, have you guys been especially good for Laura today?"

Both boys nodded vigorously, but the knowing lift of Adam's eyebrow robbed them of their initial enthusiasm. "That's not what I heard," he said to dead silence. "Officer Cooper told me you were giving Laura a hard time this morning, climbing out of your car seats, jumping around in the car. In fact, I was told that Laura was so flustered, she lost her driver's license." His gaze slid back to her, and she felt her breath catch.

That blasted police officer had actually checked up on her! Had he checked through police channels, as well? Oh,

God, what might he have told Adam? Suddenly her heart was pounding so hard she felt faint. She didn't even hear Adam ask his question the first time.

"Laura!"

She flinched. "What?"

"I asked if you'd found your license."

She opened her mouth, but before she could decide what to say to avoid trouble, Wendy unwittingly shoved her right into it, neck-deep. "Laura didn't lose her license, Daddy," she said helpfully. "She hid it under the seat."

Adam's gaze turned incredulous. "*Hid* it?"

Laura felt her face drain of color, then surge with heat. "I...I... It was..."

Adam let the boys slide down to the floor and stepped forward, his hands gripping the back of a chair. "You hid it, Laura? You hid your license from the police?"

Laura felt perilously close to tears. "I—I was afraid."

"Afraid? Why on earth—?"

"It's expired!" she gasped in sudden inspiration. "I... I forgot, and—and I let it expire!"

"You let it expire."

"Yes, and... Well, I hadn't thought about it in weeks and weeks." She gulped. "Then, this morning, wh-when I saw those flashing lights in the rearview mirror, I—I panicked. I...well, I was already upset, you understand. The boys... Anyway, Ryan had fallen and was crying like he could be hurt, and suddenly all I could think to do was stuff my wallet under the seat. It—it wasn't very smart, I know, but at the time... And it turned out okay, after all."

"Yes," Adam mused, his gaze turning inward, "it turned out okay."

Laura bit her lip, assailed by guilt and regret. Oh, if only Wendy hadn't seen her stash that wallet! How could she have been so stupid and careless? Why hadn't she just thrown the damned thing away a long time ago? If Adam should ever find out that she'd lied to him, he'd be so hurt, so angry, so disappointed in her. She couldn't bear to think of it.

"Well," he said suddenly, "you'll have to get it renewed, of course." He smiled wanly. "Can't have you driving the kids around without a proper license, can we?"

She shook her head, her gaze carefully averted. "I'll take care of it," she lied smoothly, and he nodded.

"See that you do."

She took a deep breath. "I'm sorry you had to be bothered with this."

"No bother," he murmured, idly switching a misplaced spoon from one side of the plate to another. "He, um... Officer Cooper, he didn't...get out of line or anything, did he?"

The question was so unexpected that she had to think about it. "No. No, he was very polite and helpful." She folded her arms and glanced around her. "He certainly put these characters in their places."

Adam nodded blandly. "Good." He shook a finger at the three little faces. "Let that be the end of the shenanigans in the car, or the police will be the least of your worries. Got it?"

Ryan and Robbie nodded solemnly, while Wendy, confident in her role as the lesser culprit, said brightly, "Yes, Daddy."

Adam smiled. "Fine." He rubbed his hands together. "Now when do we eat?"

Laura closed her eyes in a moment of intense relief, then reinforced her smile. "I'll ask Beverly," she said, slipping away. She didn't see the way Adam's gaze followed her from the room, or the hand that came up to skim his head in frustration.

Adam rolled onto his side and sighed, resisting the impulse to open his eyes. He really needed to get some sleep tonight. How long had it been, he wondered, since he'd slept the whole night through without waking to thoughts of Laura...Laura and her lies? She had lied to him; he had no doubt of it. She had lied to him, and he had let her. And he would go on letting her, for to call her hand might well mean ending the situation as it existed. He had known today that he wasn't ready to do that. In fact, when that brash young policeman stood in front of his desk today, grinning from ear to ear after ostensibly checking *Miss* Beaumont's story, Adam had wanted nothing so much as to knock those smiling teeth down handsome Officer Cooper's mouth. It had taken all the control developed by his years in the military to keep his seat and answer Cooper's questions smoothly. Yes, Laura Beaumont was employed as nanny to his children. She undoubtedly did possess a drivers' license. No, he could think of no reason why she might not have wanted to turn her license over to the proper authorities. Yes, it was very likely that she had simply forgotten her wallet in her rush to get Wendy to school on time.

Only she hadn't. *"Laura didn't lose her license, Daddy. She hid it under the seat." "I was afraid." Afraid.*

"What are you afraid of, Laura?" he whispered to the dark. He wished he knew. He wished he knew what Laura feared, instead of what he feared. He feared that he'd never find a business at which he could excel, a career with which he'd be happy, a life for himself. He feared that he was never again going to be content or easy, that he'd never know another night of peace, that he'd lie awake night after night wondering what might have been if Laura Beaumont had loved him. He feared whatever Laura feared, as well as her ambitions and whatever, whoever, she loved. He feared Officer Cooper, and every man who might win Laura's heart.

Somehow he'd known from the beginning why Cooper had really come into his office that afternoon. He'd waited, some part of his mind mechanically filing away Cooper's every word, gesture and expression, while another part of him dreaded what was to come. It hadn't taken Cooper long to get to the point.

"I figured she was on the level," he'd said, "working for you. Stands to reason that anyone working for the Fortunes has been checked out."

Adam had had to look away. Why hadn't he checked her out? he'd asked himself. But he'd already known the answer to that. He hadn't checked because he hadn't wanted to know if she wasn't who she said she was, what she seemed to be.

The officer had gone on. "Fact is, it's the situation I want to check out. Frankly, I take it as a matter of honor not to step on another man's toes where his woman's concerned. So I decided to come on over here and just be sure...."

Adam hadn't helped him. He hadn't said what any honest, self-respecting man in his position would have said at that point, that Laura was her own woman, free as a bird, unattached, available. He'd just lifted his chin and waited, his heart beating slow and steady, but hard enough to shake his body with every slam. Officer Cooper had cleared his throat and lost a little of his bravado.

"I mean, her being such a beautiful woman and all... And I remembered that you're single..." Adam's continued silence had obviously frustrated him, for he'd gone on to firmly point out the obvious. "She lives in your house."

Adam had smiled then. "Yes."

The satisfaction he'd felt, the relief just in knowing that she lived in the same house with him, that she'd be there when he got home in the evenings, when he woke in the mornings, was enough to tell him that his feelings had gone beyond mere physical attraction and gratitude. But for how long? The end of the semester? The end of summer? Or until some man like Officer Cooper turned her head? Adam had looked then at the tall, well-made young man before him, handsome by anyone's standards, confident, healthy, and he'd made up his mind that he was not going to stand idly by, tongue-tied, while such a man stepped between him and Laura. He had cleared his throat and put out his hand.

"Thank you," he'd said as the younger man took his hand, confusion apparent on his face. "You're a rarity these days, Officer Cooper," Adam had told him. "Most men would have pressed the lady for a date, even if they'd known another man was involved with her."

He'd felt sorry for the officer after that because of the way his face had fallen. "Then you and she are..."

Adam had taken his hand back then. He'd felt sorry for the young man, but he wasn't an idiot. "She is, as you say, a very beautiful woman," he'd pointed out, "and my children adore her. She's made an enormous difference in our household, I assure you. We'd be lost without her."

Officer Cooper was looking at the floor, his disappointment palpable. "Yes, well..." he said, "as for the children... They were giving her a pretty hard time this morning. The little boys had climbed out of their seats and were acting up. That made her weave slightly in her lane of traffic, and that's what prompted me to pull her over. She said she'd left her wallet behind in the rush to get the little girl to school."

Adam had nodded. "They can be quite a handful. Since their mother died a year and a half ago, I've had some trouble finding my way with them, but Laura's changed all that. Together we're getting a handle on it. Thank you for bringing this to my attention. You can be sure that I'll deal with the matter."

But he hadn't. Not really. He'd spoken to the boys about their misbehavior in the car only as a way to bring up the matter—and Officer Raymond Cooper—with Laura. He'd wanted to gauge her reaction to the young, handsome officer, and instead he'd gotten lost in the look of pure terror that lurked just beyond a too-bright smile and a too-level gaze. What was she afraid of? Even if her license had expired, why would she hide it, rather than simply face the issue head-on? It wasn't as if it were a truly criminal offense. No, it just didn't make sense. It didn't add up. In fact, now that he thought about it, nothing that he knew about her, little as it was, added up. He had questions about her, questions with answers that he feared. Wouldn't it be better to get it out in the open? Whatever it was, they could deal with it then. Yes, head-on, that was the only way to deal with a problem like this.

He threw back the covers and slid into the fleece pants that he kept beside the bed, then reached for his bathrobe, simultaneously stuffing his feet into corduroy house shoes. He slapped the robe together and knotted the belt as he strode across the floor. And then he was standing at Laura's door, his fist poised, his heart pounding like a steam engine at full tilt, and he could only think, *What if?* What if the truth drove them even farther apart? What if she chose to leave them, rather than face it? What if he couldn't bear it, what if he couldn't accept whatever it was? What if she hated him for forcing it out into the open? He unclenched his hand and laid his forehead against the cool painted wood of her door, wanting Laura Beaumont more than he could remember ever wanting anyone or anything.

He pulled away from the door, feeling as if he'd just averted catastrophe, and returned to his room, where he slid off his robe, kicked off his shoes and climbed into bed, fleece pants and all. It was a long time before he could sleep, a long time, but when he did, it was with the thought that Laura would be there in the morning—for now.

# Eight

Adam leaned back in his black leather desk chair and rubbed his eyes with the thumb and forefinger of his left hand while the right cradled the telephone receiver against his ear. He yawned silently, nodding his head at the comment his sister had made until he had recovered enough to speak.

"Yeah, I know. I talked to Mom yesterday. She's worried that Rocky's upset because the family hasn't formally welcomed Luke, but she's wary about getting everyone together, for Dad's sake."

"Well, you can hardly blame her," Caroline replied in her smooth voice. "Nathaniel's trying to stage a coup because of this stock business. I keep telling everyone that we should be less concerned with questioning Dad and more concerned with what Monica's intentions are now that she has the stock, but I honestly don't know what Mike and Kyle and Kristina are thinking right now."

"I don't imagine they know what to think any more than the rest of us do," Adam said absently.

Caroline's reaction was predictable. "Adam! You know Dad never does anything that isn't in the best interests of the Fortune companies. I'll admit that his reticence about his reasons is puzzling, but ultimately you have to trust his judgment and intentions."

Adam shook his head. "No one's arguing the point, little sister. Dad and I may not see eye-to-eye on a lot of things, I may even take violent exception on one or two issues, but his dedication to the family business has never been in question. I might like him a little better if it were."

"Adam!"

"Yes, I know, sacrilege from your viewpoint."

"It may surprise you to know, Adam, that until recently your dedication to the military was looking very Jake-like."

Adam smiled humorlessly. "As a matter of fact, someone else has pointed out that very thing to me."

"Really? Who?"

Adam's voice softened of its own volition. "In a manner of speaking, Kate."

A moment of bittersweet silence followed. Then Caroline cleared her throat. "I assume that you're referring to the legacy."

"Mmm-hmm . . ."

"I never quite understood why she left you a pair of photo albums," Caroline hinted.

Adam smiled to himself. "She was very wise, that's why. Actually, someone else figured it out before I did."

"Oh?"

"And that's all I'm going to say on the subject."

"That someone else wouldn't be tall and slender, carry herself like a dancer and have long blond hair, would she?" Caroline asked teasingly.

Adam frowned. "Who told you about Laura?"

Caroline laughed. "Dad was very complimentary."

Of course. "And just what did he say?" Did that sound too concerned, too proprietary?

"That the new nanny was cut from a very different cloth than her predecessors," Caroline told him. "For what it's worth, he approves."

A sarcastic retort was right on the tip of his tongue, but for some reason, Adam swallowed it, choosing to change the subject instead. "How's Nick and baby Kate?"

Caroline's chuckle told him that she knew exactly what he was doing and that she was going to allow it. "Nick's working hard and Kate's napping."

"And you?"

"Oh, I'm fine, Adam. Never better."

"Motherhood obviously agrees with you," Adam noted softly.

"Yes."

The wealth of well-being and happiness in that one word made Adam's throat close up on him, and suddenly he was assailed with a fierce longing for things he could not even identify. For a moment, he had a hard time following Caroline's continued speech.

"Just Dad," she was saying. "Well, and Monica. That's one reason I called you, brother mine. You're more detached than I am. Your viewpoint is bound to be more objective. What do you think Monica's after?"

Adam rubbed a hand over his face, trying to marshal his scattered thoughts. "Well...maybe she just wants a piece of the pie. She was the Fortune Cosmetics spokeswoman for so long, maybe she feels she's entitled."

Caroline produced a surprisingly unladylike snort. "Monica Malone has never struck me as a woman who might be willing to settle for a piece of anything."

Adam had to concede the point. "True. All right then, so ultimately she's after the company."

"Kate's company," Caroline pointed out.

"You think that's pertinent?" Adam asked.

"Somehow I do."

Adam thought a moment, then shrugged. "I don't see the point in speculating about this."

"We have to be prepared," Caroline argued.

"*You* have to be prepared," Adam retorted, then he sighed. "You said it yourself, Caroline, I'm more detached. The truth is, I've got more on my mind than Monica Malone and the Fortune companies. I have a family to raise, and I haven't the slightest idea yet how I'm going to support them."

"You know you just have to say the word and the door to the office of your choice will open at Fortune—"

"And you know I'm not going to do that," he said, interrupting her. "Look, Sis, thanks for calling. Sorry I couldn't be more help, but like I said, I've got a lot on my mind."

"Poor Adam," Caroline said lightly. "Don't worry. You'll find your place in the world."

But would he? Adam wondered. He seemed no closer now than he had the day Diana died. He sat forward in his chair, uncertain why he wanted to get off the phone so badly. It wasn't as if he had anything truly productive to do. Nevertheless, he couldn't wait to end the conversation. He tried to sound caring and busy. "Give my best to Nick."

"All right, thanks. Say, why don't you and the kids come over one weekend soon? I haven't seen my niece and nephews in ages."

"Sure thing. I'll call."

"No, you won't. Maybe I should call and make arrangements with *Laura.*"

"No!" Adam rubbed a hand over his face, aware that his outburst had been telling. "Laura's not the parent here. I am, and I'll take care of it first chance I get."

"Great. I look forward to seeing you soon, then, big brother."

"Soon," Adam promised, and dropped the telephone receiver into its cradle. He reached for the top file folder from a short stack on his desk, flipped open the cover and began to read. After a moment, he realized that he hadn't absorbed a single word and started over again from the beginning. But it was no use. He tossed the folder back onto the pile and slumped in his chair.

He was in a lousy mood. Nothing seemed to be going right these days, and he was impatient to settle in to some solid work. Yet he couldn't seem to concentrate—not that he'd found a damned thing on which he wanted to concentrate. Nothing, but nothing, appealed, and he was sick of the search. Moreover, he was sick of his own company, but he didn't want to see anyone else, except... He scowled at the very thought of Laura. He would not fall to fantasizing about the nanny, for pity's sake. It was bad enough that he couldn't control his dreams, that he woke up night after night hard as stone, thinking of Laura sleeping in her bed just across the hall. Better to think of his children.

He smiled at that. Who would have thought that he'd so enjoy those three little scamps of his? And they were scamps, no doubt about it. They needed a firm hand, those three, and yet a firm hand was what the previous nannies had tried, and in every case, the children's behavior had worsened instead of improving. What was it about Laura that reached them? Or was it Laura at all? Might it not be him? He was the one who had changed his behavior, and the children had responded in kind, more or less. Oh, he wasn't fooling himself. Every one of them would continue to challenge and try him, simply because of the exuberance of their individual natures and the history of his neglect. It was to be expected. He had it coming. But he felt certain that he could deal with it now. Considering that, what was his excuse for keeping Laura on?

She had lied to him; she was keeping things from him. Despite what she'd said, he knew that she hadn't renewed her driver's license, and he knew there had to be a reason for that. She was afraid, afraid of being tracked, of being found—but by whom? The law? He prayed that it wasn't the law, but how could he know? And, not knowing, how could he go on trusting his children to her? Because he wanted to, because he did trust her, despite everything. Because he wanted her.

That was the upshot of it all. He wanted Laura Beaumont, with a passion far surpassing anything he had ever felt for anyone else, and that desire was making him crazy. It was destroying his concentration, undermining his search for a business and career, playing havoc with his moods and emotions. Was it also compromising his judgment? Was he making a mistake by keeping her on? He wished to God that he knew.

Laura glanced across the room and laid aside her book. He was preoccupied, lost in thought, his magazine sagging to his lap. Even as she watched, he closed his eyes and laid back his head. She wondered again what was bothering him, and why he didn't talk about it. He seemed so tense lately, so worried. Quietly she got up and walked into the kitchen, pulled a snifter down from the cabinet and tipped a measure of brandy into it. She cupped the bowl of the snifter in her hand, as she'd seen Adam do, and carried it back into the den.

"Here."

Adam abruptly sat up straight and opened his eyes, focusing on the brandy snifter.

"Thought you might like a drink," she said, offering it to him.

He glanced up in surprise, then carefully took the snifter from her hand. "Thanks." He quaffed half the amber liquid in a single gulp while she crossed once more to the sofa and sat down, curling her legs beneath her. Adam gasped and shook his head as the liquor burned.

Laura folded her hands in her lap. "How was your day?"

He lifted a cryptic brow. "Pointless."

"No luck yet?"

He shook his head. "I don't know, maybe the military is the only thing I'm fit for."

"Why do you say that?"

He sipped brandy and thought. "Maybe I need someone to give me orders."

She laughed at that, her voice clear and bright. "I'd say that you're definitely better at giving them than taking them."

He smiled. "Maybe so. I've had a few superior officers who would testify to that."

Laura answered his smile with one of her own. "I think you could do any number of things," she told him.

He seemed pleased. "It's not that I can't do any of these things," he admitted. "It's just that I haven't found anything that appeals to me. I mean, how excited can you get about replacing brake pads or selling other people's property?"

"Well, for the right persons, those are fine things," Laura ventured, "but maybe you need something with more challenge."

"I guess," he muttered into his drink. Then he settled back, apparently thinking aloud. "I want to be passionate about what I do. I want to look forward to going to work every day. I want...too damned much, evidently." He sighed and laid his head back once more.

Laura sat forward, unwilling to let him fall back into the malaise that seemed to afflict him these days. "Maybe you're going about it the wrong way," she said thoughtfully. "What sort of things are you interested in? I mean, what are your hobbies?"

He grimaced. "I don't have any hobbies."

"Well, what are your favorite things?"

He shook his head, rolling it from side to side against the back of his chair. "I don't know."

For an instant, she was exasperated with him, but then she had a thought. Scooting to the edge of her seat, she said, "You like history. At least you seem to prefer historical subjects on the television and in magazines."

He lifted his head, then looked down at the magazine on his lap, flipping it closed. "That's true, but everyone likes history. It's fascinating."

"But everyone doesn't," she argued.

He frowned. "Well, they ought to. History is...well, it's us. At least it's what makes us what we are."

"I agree."

He sat forward, warming to the subject. "Maybe all the traveling I've done has given me a special perspective on history, though. I mean, this is a young country, socially. Now, you take Europe or the Orient, those societies are thousands and thousands of years old! What's really fascinating to me, though, is how slow change came until relatively modern times. For instance, people just don't realize how little the American life-style changed, say, in the century that encompassed the American Revolution and the Civil War. Honestly, just tour Washington's place, Mount Vernon, then go down and do the antebellum mansions on the River Road, between Baton Rouge and New Orleans. You'll see that there wasn't much difference in the quality of the life-style in those two periods."

"Fascinating," Laura murmured, smiling to herself as he launched into another monologue.

"You can't begin to understand how society has changed until you realize what it changed from. Now you take, oh, all the emphasis on health issues these days. In the past, nobody really worried about cancer or high blood pressure or any of those diseases we now focus so much preventive care on. For one thing, they had no idea what to do about them. For another, too few people lived long enough to suffer from them. Do you know what the major cause of accidental death for women was until this century?"

Laura shook her head. She could have guessed childbirth but he didn't give her a chance.

"Fire," he said. "Think about it. Open fire was the only method of cooking until the advent of the cast-iron stove, and that was inefficient at best. Plus, it had to be stoked. Now think about the clothing that women wore until *after* the turn of the century. You turn too fast in a small, crowded kitchen. Your long, full skirt brushes a live ember or a red-hot stove. Poof! You go up in flames. The danger of fire was why so many kitchens were built *separate* from the house—and who worked in those kitchens?"

"Women, naturally," Laura said.

"You bet. And when did that begin to change? That began to change with the advent of public utilities." He set aside his brandy snifter and shifted in his seat to face her. "Now, you take warfare. You have no idea how brutal basic warfare was until the repeating rifle came along. These days..."

Laura sat back and got comfortable. She loved to see him like this, talking a mile a minute, gesturing broadly, so very animated and involved. *If he could see his own face now,* she mused, *he'd know how passionate he can be about a subject.* Irrationally she wondered if he could ever be that passionate about a woman, and then she remembered the feel of his arms, his mouth, his hands.

Instantly, remembered sensation swept over her, heightening her senses and evoking a sudden sense of loss. Instinct told her that Adam Fortune's unrestrained touch and focused attention would reduce her to the most elemental level of her existence and simultaneously lift her to the highest plane. She knew that nothing she had ever experienced would compare to what she could have with Adam—or rather, what she might have had, were it not for the mistakes of her past. How could she have thought that she loved Doyal, or that he loved her? And now, because of him, she was no longer free to love any man, and certainly not this one, for there were the children to consider. She could not expose them to danger, which meant that her time here was growing short. Suddenly grief swamped her, tears burning the backs of her eyes.

"Hey."

She didn't even know that Adam had moved until he took her hand in his. The shock of physical contact brought her thoughts to an abrupt halt, and her eyes once again focused outward. He was sitting on the edge of the coffee table, his elbows on his knees as he leaned toward her.

"What's wrong? The history of warfare may not be everyone's favorite topic of conversation, but I don't believe I've actually reduced anyone to tears with it before."

Laura realized her eyes were swimming and hastily dashed away the moisture, forcing a laugh. "I'm afraid I wasn't listening."

He abandoned the avuncular tone. "Tell me what's wrong, Laura."

She shook her head, deciding on half-truths. "Oh, it's silly. I was just realizing that I probably won't ever know what career you choose. "I—I won't know how the children progress or if the family likes your sister's new husband or how your father fares." She used her free hand to lift her hair and smooth it back from her face. "I guess I didn't expect to get so involved."

His thumb skimmed her knuckles. "You don't have to go," he said softly. "You can stay."

Laura gently pulled her hand from his, pretending a need to shift her weight. "I know I could stay at least as long as the children need me," she said, retreating once more into the lie, "but what about my plans? My dreams?"

He straightened, his hands smoothing up his thighs. "There ought to be a way to accommodate both your desire to go to college and your wish to stay here."

She hadn't thought of that. Quickly she shook her head. "The children deserve more attention than I could give them while attending college."

He leaned forward again suddenly, grasped her upper arms and pulled her to the very edge of the sofa, so that her knees came up against his. "*I* don't want you to go. *I* need you here. Doesn't that mean—"

She pressed her trembling fingers to his mouth, stopping the flow of words before they became too much to bear. "Don't," she whispered. "Please don't make it harder than it has to be."

He lifted his chin and pushed her hand away, pulling her closer still. "Laura..." It was part plea and part demand.

She slipped off the edge of the sofa and onto her knees just as his mouth found hers, giving herself up to the moment, knowing that it must be all she would ever have of this man. For that moment, she allowed herself to kneel there on the floor, between his splayed legs, her arms sliding around his waist as he bent her head back with the force of his kiss. He pulled her up and against him, his arms locked at the small of her back, his thighs holding her firm. His tongue pushed into her mouth, testing the edges of her teeth, licking the silky arch, stroking the sensitive walls, coaxing her tongue to dance, filling her, opening her to him. She clutched his shirt in her hands, wanting all the moment could give her, reveling in the knowledge that he was trying to bind her to him, even if it was only with desire.

When his hand slipped beneath the hem of her sweater at her back and began a slow journey upward and around, she knew where it was headed, and her breast tingled with anticipation long before his fingers plowed beneath the band of her bra and covered her flesh with his, making it crest against his palm. She began to tremble as he kneaded her, his mouth possessing hers, his arm and legs holding her captive to that possession. He couldn't know how badly she wanted truly to belong, how much she wanted to give herself, to him, only to him. He couldn't know, and she couldn't tell him. It was that sad knowledge that brought fresh tears to her eyes when he tugged himself free and gathered the soft curtain of her hair into both his hands, pulling her head back so that he could look down into her face.

"Tell me you won't go. Laura, sweetheart, tell me you'll stay. I'm asking you to stay. For pity's sake, say you'll stay!"

She could only gaze sadly into his eyes and whisper, "I'm sorry. I'm so sorry."

He jerked as if she'd slapped him, and his breathing was suddenly harsh and uneven. He released her abruptly, his hands going to his knees, splayed wide. He turned his face away from her, a muscle working in the hollow of his jaw. Laura bowed her head, her arms falling to her sides as she got a foot beneath her and rose. She swallowed the need to tell him how desperately she wanted to stay, how much she had come to love him and his children, how only her fear for their safety could make her go now. She stepped carefully to the side and moved swiftly toward the door.

"I trust there will be no accusations about my immoral intentions tomorrow," he stated bitterly.

Laura halted where she was and turned back, her arms wrapping around her middle protectively. "No, no accusations, no pretending I didn't want you to kiss me, not this time."

He was suddenly on his feet, facing her. "Why did you before? Why try to make either of us believe you didn't want it?"

Her smile was self-deprecating. "No woman wants to admit she's a fool, not even to herself."

"Why does wanting to be with me make you a fool?" he asked, frustration sharpening his tone. "It's what I want. You know it's what I want!"

Laura shook her head, blinking back tears. "It doesn't make any difference, Adam. I cannot stay. I *have* to go. Only a true fool would make the leaving more difficult than it has to be."

He pushed a hand over his head, then brought it to his hip, nodding. "I'll call the agency tomorrow," he said roughly, his gaze carefully averted.

Laura lifted her chin, steeling herself. "Fine. Thank you." With that, she turned and made her escape, forcing her feet to keep a sedate pace, despite the tears rolling down her face.

"There's a Miss Wilton here to see you, Adam."

Her voice was smooth as silk and utterly devoid of emotion. He felt a flash of irritation, but then he looked up and caught a spasm of pain on her face. She mastered it quickly, lifting her chin. Nevertheless, he felt a surge of hope. He had wondered what her reaction would be when he made the appointment, intentionally arranging this interview where and when Laura was sure to be about. Now he knew. She didn't want to go. No matter what she said, she didn't *want* to go. Why, then, was she doing this? He pushed the question away, rising to meet the small, delicate, almost childlike woman who stood at Laura's side. He put out a hand, sliding into cordiality. He gauged her age at about thirty, now that he got a closer look.

"Hello. I'm Adam Fortune. Please have a seat on the couch."

The little woman nodded cheerfully and moved quickly to sit. Laura turned to go, but Adam stopped her. "No, Laura, stay. Since it's your position that Miss Wilton is applying for, she may have a few questions for you."

Laura flashed a desperate look over her shoulder, her dismay evident even as she drew herself up and stood her ground. "I—I'll help if I can," she said, unable to quite keep the tremor from her voice.

Miss Wilton seemed not to notice. She was busy tugging off her gloves and folding them together in her lap. "Well, there is just one question," she said primly, "if you don't mind."

Laura cleared her throat. "Not at all."

Miss Wilton cast a bright-eyed look at Adam that seemed to say she was embarrassed to speak in front of him, yet he had the distinct impression that she was not. "I was just wondering why you're leaving," Miss Wilton said.

Laura opened her mouth, but then she snapped it shut again and bowed her head, her facade of indifference crumbling. Adam's heart lurched. He felt her pain as if it were his own. Oh, no, she did not want to go. Why, then, did she insist on this farce? At the moment, that question was secondary to the need to rescue her from her own stubbornness. He turned smoothly to Miss Wilton, engaging her attention.

"Miss Beaumont's employment was always temporary," he said. "I assure you that her leaving has nothing to do with dissatisfaction on either of our parts. It was prearranged."

Miss Wilton seemed satisfied. "I suppose you'd like to see these before we go on," she said, extracting an envelope from her purse and extending them toward him. She seemed totally oblivious of Laura's distress, a fact that did not endear her to her prospective employer.

Adam took the envelope and pulled out several sheets of paper, which he quickly scanned. They were letters of reference, very glowing letters of reference. He pretended genuine interest, but his every sense was trained on Laura, who stood tensely by, her moroseness hanging over the room like a black cloud. He folded the papers, put them back in the envelope and handed them to Miss Wilton, saying noncommittally, "You seem to have a good deal of experience."

"Oh, yes, I should say so."

For several minutes, Miss Wilton expounded proudly on said experience, but Adam could only concentrate on not looking at Laura. Finally, sensing a break in the monologue, he quickly interjected, "That's very impressive. You've definitely given me a great deal to think about. Thank you."

Miss Wilton preened, one small hand patting her short mouse-brown hair where it flipped up, just behind her left ear. Adam imagined that the tiny flip irritated her no end.

Miss Wilton did not seem the sort to tolerate errant flips. Seeing that he'd noticed, she dropped her hand to her lap.

"I'd like to meet the children now, if you please," she said firmly.

Adam was taken aback. His smile strained, his impatience barely held in check, he quietly replied that he had decided not to bring the children into the matter until he had narrowed down the list of applicants. "They're quite young," he explained hastily. "I don't want to confuse them."

Miss Wilton stiffened at the implication that she did not yet have a lock on the position. "I see. Well, you understand, I trust, that I simply cannot accept any offer until I've met the children involved."

"Yes, of course," Adam said, resisting the impulse to grit his teeth as he got to his feet and held out a hand to assist her in rising.

Miss Wilton's slender brows rose into the fringe of her bangs. Quickly she gathered herself and her accoutrements and stood. "I can't promise not to accept another position before I hear from you," she pointed out briskly.

Adam smiled and nodded. "I understand. Thank you for coming."

Miss Wilton was frowning when he closed the door behind her a few moments later, but Adam didn't give it a thought as he turned and strode swiftly down the hall to the den. Laura was standing at the window, the curtain pulled aside so that she could stare out at the blanket of snow covering the ground. Adam went straight to her and, after only an instant's hesitation, slid his arms around her and pulled her back against his chest. "Laura, you can't pretend anymore that you *want* to leave here. Whatever is driving you away, I know it's not ambition. Tell me. Please tell me what the problem is."

She laid her head back against his shoulder and rolled it slowly from side to side. "I can't, and it wouldn't make any difference if I could."

He slid a hand upward, over her breasts and along the graceful column of her throat, to cup her chin and angle her face toward his. "Laura," he whispered beseechingly, brushing his mouth across hers. Her lips trembled beneath his, but then she turned her face away.

"Please don't, Adam. It already hurts so much."

He didn't know what to say, how to convince her to change her mind. He could only offer a silent comfort, his cheek pressed to her temple, his arms tight around her. He could only hold her, it seemed, and so he vowed to hold her as long as he could.

Laura closed her eyes and let herself feel safe, but it was an emotion she dared not indulge too long. She dared not believe that it extended beyond this moment, far worse even than the thought of going was the thought of Doyal finding her here. She knew that he wouldn't let her escape him a second time, and even if, by some miracle, his fury did not spill over onto the Fortune family, they were bound to suffer. Even if she simply disappeared one day and they were never to know how or why, they would still wonder and worry. She couldn't let that happen. They'd already lost Diana in a senseless accident. She couldn't let her own departure remain unresolved. When the time came to go, she would have to find a way to convince Adam that it was what she wanted—but not yet. Oh, God, not yet!

And so she stood, her head on his shoulder, her arms covering his as he held her. She could have this, just this, and when he found a replacement for her, she would go. She would convince him that it was what she wanted after all, and she would go. For now she would feel safe—and loved. She would let herself feel loved, just this once, just this moment. Even if real love was not quite what Adam felt for her, she would let herself believe that it was . . . for now. Just for now. But the moment Adam found her replacement, she would go. She promised herself that she would go, and she kept her promises. She always kept her promises. No matter how badly it hurt.

# Nine

Her cheeks were so cold they stung, but her nose was beginning to thaw to the point of dripping. Still, she smiled as Robbie attempted to pull off his knit mask and yelped when he also tugged a handful of hair.

"Here, let me." She went down on one knee and carefully peeled up the heavy woolen combination mask and cap. Robbie giggled when it momentarily hung on his nose. Laura pulled it off, shook it, folded it and stuffed it in his coat pocket before turning to aid Ryan. Wendy already had her pink-and-blue monstrosity off. Her fine, thin hair flew about in all directions, the barrette on the top of her skull alarmingly askew. Laura paused for a moment to smooth her hair back into place and reset the barrette before absently dropping a kiss onto her forehead. In short order, all three pairs of little arms were grappling for holds about her neck, while plumply pursed lips smacked dry kisses all over her face. Laura fell back on her rump, laughing, but even as the sound bubbled up, her throat closed around a lump of tears. How in heaven's name was she going to give up this? They loved her. They needed her. She was a danger to them. She had to go.

*Don't think about it until the time comes,* she told herself. It was the same advice she'd been giving herself for days now.

When the frenzy of affection subsided, she pushed herself up to a full sitting position, her legs folded so that her ankles were crossed, and helped Robbie off with his mittens and coat. She noticed that Ryan did not wait for help, performing an antsy dance as he shed his outerwear. She

sent the lot of them to the bathroom, with instructions for
Ryan to go first.

"I'll be back in a minute to help you wash up."

She got to her feet and removed her coat and scarf, stowed
everyone's cold-weather gear in the hall closet, then went in
search of Beverly to ask that lunch be served. She was
starved. Playing in the snow and cold took a lot of energy.

Just as she started through the dining room toward the
kitchen, the sound of laughter drew her up short and spun
her around. It was couple laughter, the harmony of male
and female voices in intimate concert. It spoke of understanding and approval, of ease and kinship, and the male
voice was definitely Adam's. Curiosity and dread pulled her
toward the den. She paused in the doorway, her heart dropping like a stone in a well.

Adam and a small, attractive woman about his age were
sitting on the couch, their bodies angled toward one another, their eyes alight with eagerness. They were talking,
their conversation so tight and interwoven that they seemed
almost to be speaking at the same time. Laura's outsider's
ears could not even comprehend the words, but she understood all too well Adam's relaxed smile and enthusiastic
nods. When he reached out and took the woman's hand in
his, laying both casually upon her slender knee, Laura felt
the kick of jealousy in her midsection. It was so fierce that
her stomach churned and threatened to heave. She clamped
a hand to her belly, literally sick. That was the very moment when Adam seemed to notice her. He beamed at her
across the room.

"Oh, Laura, there you are. This is Jane. Jane, Laura."

The woman beside him turned a smile in Laura's direction. She was quite pretty, with large, intelligent slate-blue
eyes and long light brown hair, shot through with ginger and
curling softly about an elegantly featured face. Her eyes
sparkled with secret knowledge, or some delicious joke.
"Hello, Laura," she said richly. "I understand you have
tamed the heathens."

"What?"

Adam chuckled. "The children, where are they? Jane wants to see them."

Laura's heart hit rock bottom. So this is it, then. She gestured absently, murmuring, "I'll get them."

"Thank you," Adam said dismissively, turning back to Jane.

Laura reeled inwardly. Outwardly her legs and arms moved by rote. She collided with the walls in places, but somehow she made her way down the hall to the bath the children shared. She heard the sound of running water and giggles. She opened the door. The three of them were standing on two stools and bending over the same sink. Soap bubbled beneath running water. They were dipping their hands and smacking one another with the bubbles, aiming for the face. Any moment now, someone was bound to get soap in the eyes.

"Stop that." It came out dull and lifeless, mechanical, but all three stopped and looked up expectantly. It was then that the tears came. Laura jerked around, blinking rapidly. "Your father wants you in the den. You have company."

"Company?" Wendy squealed, delighted.

"Who is it?" Robbie demanded.

Laura turned back, smiling despite the telling sparkle of her eyes. It was the least she could do for them. "A lady, someone you'll like."

Robbie groaned, and Ryan joined in a heartbeat later, but Wendy was climbing down off the step stool, her curiosity evident in the jerky swiftness of her movements. The twins caught a whiff of it and were after her in a blink. Laura stepped aside and let them go, their little legs pelting down the halfway. She knew she ought to remind them of their manners, but she couldn't bring herself to do it. Let those kisses in the foyer be their last solid memory of her; they would be hers of them.

A misery unlike anything she'd ever felt in her life enveloped her. She lifted a hand to her mouth to stifle a sob and turned toward her room. This was the way it had to be, and she had vows to keep. She knew in her heart that Jane was a woman who would recognize the preciousness of those children. Adam was right to settle on her. She would be an excellent nanny. Her charges' misbehavior would not deter or fool her. She would be loving and firm, but she would also laugh with them and kiss their tiny wounds and keep them close to their father.

Their father. That was the real problem. Laura had seen in Jane's eyes a deep and understanding appreciation of Adam Fortune—and it had been mutual. Those two knew each other on some fundamental, elemental level. He was not wary with Jane. He was not tied in knots with her. There would be no danger to keep them apart. Oh, God. Laura sat on her bed and wept with silent, ferocious pain.

In sheer desperation, she began to tell herself that Jane might well be married or engaged to be, though it wasn't likely. Nannies were a solitary lot, dedicated to living in other people's houses and raising other people's children. An engaged or married woman would not be taking on a brand-new job. Perhaps it would be best if she was available. She did not want to think of Adam always alone. Much better that he be with someone like Jane. She wanted to think of him happy and well. She *needed* to feel that he would be all right, that his life would be satisfying and complete, even though she knew instinctively that hers would never be. It was then that she knew that she loved him. Suddenly everything she'd believed she felt for Doyal Moody was revealed, not only as ignorance, but as immature and, to her shame, quite desperate.

It was hard to admit how needy she had been—and perhaps still was. To have no one, no relative, no true friend, no lover, was a desperate and lonely and frightening thing. She had wondered sometimes after Sister Agnes's death if she really even existed. If a tree fell in a forest and there was no one around to hear, did it really make a sound? If a person lived but no one recognized that fact, did she really exist? Since going on the run from Doyal, never staying anywhere too long, trying to hide herself in plain sight, she'd often felt that same shattering sensation, but not since coming to the Fortune house. Here she was real and wanted and substantial. Here she was part of something, a necessity to the lives of others. Until now.

She closed her eyes and hoped it wouldn't be long. She didn't want the parting dragged out, the wound prodded. With that in mind, she got up, pulled her nylon duffel from the closet and began systematically packing her clothes. There were more, she noted mistily, than when she had arrived. Somehow Adam always found things she "needed." She made a thorough job of it, organizing, folding, stacking. Her bed was littered with tidy piles of clothing when someone tapped on her door.

"Laura?"

She froze. He had come to tell her straight away, then. Despite the tears starting in her eyes, she was glad, truly. The sooner done, the better for all concerned. She turned to stand at the foot of the four-poster bed facing the door, one hand clutching a pair of pink panties. "Come in."

Adam opened the door and stepped inside. He was smiling. "We're waiting lunch on you. The kids are so hungry they're threatening to eat their napkins. They—" He stopped and stared at the bed, his smile vanishing. "What are you doing?"

She turned her back, quickly folded the panties and thrust them atop a pile, stating the obvious. "I'm packing."

For a long moment, he said nothing. Then she felt him step up to her back. His voice was close to her ear when he said, "*Why* are you packing?"

She turned a pair of socks right side out and cuffed them together. "Let's don't pretend, Adam. She's absolutely perfect. I watched her for about two minutes, and I knew she was the one." She attempted a smile, a look into his eyes. She saw amusement and bleakness. She rejected both. "If you haven't accepted her already, please do so right away. Jane will work out, I promise you."

"You little idiot," he said softly, lifting his hands to cup her forearms and lightly pull her back against him. "I called the agency and told them to forget it."

"You what?" She pulled away and turned to face him, fighting the trembling warmth that being close to him brought.

"I called the agency and told them not to send over any more applicants."

She looked down, not wanting him to see the suspicious brightness in her eyes. "Then you agree that Jane is the right person to replace me."

He seized her shoulders and shook her. "I did it *before* Jane came to visit!" he declared. "I couldn't cope with it! I couldn't let you leave." His hands slid over her shoulders and up her neck, to cup her face. "Jane's my cousin. She's leaving Minnesota. Grandmother left her a house in Maine, and she's decided to move there with her son, Cody, before the new school year starts. She came to say goodbye."

A reprieve. The relief of it weakened her knees and sent her breath out in a whoosh. "Your cousin?" she repeated weakly.

"My cousin," he confirmed, sounding quite happy about it.

She closed her eyes and laid her head against his shoulder, wondering how her arms had come to be around his waist. She felt his lips in her hair and the strength, the possessiveness, of his hug. He held her for a long, sweet moment, then stepped around and turned her toward the door, his arm locked securely about her shoulders.

"Come and eat," he told her. "Then, later, you can put that damned mess away. You're not going anywhere yet."

Not yet. She wasn't leaving him yet. He couldn't cope with it. Yet. She realized that her arm was still about his waist, but she didn't remove it until they had almost reached the dining room.

They usually took lunch in the kitchen, but that table only sat four comfortably. As long as the twins were small enough to share one side of the table, it was homier to eat in the kitchen, but company would naturally dictate that they use the larger table in the dining room.

Laura put on a smile and stepped out of the curve of Adam's embrace, nodding companionably at Jane, *cousin*

Jane. "Sorry to keep you waiting," she said, as Adam pulled out her chair and she lowered herself into it.

"No problem," Jane said from across the table. "I've been visiting with the children." She smiled at the children, then turned back to Laura. "I've heard a deal about you, you know."

"Oh?" Laura turned a questioning gaze on each of the children, then on Adam.

Jane laughed lightly. "It was all good, I promise you."

"Oh." Laura felt herself blush. "Well, I love children, and Adam's so easy to work for."

"*Adam?*" Jane goggled, a slender hand flung against her chest. "*Cousin* Adam?" She laughed. "Adam The-Military-Is-Too-Soft Fortune?"

"Very funny," Adam said dryly. "Let me tell you something, Jane dear. I'd as soon take on Saddam Hussein single-handedly than try to muster these three commandos of mine alone. I bow to Laura's superior strategy. In short, she's the general in this operation. I'm the captain."

"Well, I am impressed." Jane sat back in her chair, her lively eyes moving thoughtfully between Laura and Adam, her slender hands flanking her plate, which contained a flaky croissant stuffed with turkey and cheese and a small bowl of cream of broccoli soup. It was Laura's favorite, and suddenly she was starving.

"Lunch is getting cold while we're having this silly conversation," she said lightly, and picked up her spoon.

It was all the signal the children needed. They fell to like starving soldiers, which made Adam laugh and Jane shake her head, smiling. Twenty minutes later, Adam had cleaned his plate, Laura had eaten all but a sliver of her sandwich, the children had picked out their favorite portions—cheese and bread for Robbie, turkey and cheese for Ryan, only the soup and the turkey for Wendy—but Jane had hardly touched a thing. *She eats like a bird,* Laura thought.

Adam asked, "Something wrong with your lunch, Jane?"

She dabbed a napkin across her mouth. "No, of course not. It's just that I had breakfast with Mother this morning."

Adam rolled his eyes. "Sheila's still trying to fatten you up, is she?"

Jane's smile grew brittle. "Naturally. Why, didn't you know? The reason I don't have a man is because I'm too thin."

Laura snorted. "That's nonsense. You're not too thin."

Adam and Jane burst out laughing. Laura noted that Adam reached out to cover Jane's hand comfortingly. The children laughed, even though they didn't have any more clue than Laura what was funny. When the hilarity had died down—if that was what it had been—Adam pushed his plate back and said to Laura, "Jane's given me a lot to think about. I'd like your opinion on it."

Laura shrugged, feeling both uncomfortable and terribly important. "I'm not sure I'll have an opinion."

Adam ignored her demurral, leaning toward her excitedly. "Remember what we were talking about the other night?"

Laura could only shake her head in puzzlement.

"You know, you asked me what interested me most."

"History," she said instantly, and he beamed at her.

"Okay, well now, think about this. Jane's inherited a house in Maine."

"A very interesting old house," Jane put in.

"She and Cody have decided to move there to live."

"Cody's my son," Jane said, her voice imbued with maternal love. "He's six." She sent an apologetic look to Adam. "I'm afraid his grandmother is monopolizing him just now. It's funny. Usually she doesn't have time for him, but now that I've determined to go, she's trying to convince me how cruel I'm being by taking him away from her."

"Sheila can't understand anyone who would willingly leave the Fortune fold," Adam commented wryly.

"As you well know," Jane said. She turned her gaze on Laura again and confided, "We're the black sheep of the family, Adam and I. Well, he's the gray sheep. I'm the black one.''

*Well, that explains the camaraderie,* Laura thought. *Two Fortunes who've opted to make their own way.* She wondered what Jane had done to get herself painted the blackest of the sheep.

Adam sent Jane an irritated glare before turning back to Laura. "Now, here's the thing. Jane has a business here, her own business, independent of the family."

"I want to sell," Jane said. "It will be easier that way. I'll simply open a new shop in Maine."

"A shop," Laura echoed.

"An *antiques* shop," Adam explained.

Antiques. History. Laura reached out blindly, unaware that she grasped Adam's hand. "It's perfect!"

Adam flashed her a bright smile, but then he sat back, sobering. "Wait a minute now. Let's think about this clearly. I don't actually know anything worthwhile about antiques."

"You know more than you think, Adam," Laura insisted enthusiastically. "Remember what you were telling me about the life-styles of the eighteenth and nineteenth centuries?"

"You're certainly well traveled," Jane added. "You're bound to have picked up something worthwhile in Europe."

"And you can study," Laura pointed out. "A great deal has been written about antiques. The public library ought to be a gold mine."

"Don't forget college resources," Jane said. "I know of at least one seminar you can attend right away. And never underestimate Hollis. That old gentleman has taught me everything I know, Adam, and I consider him a primary asset of the shop. I'm absolutely certain he'd stay on."

Adam sat back in his chair, obviously thinking it all over. "We'd need appraisals," he murmured, "property, inventory."

"Already in the works," Jane informed him. "You'll want an audit of the books, too. Why don't you speak to your CPA about it? Let him make a recommendation."

Adam shook his head. "Oh, I don't think we have to worry about that."

"I insist, Adam," Jane said flatly. "I've made it a condition of the sale."

"Your agent," Adam said suddenly. "How will she feel about you bringing in your own buyer?"

Jane smiled. "I'm a Fortune, Adam. Business is in my blood, even if it isn't the family business. I negotiated a fair contract with her. If I find my own buyer, I pay her expenses and she bows out quietly—saving me a hefty commission, I might add. Now, what do you say?"

Adam rubbed a hand over his chin, then shook his head. "Let me mull it over a day or two."

Jane smiled and leaned toward Laura, saying conspiratorially, "I've got him!"

Adam laughed and cuffed her lightly under the chin. "I said I'd think about it, imp. Don't check your bank balance until the deposit's made."

"He'll do it," Jane said to Laura. "I know him. He always makes a decision, then he second-guesses it, then he convinces himself that he was right all along. You'll see."

"That's the problem with family," Adam said, folding his arms. "They think they know you so well."

Jane winked at Laura, who smiled back. Laura had been right about this young woman. She was delightful, insightful, strong in a graceful, elegant, quiet way. She would have made Adam a wonderful nanny and partner. Laura was shamefully glad that she was Adam's cousin.

With lunch finished, they adjourned to the den. Laura got out crayons and coloring books for the children, then lay on her belly on the floor with them, encouraging them to play quietly while Adam and Jane talked. The conversation turned to their fathers. Jane, it seemed, was as puzzled by Nathaniel as Adam tended to be by Jake. Laura left the room to put the twins down for a nap. Wendy was tired, too, after romping in the snow all morning, so Laura took the time to read her a story, during which she nodded off peacefully. When Laura got back to the den, she found Adam and Jane deeply involved in a discussion about Jake's sale of company stock to Monica Malone. Feeling like an interloper, Laura turned to go, but Adam caught her eye and waved her over. He moved over, making room for her on the end of the sofa, and draped his arm loosely around her shoulders after she sat down, all without pausing in his conversation with Jane.

Finally, the topic seemed exhausted, and Jane sat forward, gathering up her pocketbook from the coffee table. "Well, this has been wonderful," she said, "but Cody's bound to be wondering what's happened to me by now. He's very good with Mother, but even his patience is not inexhaustible."

"He must be very mature for his age," Laura observed idly. "You make him sound like a small adult."

Jane smiled fondly. "He's an unusually intelligent little boy, and frankly, in some ways, he's years more mature than Mother."

Laura was taken aback, and slightly embarrassed to have received such information, but Adam patted her knee reassuringly. "You'd have to know Aunt Sheila," he said dryly.

Jane laughed. "Yes, it requires firsthand experience. You'd think we were lying if we tried to tell you all of Mother's foibles. But then, she'd be the first to say the same about me." That last was delivered with poorly disguised sadness and, to Laura's amazement, more than a little guilt. Jane stood abruptly. "I really have to go."

Adam got up to walk her out. "It's been great to see you." He took her in his arms for a bruising hug. "I hate to see you go away."

"But you understand," Jane said confidently. "I really need to be on my own."

"I understand," Adam assured her.

She hugged him once more, then pulled back, thrusting a hand down at Laura. Her eyes seemed to sparkle with some secret knowledge. "It's been a pleasure, Laura. Don't let him beg off the shop. We know it would be good for him, don't we?''

Laura started to protest that she had nothing to say about it, but at the last instant she swallowed the words and merely clasped Jane's hand, saying, ''I hope you'll be very happy in Maine.''

''Somehow I think we will,'' Jane said. Then she went off, arm in arm with Adam, to take her leave.

Laura felt somehow that she had been complimented. Jane obviously felt that she had some influence with Adam, but she was only the nanny, after all, and temporary at that.

*I couldn't cope with it. I can't let you leave. Yet.*

She focused on that *yet,* telling herself that she must not forget that today was a reprieve, not a pardon.

Some minutes passed before Adam returned. He seemed in a thoughtful, reflective mood, one hand idly smoothing the short hair above his ear, the other tucked into the pocket of his pants. ''What do you think?'' he asked, sitting down beside her again.

She lifted a brow. ''If you mean what do I think of Jane, I think she's lovely.''

He smiled. ''Oh, yeah. She's something, our Miss Jane Fortune. Of all the family, I think I like her best.''

''Kindred spirits and all that.''

He nodded. ''You could say that. Jane never wanted any part of the family business, either, and for the same reasons, I think. Her father is certainly as consumed by the Fortune companies as mine is. Then there's her mother. Nathaniel divorced Sheila years ago, but she clings to the Fortune name as if she's due it, and everything else that comes her way.''

Laura cocked her head. ''I'm surprised, then, that Jane took back her maiden name.''

''Took back?'' Adam repeated. He shook his head, his smile turning sad. ''You're assuming that she's divorced.''

''Well, yes, I . . .''

His mouth turned down. ''You remember that she called herself the blackest sheep in the family?''

''Certainly, but I just assumed—''

Adam took her hand. "She was never married to Cody's father."

Laura felt a wave of regret. "Oh, my. The poor thing."

Adam squeezed her hand. "I knew you'd understand. The crumb left her when she told him that she was pregnant."

"But she had her child anyway," Laura added mistily, "and kept him. It must have been very difficult for her. I imagine it still is."

Adam nodded. "Not that the family abandoned her or anything."

"Of course not."

"Truthfully, Sheila was the worst."

"Her own mother," Laura marveled.

"You'd have to know Sheila," Adam said again. "At first she all but put out a hit on Cody's father, but Jane wouldn't have it. She was terribly hurt by his abandonment, but she took all the responsibility herself. Deprived of her preferred target, Sheila took her venom out on Jane for a while."

"All that nonsense about Jane being too skinny to keep a man!" Laura exclaimed. "Somebody ought to point out that Sheila couldn't keep Nathaniel!"

"That would have been Kate," Adam said, smiling. "But Sheila's not exactly the sensitive type."

"So I gathered. Sounds to me like Nathaniel's better off without her—and Jane's better off without Cody's father."

"Agreed," Adam said, "but I wasn't really asking what you thought about Jane. I was asking what you think about the idea of the antique shop."

"Ah." Laura folded her arms. "Well, it's really none of my business."

He cut her a look. "Don't make me haul out the military attitude, Beaumont. When I give an order, I expect it to be carried out. Now tell me what you think."

"I thought I was the general," she said teasingly.

He threw an arm around her shoulders and squeezed her to his side. "I'll get it out of you yet." Then his embrace gentled, and he leaned his head close. "I value your opinion, you know, and that makes you a genuine rarity."

Laura smiled, going all soft inside. "So far as I've seen, nothing else has intrigued you like the possibility of the antique shop, Adam. Isn't that right?"

"I suppose. It's just that I'd be going into it cold."

"No, not really. There's your love of history, your respect for antiquity."

"All right."

"You said that you wanted to do something that you could be passionate about," she reminded him.

He nodded. "So?"

"So, I think you should follow your heart. That's where true passion begins, isn't it?"

"You think I should follow my heart?" he murmured, curling a finger beneath her chin. She nodded, even as he turned her face up to his, her heart beating with strong, rapid strokes. "Following your heart can be dangerous," he whispered, and to prove it, he brushed his mouth across hers.

Laura gulped. "Y-yes, but anything w-worth—"

"Do you know what you're worth, Laura? Do you have any idea how I value you?"

She made a small sound of distress and surrender as his hand settled on the curve of her jaw and neck. To be valued. To be held dear. She lifted a hand to his arm, as if intending to push him away, but she didn't have the strength or the desire. Then he began to kiss her, and it was too late.

His mouth tasted hers repeatedly, and with such tender enjoyment that she let her head fall back and gave him unrestricted access. His arm folded her close, and he plunged his tongue into her mouth over and over, his hand sliding down her throat and across her chest, to her breast. He covered her and squeezed gently. Laura clutched the front of his shirt, her breathing ragged, as his hand molded her and his tongue plunged and plunged.

Abruptly he broke their mouths apart, his hand dropping to the bottom of her sweater. "I have to touch you." His gaze held her as his hand burrowed beneath her sweater, tugged her undershirt from the elasticized band of her knit pants and slipped beneath it to skim her torso. He tugged the strap down and folded back the cup of her bra. She caught her breath as his hand covered her bare breast. He closed his eyes and lowered his head to the curve of her shoulder, breathing, "Oh, God, Laura. I need..." His hand convulsed around her breast, then left it to travel lower.

She jerked when his fingers pushed beneath the band of her leggings, but he caught her mouth, stifling any protest with the plunge of his tongue. She dug her fingers into the top of his shoulder, uncertain whether she meant to push him away or pull him closer. He was trembling even harder than she was, but his hand pushed lower, slipping beneath the narrow edge of her panties. The muscles of her stomach rippled, but she fought the urge to lift herself against him. He plunged his hand between her legs and cupped her. She cried out, feeling her own damp heat. He took the sound into his own mouth, shuddering as he parted her with the tip of one finger and pushed up into her.

It was too much. Laura turned her face away, gasping at his invasion. Instantly he withdrew. Pressing his cheek to hers, he brought back his trembling hand, whispering, "I just had to touch you. Laura... Laura, look at me."

Timidly she turned her head and slowly lifted her gaze, breathing roughly through her mouth. He stroked her cheek lightly with the backs of his knuckles. "I want you so much."

She closed her eyes, unable to bear the way his desire for her softened his features and warmed his eyes to glowing golden lights. If she looked again into those eyes, she would surrender everything, and that would be the most selfish thing she could possibly do. Yet she couldn't suppress the rising surge of joy that filled her. He laid his forehead against hers, and she let her arms encircle him. He kissed her eyelids and her nose.

"Have you put away your things?" he asked softly.

She shook her head. He pulled back. "Do it. Do it now. Go and put everything away."

She let her arms fall away, and slipped out of his embrace, moving to the very edge of the sofa. There she paused. She didn't want to say it, but she had to. She bit her trembling lip. "Adam . . ."

He took her hand in his and stared at it, telling her that he didn't want to hear what she was going to say. She said it anyway.

"This doesn't change anything. I'll have to go sooner or later."

"Later, then," he said harshly, his gaze flicking upward to scan her face.

She wanted to tell him that she couldn't delay very much longer, that time was catching up with her. She could feel it. She just couldn't force the words from her mouth. It would mean taking another step along the way out. It would mean explanations and lies, for she certainly couldn't tell him the truth. He'd know what a dunce she was if she told him about Doyal. She'd hate that. She wanted, needed, for him to think well of her. Impulsively she leaned back and kissed him quickly on the mouth.

His smile flashed, and he reached for her, but she popped up and moved out of reach, smiling as she shook her head. She hurried away, pausing only when she drew near the foyer to lean against the wall, hug herself and calm her hammering heart.

*I want you so much.*

And now he knew that she wanted him, too. She couldn't regret that, and yet, as she'd told him, it changed nothing, except perhaps to strengthen her resolve to protect him and his children in the only way she could. As badly as it hurt, when the time came—and it was coming soon—she would go. God help her, she had to do it before it was too late.

# Ten

"I insist."

Laura looked at Adam, shocked by the steely edge of his voice. "B-but it's a family thing."

"I'm well aware of that."

"I have no place at a family visit."

"I disagree. I want you to go. Therefore, you have a place. Now get changed, or we'll be late."

She stood for several seconds with her mouth agape, puzzled by his implacable insistence. Well, two could play this game. She squared her shoulders. "I'm not going, and you can't make me."

To her irritation, he chuckled and shook his head. "Laura, you're beginning to sound—and act—like the children." He sat forward on the edge of his chair, all earnestness. "There's nothing to be afraid of, you know. My mother's a lady. She never bites."

"I'm not afraid!" Laura declared. "I just prefer to stay home alone. I hardly ever have any time to myself. This is a perfect opportunity."

Adam slid back in his chair with a sigh. "You can have the whole of tomorrow evening off. Go where you like, do what you like. The kids and I will enjoy some quality time."

"No! You don't understand. I want to be *home* alone. As long as you and the children are in the house, I'll be…well, I'll be…not alone."

Adam made a visible effort to relax, but the muscle in the hollow of his jaw flexed tellingly. "I'll take the kids out tomorrow night. You can have the whole house to yourself. Satisfied?"

It was all Laura could do not to stomp her foot, but that crack he'd made earlier had hit home. She made herself relax, exhaling slowly, smiling casually. "Adam, your mother doesn't want to see me. Your mother wants to see her son and grand—"

"Oh, but she *does* want to see you," Adam said smoothly, interrupting her. "In fact, she wants very much to see you."

Laura threw up her hands. "That's absurd!"

"I don't see why. You do take care of her grandchildren. It's only natural that she'd want to meet you, don't you think?"

Laura folded her arms and narrowed her eyes. "I think you are being unreasonable," she said, "and I can't help wondering why."

Adam passed a hand over his eyes. "Fine. If you choose to think that I'm unreasonable, so be it—but be ready to leave in ten minutes. I'll see to the children myself."

Laura made a sound in the back of her throat that clearly communicated her frustration, but Adam ignored her, brushing imaginary lint from the gray wool tweed sleeve of his sport jacket. "Adam," she implored.

He flicked his gaze up. "Nine minutes," he said, "and counting."

Obstinately Laura plopped down on the coffee table, daring him to move her. He catapulted up out of his chair, but then he merely straightened his cuffs and rippled his shoulders and craned his neck, as if trying to get comfortable inside his navy blue shirt and tie. "Fine," he said with an air of boredom. "Mother will, of course, be wearing a dress, but she'll forgive you your...pants."

With that, he reached down and grasped her forearm, pulling her to her feet easily. She knew when she was beaten. Not being childish enough to dig in her heels, she allowed him to haul her out of the den and down the hall. When they reached the foyer, he began pulling coats out of the closet and calling the children. Laura ran down the hall to her bedroom, calling over her shoulder, "Five minutes!"

"You can take six!" Adam called after her. She didn't see his smile.

With six minutes to transform herself, Laura didn't waste time bemoaning her situation. She ripped her only skirt from its hanger and began tossing things out of drawers. Next, she stripped down to her panties and bra, then wiggled into heavy black tights and her one and only slip. After that came a white cotton shirt with short sleeves and a Peter Pan collar. In her haste, she buttoned the top two buttons and didn't bother with the rest. Quickly she pulled on the black wool gabardine skirt that ended in a row of pleats just inches above her ankles, stuffed in the tail of her shirt and zipped up. She pulled a closely fitted long-sleeved black imitation-angora sweater over her head, flipped her shirt collar out over the edge of the sweater's straight neckline and jammed her feet into half boots with stacked heels. She whipped a narrow black belt around her waist and buckled it, tugging the hem of her sweater smooth. Finally she whisked a brush through her hair, tucked one side behind an ear and plopped a small black beret on her head at a jaunty angle. Hands shaking, she jammed a wide filigreed-silver ring onto the index finger of her left hand, then grabbed up tiny black-and-silver button earrings from a dish on the top of the bureau. She was fixing the back of the second earring when she drew up in front of Adam in the foyer.

"My goodness," he said, raking an appreciative gaze from her head to her toes and up again. "What might you have done with the full ten minutes?"

"The very same," she said, tilting her nose and sticking her arms in the sleeves of the coat he held open for her. "This is the only 'dress' I own."

He pulled the coat up over her shoulders and settled it into place. "Then we'll just have to get you another," he said, his soft voice in her ear.

"I don't need another," she said, ignoring the tiny shivers that coursed through her body.

He turned her to face him and looped her scarf about her neck. "You will," he said, and then he turned her toward the garage door. "The kids are in the car."

"Already?"

He smiled as he escorted her out the door. "I can work wonders in minutes, too."

She rolled her eyes. "Yes, but you do it the easy way. You give orders!"

He put his head back and laughed at that.


Erica smiled at her son. He flipped a little wave at her, dusted off Ryan's bruised knee, patted the boy's shoulder, then watched as Ryan disappeared into the lush greenery of Erica's garden room, his latest scrape forgotten in the heat of his brother's shouted challenge: "Ready or not, come hide-and-seek me!"

Adam straightened and strolled back to the chair positioned next to Erica's chaise, laughing. "Well, he's got the terminology down. He just hasn't quite figured out who's the hider and who's the seeker."

"Children are so funny," she said. "Still, I haven't seen you laugh so much in years."

Adam quirked a brow and crossed one knee over the other, pinching the crease of his navy blue slacks with thumb and forefinger. "The kids are at an age to be lots of fun," he said finally.

"Umm..." She caught and held his gaze, saying very deliberately, "I'm surprised you've noticed. I don't suppose the lovely Laura has anything to do with that."

Adam considered pretense, then quickly abandoned the idea. He smoothed a finger over the edge of the small, round glass-topped verdigris table placed near to hand. "She has utterly changed my life," he said. "Now if I could only figure out how to keep her."

Erica opened her mouth, but before she could comment, the object of their conversation appeared, ducking beneath the lush fronds of a potted palm. Her beret was askew, and she was brushing tiny brown tendrils from her skirt. She strolled over to the table, a nervous smile on her face, and picked up the glass of water she had requested earlier, at Erica's urging. She took a long drink, fanning herself with her hand.

"This garden room is so great," she said, putting down her glass and straightening her hat. "I'd almost forgotten what it was like to feel really warm."

"This room is my refuge in wintertime," Erica told her, "and the older I get, the more I appreciate it."

Laura looked around her, still slightly awed. "It's just so wild to find tropical plants growing in all this snow."

The snow, in fact, was piled four and five feet deep in drifts against the glass wall of the hothouse, but inside it was a toasty seventy-five degrees. That being the case, Grandmommy's hothouse was and always had been a favorite place for the children to play. The twins were zigging and zagging through the potted ferns at that very moment, while Wendy was playing kitchen with a collection of empty plastic containers and various tools from the potting shed. Laura had just returned from inspecting Wendy's imaginary concoctions. The very moment she sat down in the chair facing Adam, Ryan stuck his head out of a leafy hole and bawled, "Wau-ra! Wau-ra, come see!"

Laura immediately popped up again, but Adam leaned forward and snagged her hand, pulling her back down. "You've run Laura ragged," he called out to Ryan. "Play on your own for a while, and let Laura sit down!"

Ryan stomped out of his hiding place, arms rigid at his sides. "Aw, Dad," he complained.

"Don't 'Aw Dad' me," Adam replied calmly. "Just go on and play. Laura will be right here with me."

Ryan flattened his lips in disgust, his brows drawn together, but he stomped back into his play place amid the greenery. Almost instantly they heard a growl, followed by a loud "Ow!" and Ryan tumbled out of the plants again. His twin could be seen dashing through the rows of potted growth.

Laura jumped to her feet. "Robbie!"

Adam stood and pushed her down again, his hands on her shoulders. "I'll deal with this," he said, advancing on

Robbie's hiding place. He stopped in the aisle between the rows of lush greenery and stooped to assess Ryan's injuries. There were none, of course, just a few crocodile tears and a trembling lip worthy of a prize-winning actor. "W-W-Wobbie 'tacked me!" he exclaimed.

Adam picked him up and dusted him off. "You're not hurt. Why don't you go play with Wendy? I'll take care of Robbie."

Ryan nodded and smugly took himself off to pester his sister. Adam stepped into the potted jungle and looked in three different directions. He stepped out into the aisle again and brought his hands to his hips. "Show yourself, Rob. Robbie? Come out here, son. Now." The only reply was a rustle of fronds. Adam took a look over his shoulder. Laura appeared to be conversing politely with his mother—until she cast a worried glance in his direction. Adam jerked his head around, thrust back his shoulders and pitched his voice in the direction of that suspicious rustling. "Robbie, if you don't want to find yourself on TV restriction for the next *week*—and I mean no TV at all—you'd better present yourself, front and center, within the next three seconds. I'm counting. One... Two..."

Robbie pushed aside a huge green leaf and stepped out into the aisle, chin down, shoulders drooping.

Adam carefully covered a smile with a stern face and beckoned his son with a crooked finger. Robbie dragged himself over, managing to avoid stepping on his bottom lip. Adam went down to the child's level, his weight balanced on his toes.

"Now then, why did you 'attack' your brother?"

"I'm the lion!" Robbie explained in a deep, growling voice.

So it was all a game that got out of hand. Adam nodded. "Well, the lion is going to find himself caged if he doesn't stop attacking people. Tell you what, you go over and apologize nicely to your brother, and we'll forget about it this time. All right?"

Robbie instantly perked up. "Sure."

"Get at it, then."

Arms swinging, Robbie strolled over to his brother, looked him in the face and said, "I'm sorry I tried to eat you, Ryan."

Ryan patted his shoulder generously. "I be the wion this time!" he exclaimed, and the pair trotted off toward their make-believe jungle again.

Wendy rolled her eyes, rapidly stirring a pot of dirt. "Boys!" she muttered.

"Be a nice lion!" Adam called out.

"Aw wight!" Ryan conceded. "I be a nice wion! I won't eat people!"

Adam shook his head, laughing softly, and walked back to the table. "Never a dull moment," he commented, re-taking his chair.

Erica chuckled. "As if I didn't know. You kept me hopping day and night, not to mention your sisters!"

"Oh, I was a joy," he teased. "You've told me so repeatedly."

"You were a joy, all right," Erica conceded, "but a very busy and very easily offended one."

"The busy part sounds like the twins," Laura said, tapping her chin with a finger. "Which one of them would you say is most like his father?"

Erica smiled. "Wendy is most like her father," she said. "All too aware, quick to take offense, long to hold a grudge, but very, very loving."

"I don't hold a grudge!" Adam objected.

"No?" Erica said. "Perhaps we should ask your father."

Adam frowned. Had he been holding a grudge all these years? He shifted in his chair. "How is Dad?"

Erica stared. "Why ask me? He doesn't tell me anything anymore. We're separated, remember?"

Adam sighed. "When is this nonsense going to stop? You and Dad belong together. Dad belongs at the helm of the Fortune family business. Rocky and Luke deserve a family reception, and while I'm ordering the world, Kate ought to be here. If Kate were here, none of this would be happening. You know that, don't you?"

Erica smiled wanly. "Indeed I do. Our Kate had a way of willing this family into order." Her eyes glazed with tears that she attempted to smile away. "I think I miss her more now than ever. I know your father does."

"Kate was our rudder," Adam said in a husky voice. "Without her, the family in general just seems to flounder."

Erica turned her gaze on Laura. "I wish you could have known her, Laura dear."

Laura replied graciously. "I'm sure she was a very wise woman. Just the legacy she left Adam is enough to tell me that."

"The legacy?" Erica asked, slanting a look at her son. "I always wondered about that pair of photo albums."

With an abashed look, Adam briefly explained about the photo albums, neither of which contained a single photo of a father with his children. "Laura figured it out," he added. "I don't have any doubt that Kate was trying to tell me how in danger I was of doing the very thing I resented Dad for."

"How like Kate," Erica mused, and then she turned a thoughtful gaze on Laura.

Adam sat up straight, suddenly catching his mother's thought. "Yes," he agreed, "very like Kate."

Laura seemed not to understand their conclusion. She was busy with thoughts of her own, and Adam didn't have to wonder long what was on her mind. "You know," she said, abruptly sitting forward, "it isn't hopeless. You simply must think and do what Kate would have done. Someone must talk to your father, someone whose words and opinions matter a great deal to him, someone like . . . you, Adam."

Adam recoiled. "Me? I'm the last person Dad would listen to."

Erica cut in. "Oh, no, for all your differences, do you think your father would pressure you to come into the company if he didn't trust, even covet, your judgment and opinions?"

Adam felt a pang near his heart. "But, Mother, the fact remains that I have no intention of getting involved in the family business, and you know Father has always kept his own counsel.''

"I'm not suggesting that you give him business advice," Erica countered. "Just tell him that you care, that the family fears, in one way or another, that we're losing him. It's what Kate would have done. It's exactly what Kate would have done."

Adam couldn't argue with that. He knew at soul level that his mother was right, and yet... He turned a newly appreciative gaze on the young woman who had so changed his life. The idea, the impulse, the intuition, had been hers, and God knew it wasn't the first time. If not for Laura, he realized in a flash of insight, he'd still be stumbling around in the dark, wondering why his children didn't love him, searching for his life's work, resenting and holding at arm's length the very man whose love and approval he had craved since childhood. If not for Laura... He shuddered to think of it.

"I'll call Dad and invite him to lunch tomorrow."

Snippets of conversation floated up from the mouths of chatting, laughing diners, but Adam ignored them as he looked over the opulent room, searching for his father. His gaze snagged on a black-garbed figure seated at an out-of-the-way table behind a column near the middle of the room. Something about the heavily veiled woman seemed familiar, but before Adam could analyze what, a movement at the edge of his vision distracted him. He acknowledged Jake's wave with a nod of his head and began weaving his way through the tables and chairs.

Jake was early—a testament to his eagerness for this meeting. Adam felt a simultaneous lift of spirits and a pang of guilt. He'd recognized the delight in his father's voice when he phoned for the appointment, and it warmed him to know that a simple thing like an invitation to lunch from him could so please his father—warmed and shamed him, for it was an absurdly easy thing to do once the decision was made.

As he approached his father's usual table at the familiar restaurant, he unbuttoned his suit coat and smiled. Jake looked up, caught sight of him and leaped to his feet, both arms extended. Adam gave himself over to a hearty handshake and a back-pounding. It occurred to him that he had received more of those over the years than he had realized. Perhaps his father was not as undemonstrative as he had believed.

"I'm afraid to even guess why you've invited me here," Jake said once they'd taken their chairs, glanced through menus over a coffee for Adam and a drink for Jake and ordered. "Dare I suggest that you're interested in the Fortune companies after all?"

Adam chuckled, amazed to find that his temper did not ignite—his usual reaction. He shook his head. "Sorry, Dad. The Fortune companies will have to struggle on without me. The fact is, I have a job, or at least I will as soon as the sale goes through."

Jake accepted this news with unusual aplomb. "What sort of business are we talking about?"

Adam smiled to himself. "I've recently discovered a latent passion for antiquities." He went on to explain, at some length, that he had decided to buy Jane's business, and why. To his surprise, Jake seemed to accept, even to approve on an elemental level, his decision.

"I've never seen you so enthusiastic. In fact, I'd venture to say that you're actually happy these days."

Adam could only shake his head. Did he have it written on his forehead? *Life is better than I expected.* Or had he been so bitter in the past? "What do you mean, 'these days'?"

Jake cocked his head as if deciding how much to say. He apparently decided that it was safe to say it all. "You look...whole, Adam. I know Diana's death shook you up, but I know, too, that you were never happy with Diana. I always figured the military was just your way of escaping your marriage."

Adam was rocked. "That's utter nonsense."

Jake shrugged negligently. "I don't think so. I know what I'm talking about, son. I know how a man in love looks, how he behaves, what his priorities are. And your marriage was not your priority. Oh, you did everything that Diana expected of you, but neither of you worked very hard at that marriage. I even told Diana once that she shouldn't let you escape the relationship so easily."

"And what did Diana say to that?" Adam asked lightly, pretending little interest.

Jake sighed. "Diana said that her life pleased her greatly, that if you were escaping anyone, you were escaping me."

Adam managed a kind of smile, but his voice was tinged with bitter sadness. "Well, I'm glad she was happy. As for this notion that I was escaping via the military—"

"You don't have to justify anything on my account," Jake said roughly. "I was just making a point."

"That point being . . ."

"You weren't in love with Diana, but you're in love with someone now."

Adam couldn't have been more shocked. "Why on earth would you say something that absurd?"

"I told you. I recognize the look."

Adam arched a skeptical brow. "Oh? How so?"

Jake slid him a quelling look. "Well, because of your mother, of course."

Adam jumped at the chance to turn the tables. "So you're in love with Mom? You've a funny way of showing it, moving back to Grandmother's house."

Jake's expression was resigned. "My feelings for your mother have nothing to do with my leaving."

"Then why leave?"

Jake shook his head, looking as if the weight of the world rested on his shoulders. "I can't explain it to you, any more than I could explain it to her."

"You could try."

Jake seemed to find that almost amusing. "You don't trust me to do what's best for everyone any more than she apparently does."

Adam knew instinctively that the time had come to change the course of his relationship with his father. The words he would have said just yesterday were on the tip of his tongue. He was ready to go, eager for battle, but somehow a new spirit had gradually taken over. Adam didn't want to fight anymore. He no longer felt compelled to jockey for position. He didn't want to escape. He just wanted . . . peace.

Impulsively he reached across the table and grasped his father's wrist. He sensed somehow that words would not be enough. "I do trust you, Dad," he said slowly, evenly. "I have no doubt at all that you'll do what you think best for everyone. I guess that's what I came here to say, that and..." This was harder to get out than it should have been, but he cleared his crowded throat and went on. "That and I—I love you."

Jake Fortune looked as if he'd been poleaxed. Then the shock passed and his whole face began to tremble and twitch. He turned his arm beneath Adam's and returned the grasp with the fervency of a death grip. He shifted in his chair, not once but several times. Gradually he wrestled his emotion into abeyance and retreated into gruffness.

"Of c-course you do! Just as I . . . love you." He rushed those last two words out, as if fearing they might get lost on the way. Relieved to have mastered them, he adopted a studied nonchalance, at last releasing Adam's wrist and waving his hand negligently. "That was never in question." He ducked his head, fiddling with his napkin and trying not to sniff.

Adam felt a suspicious burning at the backs of his own eyes and a lump rising up in his throat, but he beat down such emotional display and drew a calming breath. "Well," he said, in a businesslike tone, "now that that's out of the way, may I stick my nose in far enough to suggest that you go home, or at least call Mom and talk?"

Jake made a face. "I don't have anything to say to her, Adam. I mean, nothing's changed."

"You might tell her what you just told me," Adam suggested, "and then you might help her plan a reception for

Rocky and Luke." Jake made another face, but Adam pressed him. "Luke deserves an official welcome into the family, Dad, and Rocky deserves our blessing. Besides, I've been thinking that this just might be a good opportunity for the family to show the clan at large that our confidence in you hasn't waned."

Jake looked long into his son's eyes. His voice rattled tellingly when he said, "You'd do that for me?"

Adam smiled his brightest. "We all would. I spoke to Caroline about it just the other day. She and Nick are solidly in your corner, and she tells me that Allie is, too. I'm sure Natalie and Rachel feel the same way. And if you think it will help, I'll even call Aunt Lindsay and Aunt Rebecca, too. It can't hurt to let them know we expect their support."

Jake was nodding his head, but his expression remained solemn. "I don't know that it will make a difference, Adam. Nathaniel's really got the bit between his teeth this time. But you can't know how much I appreciate..." His voice broke, and he dropped his gaze, but it wasn't necessary to say anything more.

Spying the waiter bringing their orders over, Adam shook out his napkin and smoothed it across his lap. "Will you call Mom and tell her the reception's on, or do you want me to do it?"

"I'll do it," Jake said after a long moment, "but, Adam, you've got to tell me something. What's changed you? Where is this new attitude coming from?"

The waiter arrived just then, bowing and scraping and preparing to serve them. Adam felt the oddest urge to look at that veiled woman again. He slid a glance over one shoulder, but the woman's chair was empty.

Adam shook his head, smiling to himself, and merely said, "Eat your lunch, Dad, and I'll tell you what your grandchildren have been up to."

Jake opened his mouth as if to argue, but then he closed it again and nodded. "I'd like that."

A pleasant half hour passed. When the waiter brought the check, a good-natured wrangle ensued, which Adam—for the first time—actually won. He could tell that it irritated Jake mightily to have his son buy him lunch, but he swallowed his pride and let it go. Adam got up to leave, Jake saying that he would wait for another appointment to appear shortly. At any other time, Adam would have merely nodded and hurried on his way, but he could admit to himself now that his father's affection was important to him. Uneasy as all get-out, he took the initiative, walking around the table in search of an embrace. He began to think that Jake was not going to cooperate, but at the last moment, Jake shot to his feet and stuck out his hand. Adam grasped that hand, then threw caution to the winds and wrapped his free arm around his father's broad shoulders, leaning into him for the classic male hug.

When they separated a moment later, Jake seemed to be having a little trouble clearing his throat, but then he looked up and spied his appointment arriving early. To Adam's surprise, Jake's self-possession returned in a blink of an eye. His face broke into a smile, and he wrapped his arm around Adam's shoulders, holding him in place at his side, without the slightest show of discomfort. When his business appointment drew near the table, Jake announced in a hearty voice, "This is my son, Adam. He just bought my lunch!"

The middle-aged man who nodded in acknowledgment of the introduction was a stranger to Adam, but he obviously knew Jake well enough to speak about family, as well as business. He looked Jake in the eye and said, "I envy you. The only thing my son ever bought me was difficulty, the spoiled, lazy brat."

Jake pounded Adam on the back. "Ho, not my boy! This is a military man, retired now and about to bite off a brand-new business career. And you ought to see the kids he's got—perfect angels!"

Adam started to laugh. "Hardly, but they keep me hopping."

He withstood another back-pounding and took his leave, feeling light as air. He was working his way through the tables again, grinning from ear to ear, when a funny feeling skittered up his spine. He stopped in his tracks and put a hand to the back of his neck, looking around him in confusion. He spied the woman all in black, standing against the wall behind a huge potted plant. She was wearing a rather large felt hat with a heavy veil attached, totally obscuring her face and hair, and yet Adam felt a definite tingle of familiarity. She seemed to be weeping. The white handkerchief clutched in her black-gloved hand made frequent trips beneath the heavy veil. He couldn't help staring, but when she stiffened, he saw that he was making her uncomfortable and moved on. If anyone understood grief, it was him. It was only as he nodded at the maître d' on his way out that he realized who that woman reminded him of. Something about her, the way she held herself, the way she moved her hands, was just like Kate.

Kate. He shook his head. In addition to softhearted, he was getting softheaded in his dotage. Must be an effect of civilian life. Or maybe it was just that Kate would have been pleased by what had gone on here today. In a way, she had started it all with those photo albums. He hoped she knew how it was all turning out. He hoped she was looking down on them, watching and approving, pleased that her legacy of love was outliving her. God willing, it would outlive them all.

Laura was on pins and needles. Adam's lunch with his father must have lasted well over two hours, and then there was the travel to the city and back and... Even at a distance she recognized the sound of the garage door opening—one of the rollers had started to screech annoyingly—and she couldn't bear to wait patiently for Adam to make his way back to the den. With the boys down for naps and Wendy engrossed in a picture book, Laura could not make herself keep her seat. She popped up and all but ran down the hall, arriving in the foyer at the very moment Adam opened the door from the garage. His face lit up at the sight of her.

"Can't wait to find out the results of your meddling, eh?"

Laura let her weight roll back onto her heels and defended herself. "I didn't meddle! I simply made a suggestion—one your mother agreed with, I might point out. It was a most reasonable suggestion, too. You even thought so at the time."

He had shrugged out of his coat and was stowing it in the closet. "I still do."

"Oh?"

"Mmm-hmm ..."

"Well, then ..."

He shrugged, feigning nonchalance. "Well, what?"

Laura stomped a foot, shaking her hands as if to hurry him. "Adam! How did it go?"

To her consternation, Adam poked his head into the hallway and looked first in one direction, then the other. Apparently satisfied, he drew into the foyer, rubbing his hands together as if in anticipation. Laura put her hands to her hips, out of patience, but before she could admonish him again, Adam reached out, hooked a hand in the bend of her elbow and jerked her to him, his arm wrapping around her waist as she collided with his chest. "You were right," he said smoothly, bringing up his free hand to grasp her chin and tilt it. "It went wonderfully. Thank you."

Laura blew out a gust of breath, aware suddenly of how her breasts were flattened against his chest. "Uh, I'm awfully glad everything worked out, Adam. Somehow I knew—"

"Oh, shut up," he said, grinning as his mouth descended to hers. The grin faded as their lips melded.

Laura knew that she ought to push away, but for the life of her, she couldn't seem to manage it. Her hands came up to his chest, then kept right on going until they had circled his neck and invaded the bristly hair at the back of his head. She felt him shift his weight, widening his stance as his hand slid down to her bottom, pressing her against him, and in short order she felt his lengthening hardness against her middle. Oh, what she wouldn't give ...

Adam seemed to be on the same wave-length. He moaned in frustration, even as he thrust his tongue into her mouth and flexed his lower body against her.

"Daddy?"

Reeking with censure, that little voice cut the mood as nothing else could have. Adam and Laura exploded apart, reeling in opposite directions. Laura recoiled with such force that she bounced off the wall, and Adam had to reach out and grab her wrist to steady her. Wendy folded her arms and tapped her foot impatiently.

"Daddy, what are you doing to Laura?" she demanded with little-girl sternness.

Adam sent a look at Laura. He was smiling, a devilish glint in his golden eyes.

"Adam, don't you dare!"

He ignored her and bent at the waist, bringing his face level with his daughter's. "I'm kissing her," he said flatly. Then, straightening, he gave Laura's arm a yank. She yelped and stumbled against him. He wrapped both arms around her and planted a solid kiss on her mouth before switching his gaze back to Wendy. "And doing a very good job of it, too. Now *go away.*"

To Laura's everlasting amazement, Wendy shrugged her little shoulders and grinned. "Okay!" She skipped away, singing.

Adam put his head back and laughed. "I think she approves," he said to a stunned Laura. Before she could get her mouth closed, he covered it with his, using his tongue and lips to manipulate the fit and seduce her into compliance.

Laura let herself relax against him, her hands sliding up and around his neck, but she could not so easily quell the alarm bells ringing inside her head. She made an effort to pull away.

"Adam. Adam, we shouldn't. Soon I'll have—"

He seized her by the upper arms and shook her, just once. "Don't! Not now. Just let me be happy. For God's sake, just once, let me be happy!"

Not even the firmest resolve could have withstood that plea, and Laura's resolve was not very firm. She lifted a hand to his face, her eyes roaming over it with hot pleasure until she came to his mouth. With a groan, he brought her hard against him once more and engaged the kiss with such

poignancy that the alarm bells effectively stilled. For the
first time in ... it felt like forever ... the fear left her. She
hugged him tight, letting passion take her where it would for
once, knowing that it wouldn't take her too far ... yet. But
perhaps it took her further than she realized, for a thought
never before dared began to form. Perhaps she wouldn't
have to go, after all. Doyal didn't have to find her. Perhaps
he had even tired of looking. She could be giving up everything she'd ever wanted by leaving here, and for nothing.
How could she give up Adam and the children for the mere
possibility that Doyal might find her? How could she ever
give them up?

# Eleven

"Hello, darlings!" Erica paused in the dining room door and smiled down on her grandchildren. She looked small and elegant standing there, her upswept hair glowing with streaks of silver at her temples. Her classical features were as composed and serene as usual, but Laura sensed a barely leashed excitement behind those shining green eyes.

Amused—everything seemed to amuse him lately—Adam stood and lifted an arm in welcome, indicating a chair on the near side of the table. "Would you care to join us for dinner, Mother?"

Erica glanced around the table as if enjoying the sight of the family at dinner, but she shook her head. "No, thank you, dear. I only came to let you know that our little plan worked. Your father has agreed to the reception."

Adam's eyes twinkled. "Yes, I know."

Erica turned her bright gaze on Laura. "And I wanted to thank you, Laura."

Laura was a little confused. She hadn't done anything. "For what, exactly?"

Erica smiled, her rather exotic gaze sliding to her son. "Oh, for a great deal, actually." Her attention snapped back to Laura. "But especially for convincing my son to make peace with his father." Her gaze shifted to Adam again. "I've never seen him so...emotional. You've helped him a great deal."

Adam bowed his head, clearing his throat. "Yes, well, he does seem to be...softening in his middle years."

Erica put her head back and laughed, the husky sound one of potent knowledge. "We won't tell him that you said so!"

Adam chuckled. "No, perhaps we'd better not."

Erica brought her hands together in a graceful gesture that signaled a change of subject. "Now, about the reception... I'm thinking that an island theme would dispel some of the winter gloom. Your father suggested barbecue, God help us—or, worse yet, chuck wagon! I reminded him that Luke is a doctor, a physician, however he may display his heritage. But of all the family, Adam, only you know Luke well enough to advise me. What do you think?"

Adam shrugged. "I don't think it makes any difference, Mother. Luke's just a man with a colorful heritage and a deep sense of responsibility. Frankly, I think he's going to be rather uncomfortable no matter what you serve."

"I see." Erica bit her lip thoughtfully. "Well, perhaps I'd better stick to hors d'oeuvres, then. Nothing too ostentatious, of course."

"Well, if I know you," Adam said, drawing her near to kiss the top of her head, "it will be a very elegant affair."

"Elegant but relaxed," Erica promised. "Now sit down and eat your dinner. I just want to hug my grandchildren before I go."

Adam escorted her around the end of the table, then took his seat, spreading his napkin across his lap while his mother floated down to wrap her arms around a giggling Ryan. "Mmm-hmm... How is Grandmommy's little man?" Ryan twisted in his seat to give her a prim kiss, his little mouth puckered tightly. Erica chuckled and patted and moved on to Robbie, whom she called her "darling mischief-maker." He made her work for her hug and kiss, but not too hard, and his eyes were sparkling with delight the whole time. Wendy got up on her knees and turned around in her seat in anticipation. Her hug included a whisper in her grandmother's ear. A sleek blond brow lifted in response as Erica's gaze slid between Adam and Laura. "Oh, he did, did he?" then she gave that throaty chuckle again and whispered something in her granddaughter's ear.

Laura felt her face glow hotly. She had very little doubt what secret Wendy had just imparted, and just the thought of that little interlude in the foyer brought back every sensation of Adam's kisses, intensifying her blush. Actually, *kiss* was an inadequate term for what they had shared in the foyer. Only the boys' waking from their naps had kept things from getting entirely out of hand. She'd have to be very much on her guard when he kissed her again, and he *would* kiss her again. She knew it as well as she knew her own name, and Adam's unwavering gaze was promising it. He covered her hand with his, squeezing tightly.

Erica kissed Wendy and moved to Laura's side, her green eyes glowing approvingly. "Jake says you're a miracle worker," she told Laura gently. "I believe he's right." And, to Laura's profound shock, she bent and laid her smooth cheek next to Laura's, hugging her lightly.

Laura could only gape at Adam, who smiled secretively.

Erica withdrew regally. "Well, I really must run. Enjoy your dinner, darlings." She patted Adam's shoulder and briefly touched her cheek to his as she floated by. "Keep your calendars open. I'll call you with a confirmed date soon."

"Absolutely," Adam promised, starting to get up again. "I'll see you out."

"Oh, no," Erica protested, moving toward the door. "Eat your dinner. I'll see myself out." She blew a kiss and floated quickly out of sight with a last wink for Wendy.

Laura looked at Adam. "You've made her very happy."

"Me? You're the miracle worker."

"Don't be silly."

"Who's being silly? No one knows better than me what a difference you've made in this family."

Laura shook her head. "Adam, you're the—"

He laid a finger against her mouth. "And who do you think has made the difference in me? Who pointed out what everyone else seemed to know but for one reason or another wouldn't say? Not that I'd have listened. Who helped me see where my real interests lay? Who showed me that a little honest affection is good for the soul?" He flipped a meaningful glance at his children and dropped his hand. "Who saved me from utter chaos?"

"You're not giving yourself enough credit," she argued.

He smiled and turned his attention to his dinner, switching topics pointedly. "I'm actually looking forward to this reception. We're going to have a lot of fun."

"I'm sure you will," Laura murmured, yielding the argument only reluctantly.

Adam put his knife and fork down once more. "No, *we* will."

"We?" Laura echoed in surprise.

Adam cocked his head. "You don't think I'm going without you, do you?"

Laura was stunned. "Oh, but... Adam, it's a family gathering. I'm sure your mother never meant for *me* to be included, and it's all right. I understand perfectly."

"Of course she means to include you, and if by some quirk of logic she hadn't, I would have included you myself."

"But Adam, I can't—"

He leaned back in his chair. "You can, and you will. Surely you wouldn't disappoint her after setting me on Dad. I convinced him to go through with the reception, if you'll recall, at your urging. I wouldn't dream of not going now. Besides, Rocky is my baby sister, and I know Luke. He'll be wanting a friendly, familiar face in the crowd."

"Well, of course *you* should go," Laura said dismissively, "but I'm not family, Adam. I don't belong at a Fortune family *gala*."

"Well, all the same, you'll go," Adam said flatly, shifting in his chair and picking up his eating utensils again, "because I'm not going without you." He cut a piece of Beverly's basil-roasted chicken and popped it in his mouth, chewing with a vengeance.

She stared at him, completely disbelieving what she was hearing. "But, Adam!"

He leaned toward her suddenly. "I'm not going to argue with you about this. I want you with me, and my mother *expects* you to be there, I'm certain. Dad, too, unless I miss my guess, and I don't think I do." He grinned and tapped her chin. "You little miracle worker, you."

Laura couldn't resist a wry smile. He wanted her with him, and if neither of his parents was going to be shocked or disapproving of that, well then, there was only one problem, and she hated to broach it. Still... She bit her lip and said softly, "Adam, I don't have anything to wear."

He waved a hand negligently. "Oh, that. Don't worry about a thing. We'll go shopping."

He dismissed the problem completely, but it was no small thing to Laura. She liked the feeling of couplehood that he seemed bent on fostering, but she wouldn't embarrass him in front of his family, and she didn't like the idea of taking his money for anything so frivolous as a party dress. She wondered if she might have saved enough to buy something appropriate for herself.

"I guess I could do that," she mused. It occurred to her that she might call Jane or even Erica and ask for advice on the proper thing to wear. No doubt she'd have to go into the city to find something. The old fear about exposing herself to Doyal reared its ugly head momentarily, but Laura fought it. The Minneapolis-St. Paul area was large enough that she wasn't apt to stumble on Doyal or anyone else she knew there. Besides, he might not even be looking for her still. Surely he realized that if she hadn't gone to the police by now, she wouldn't, if only for fear of exposing herself to him.

Adam's hand found hers, jolting her from her reverie. "Hey, it's all right. No one's going to bite you...except me." He lifted her hand and playfully nipped the back of it. Electricity shot through her. His eyes holding hers, he pressed a kiss to the very spot he had grazed with his teeth, and Laura shivered with repressed passion.

Then Wendy shouted down the table, "Kiss her again, Dad!"

Adam abruptly dropped her hand. Color flooded Laura's face. Ryan slapped both hands over his mouth, as if fearing Adam's kiss might somehow find its way to him, while Robbie screamed and collapsed in giggles, making smacking sounds with his mouth. Adam shot an apologetic glance at Laura, his hand dropping beneath the table to find her knee before he turned a censorious gaze on the children, effectively silencing them.

"Eat your dinner," he instructed flatly, then winked. Three smug gazes switched back to three barely touched plates. Adam leaned close to Laura, lifted his free hand to shield his mouth and whispered in her ear. "Kisses are for later."

Anticipation tingled along her nerve endings, heightening her color once more. His mouth quirked in a knowing smile, despite the gaze trained studiously on his plate. She wanted to poke him in the ribs, the wretch! This was all his fault. If he'd just stop looking at her as if he could eat her alive, if he just wouldn't touch her with that leashed lightning, if he just didn't set fire to her skin with a glance... If he just hadn't made her love him.

That was it. That was the real rub. No matter how hard she tried, she just couldn't stop herself from loving Adam Fortune, and it was going to take a real miracle to keep her from getting her heart broken over it.

Laura decided that calling Adam's mother might foster the notion that she was cultivating favor, but by the time she came to that decision and worked up her nerve to call Jane, the dress she had dreamed in her head was a ball gown that would have made Cinderella green with envy. Jane punctured her dream bubble with casual ignorance. "Oh, I'll probably wear a pair of dressy slacks and a silk blouse or something," she said dismissively. "Frankly, I hadn't thought about it."

Laura blushed to think that she hadn't thought of much else. Despite her better judgment, she'd been absolutely captivated by the idea of appearing on Adam's arm in the very bosom of his family, dazzlingly beautiful in her dazzling dress, which she would absolutely acquire for a bargain basement price. Jane was good enough to suggest three different stores where Laura might find what she was looking for—or what Jane assumed she was looking for.

To Laura's chagrin, Adam nixed Jane's suggestions, saying that he had in mind a certain upscale department store.

"I want to pick up some things for the kids, too," he explained. "We'll want to turn them out in their best in honor of Rocky and Luke."

*We* again. His use of that word never failed to warm her. She knew that she was playing with fire, but when he looked at her with that sparkle in his eyes, she reached blindly for the flames again. True, Adam was happy with her now, but even if Doyal didn't eventually find her, there were no guarantees for the future. Once Adam had his feet firmly on the ground, business-wise, he might very well find himself ready to embrace other areas of his privileged life-style. There were bound to be plenty of women from the upper echelons who would love to get their hands on a man like Adam Fortune, children and all, women with families of consequence and diplomas from all the right schools, women with closets full of the right clothes, women whose closest contact with a drug dealer was in the movies. Oh, yes, she was definitely riding for a heartbreak, but the ride itself promised to be the grandest thing in her miserable life.

She assumed that since Adam wanted to buy for the children, they would be taking the kids with them into the city, but Adam surprised her by getting his aunt Rebecca over to the house to baby-sit. Rebecca surprised her by being young, very near Adam's age, in fact, and not the least bit old-maidish, with her long, curly auburn hair and striking features. Laura found her as fascinating as the mystery novels she wrote, and extremely intuitive.

"She'll want something dazzling," she told Adam after giving Laura a thorough scan. "With her looks, that shouldn't be difficult, even for you."

Adam wiggled a brow at his aunt and turned Laura toward the door. "She's dazzling already," he said.

Rebecca folded her arms and smiled mysteriously. Her gaze seemed to say, *She's dazzled you already*.

Laura closed her eyes as Adam led her out into the garage, praying that it was so.

They made the trip into the city in the truck, just in case the four-wheel drive was needed to cross a patch of ice or snow. Adam surprised Laura by playing a classical music tape along the way, Tchaikovsky being his favorite. She was a Mozart freak herself, thanks to Sister Agnes, but she'd left the only tapes she'd owned behind in Colorado. She hadn't realized how much she missed them until now. Adam caught her tapping her toe and waving a finger in the air.

"It's infectious, isn't it?"

She laughed at herself. "Obviously."

He hummed along a moment, then said, "Diana was a pop fan. You know, light rock, a little jazz, some oldies. I couldn't get into it. I like something with a little more... challenge."

She laughed again. "Yep, that's you, all right."

"You're a challenge," he said, his gaze darting between her and the road. "Too much of one sometimes, I think."

She felt her heart beating slow and hard, and somehow her gaze didn't want to go anywhere but her lap. She thought carefully about what she wanted to say, and then she said it.

"I don't mean to be. I guess you scare me a little."

"How so?"

She shrugged, trying to put it into words. "This is the closest I've ever come to having it all, Adam. It feels... too good to be true."

He sent her a piercing gaze. "What do you mean by 'having it all'?"

"A family, a home... someone of my own."

He licked his lips. "That's not scary, Laura. That's security. That's love."

*Love.* The word hung there between them, a symbolic brass ring, so close yet so far. Would it jerk out of reach if she tried to grab it? She didn't have the courage to try just yet.

They rode on, surrounded by the alternately fierce and lilting orchestral music, wrapped in thoughts too fragile and frightening to give voice to. Almost before she knew it, Laura found herself looking up at a gleaming granite building in the heart of the city. An upscale department store, he'd said, but Laura had never shopped at any department store with valet parking and elevator attendants. She had the sickening feeling that she was in way over her head, even before the "shopper's guide," a thin, haughty middle-aged woman far better dressed than Laura, ushered them to a private alcove, seated them and commenced interviewing them.

Laura noted that the Fortune name meant as much in the city as it did in little old St. Cloud. Her own obviously evoked no fawning, however. The woman shot her a stern, rather disapproving look as Adam explained that Miss Beaumont was in need of a special dress.

"Nothing too formal," he said offhandedly. "Something suitable for a family reception."

Ms. Hauteur Personified was all grace when she turned back to Adam. "Is there a theme, perhaps?"

He waved a hand. "Nothing definite. Think elegant."

"Ah." She turned back to Laura and signaled that she should rise. Looking Laura up and then down, the woman said to an assistant hovering in the background, "A size eight, I think. Perhaps a six in a strapless." She stared pointedly at Laura's chest for a moment, then sniffed and shook her head. "No, the eight would be better, even if we have to take it in in the waist." With that she clapped her hands, and two things happened: Coffee and tea appeared and a staff of silent, obsequious clerks began bringing the store to them.

Laura had never seen so many lovely clothes in her life. Some were absurd, but most were breathtaking—and none of them were right. She knew it, and Adam knew it. After nearly an hour, he got up and pulled Ms. Hauteur aside. A whispered conference with much gesticulation followed. Ms. Hauteur clapped her hands and all the pretty clothes disappeared—the ball gowns, the beaded numbers, the tulle and the lace and the sleek satin prints.

When Adam reclaimed his seat, Laura leaned close and whispered, "What's going on?"

He merely smiled and patted her knee. "You'll see."

The fashion show that began then had Laura on the edge of her seat. A quartet of tall, leggy models strolled the lush carpet before them, swirling and swaying and showing off one scrumptious costume after another. It was all too much for Laura to take in. She had stopped trying to picture each and every creation on herself and was just enjoying the show when Adam suddenly exclaimed, "That's it!"

Laura's mouth fell open. She wasn't sure which of the exquisite creations currently being shown had captured his imagination, but she was absolutely certain that none of them would look as good on her as they did on the models. The salesperson knew. She waved away two of the girls and brought another forward. Laura gaped. It was a short, strapless number with a fitted and draped bodice and a sarong skirt that tied in a pretty knot at the waist and fell open to the hem, which ended several inches above the knee—too many inches, to Laura's eyes.

"That's the dress," Adam said, "but the color's wrong."

The saleswoman lifted a finger, indicating that she would need a moment for a brief conference with her assistants. After surprisingly few words, they scattered like quail flushed from the nest. In short order, they were back again, flourishing not just several dresses, but everything that could possibly go with them: shoes, stockings, even underwear—shockingly brief and sexy underwear, bras with scraps of lace for cups and panties made with less fabric than a self-respecting hankie. They all came in precise shades of white, yellow, blue, green, pink and the original black.

"White," Adam decided, dismissing the clear, deep rose color that was Laura's secret favorite.

"An excellent choice," cooed the saleswoman, "not precisely in season, but certainly acceptable. The style is a dream. I suspect that no alteration will be necessary, since the sarong may be wrapped and tied just enough tighter for that narrow waist." She looked down her long nose at Laura and added, "If you will just follow me."

Laura got up and trailed along after the woman hesitantly. She found herself shoved into a dressing room already filled with people, where she was summarily stripped, then hooked, smoothed and zipped into the white dress and the necessary underpinnings. She had on the opaque sparkle hose before she even knew what had hit her, and hated them on sight. From her perspective, they made her legs look fat and ugly, but when she indicated her dislike, Ms. Hauteur merely sniffed and announced, "We'll let Mr. Fortune decide."

Laura strode out, teetering on three-inch heels, her waist properly cinched, and smiled apologetically at Adam. "I hate the stockings, and if I have to walk another yard in these shoes, I'll break my neck."

Adam smiled at the saleswoman. "Ditch the stockings and the shoes."

Laura wanted to kick the saleswoman when she all but groveled in doing as he bade. She agreed, of course, but Mr. Fortune had the final say. Laura rolled her eyes, her hands at her hips. Then it was back to the dressing room for sheer white stockings and a pair of simple, and thankfully comfortable, shoes with sensible two-inch heels.

Adam made an approving sound, but Laura saw the doubt in his eyes. "I want to try on the pink," she announced forthrightly. The "shopper's assistant" did not so much as flicker an eyelid until Adam nodded in agreement.

Laura did not allow herself to be propelled, pummeled and poked this time. She stood her ground and insisted on seeing a greater selection of shoes and stockings. After quick consideration, she chose a sheer beige stocking with a rosy hue and a shoe with a slender, flared heel and a draped effect on the toe that echoed that of the bodice of her dress. The color was not exact, but one of the assistant's assistants whispered that the shoes could be dyed in a matter of hours. Laura thanked her with a smile and entered the dressing room alone, emerging minutes later with the natural confidence born of feeling perfectly turned out.

Adam approved heartily. The clerk then sold him on a cream-colored satin wrap coat with a pink lining and a pair of dangly earrings and a matching bracelet made of synthetic stones known as "pink ice." Laura insisted sternly that she didn't need the coat or the jewelry, but Adam ignored her and bought it all, the purchase handled as discreetly as a state secret.

. Laura allowed herself to be herded back to the dressing room, her pride at war with the feminine need to look her very best for her man. Surely she could cover the cost from her savings. The woman had said that the coat was on sale, and Laura took heart from that, but standing there in front of that dressing room mirror, she turned this way and that, sure something was wrong, and then she knew. It was her hair. It was the same old hair she wore every day, long and straight as a board. She bit her lip, wondering what Adam would say if she asked his opinion, then shook her head. She ought to manage this much on her own, but what to do? She supposed she could ask Jane or Erica or even Rebecca, but she doubted they'd give her an honest opinion, for fear of hurting her feelings. She turned to the haughty salesperson instead. Here was one who respected nothing but the almighty dollar. She need not fear having her feelings spared at the cost of truth.

It took some nerve to ask, but to her surprise, the woman merely gave her a frank look, then stepped behind her and swept her hair up with a few swift, economical movements of her hands. She curled it in one smooth twist up the back of Laura's head and anchored it with her fingers at the crown. It was a sleek, chic, elegant style that Laura immediately knew suited her well. Her bangs were a little overlong, but Laura combed them into place with her fingers, liking the way they framed her face.

"You'll need a bit of shadow in the folds of the eyelids," the sales consultant instructed smoothly. "I should think a soft shade of taupe, and of course you'll want to use a dark brown mascara before curling your eyelashes. Then I think a mauve lip pencil, followed with a clear pink lipstick. Hmm . . ." She cocked her head, studying Laura's face, and announced, "Or you could go red, but no blush, I think. Your natural coloring is adequate."

Laura thanked the woman, who deigned to lift an eyebrow before striding from the room, letting Laura's hair fall to her shoulders. Laura quickly twisted it up again and smiled at her image. Yes, it was exactly right—the dress, the shoes, the hair, even the stockings. Whatever the cost, she would pay it to know that Adam could escort her proudly.

It didn't work out quite that way, and she got her first inkling that it wasn't going to when she priced some of the articles of clothing in the children's department. A hundred and seventeen dollars for a child's dress! Adam chose a simple jumper of yellow-gold velveteen and a lacy blouse and petticoat to be worn beneath it. Laura suggested white tights, having noticed runs and snags in those Wendy already possessed, but balked at buying shoes without Wendy there to try them on, even though Adam had traced patterns of the children's feet on plain white paper.

"How about these?" Adam asked, picking up a pair of soft ballet-style slippers with elasticized edges.

Laura conceded that those might well work, but shopping for the boys proved a little more difficult. Boys' shoes didn't come in soft elasticized styles. After some wrangling, however, they managed to agree on identical pairs of short navy blue coveralls, white long-sleeved shirts with little red bow ties and navy knee socks. The shoes would have to be purchased in St. Cloud.

At the last moment, Adam picked up a tiny leather handbag for Wendy, and for the boys zippered wallets embossed with the faces of favorite cartoon characters. Then, to Laura's everlasting amazement, Adam steered her to the men's department, where he proceeded to buy himself a classy double-breasted tuxedo, pin-tucked shirt and black silk cummerbund and tie, military dress uniform no longer being appropriate. It was such fun, especially when Laura managed to sneak in the purchase of a white cashmere scarf for him without his knowledge. She teased him while he stood with arms extended and legs spread as no fewer than three tailors buzzed around him with tapes and chalk and lethal-looking straight pins, each fervently promising that the alterations would be completed by the end of the working day.

Adam then whisked Laura off for a late lunch in an expensive restaurant, where he flirted with her over medallions of veal and pasta primavera. Laura was feeling relaxed and happy by the time they collected their parcels and headed for home. As Adam expertly merged their vehicle into traffic, she reached across the armrest separating the seats and laid her hand on his forearm.

"I have a favor to ask you."

He shot her an intrigued look. "Anything."

She smiled. "You're extremely generous, but this is very important to me."

His gaze swept over her face, lingering briefly on her mouth. "Just ask."

"I want you to let me pay for my own clothing."

He flipped a hand. "Done. From here on out, whatever you buy, you pay for."

"I mean the clothing we bought today."

Adam shot her a surprised look and shifted uncomfortably in his seat. "Laura, honey, I don't think that's such a good idea."

"Adam, please. I was serious when I said that this is important to me."

He shook his head. "Baby, you don't realize... That is, I'm not certain you can... Just take my word for it, sweetheart, now is not the time to assert your independence. Let it go this once. Next time—"

"Next time you'll say the very same thing," she argued. "I know you, Adam Fortune, you won't let me pay for a thing!"

"Word of honor, hon. Besides, this particular purchase was instigated completely by me."

Laura sighed. "Adam, I want you to be proud of me, but—" she began softly. Suddenly the truck jerked over to the side of the street, ran up onto a curb and came to an abrupt halt. Adam jerked the emergency brake and reached for her, pulling her close.

"Have you got it in that brain of yours that I'm somehow *ashamed* of you?"

"Well, no, not exactly."

"Not at all!"

Her heart swelled to the bursting point. "Oh, Adam, I fought so hard against falling in love with you. Now, I need you to know that it isn't the money or the job, and certainly not the name. It's you, all you, and I don't want there ever to be any doubt about that. Whatever happens, I want you to know that what won my heart was *you.*"

"Laura." He wrapped a hand around the back of her neck and pulled her closer still, his mouth seizing hers with possessive intent. "Laura, my Laura. You'll never know what that means to me. God, you light up my life like nothing and no one else ever has before. What would I have done if you hadn't come along?"

"Well, you wouldn't have bought that dress, for one thing!" she teased, beaming.

He laid his forehead against hers, laughing huskily. "Pay for the damned dress, if that's what you want to do. Just remember that I'd buy anything, do anything, say anything, to keep you with me!"

She didn't tell him then that she'd stay, but in her heart she knew that only one thing could ever make her go.

# Twelve

Life was good.

Laura sat curled up on the couch, thumbing through a magazine and listening to Wendy hum softly to herself as she lay on her belly on the floor, wielding a crayon against a page in her new coloring book. Her little feet drummed lightly in time with her tune, and her head wagged slightly from side to side as she concentrated on her coloring, her tongue poking out the side of her mouth. She was the picture of a contented child, and Laura felt a warm glow of pride because it was so.

Adam came into the room. He was walking blindly, his nose stuck in a book that promised to be the definitive study on American Empire furniture. He bumped his shin on the edge of the coffee table, but merely grunted and shifted course, finally lowering himself gingerly into his chair. No sooner was he settled than he turned the page and crossed his legs.

Laura smiled to herself. She would not have ventured to say that he was contented, for a finely drawn sexual tension had developed between them, an awareness and a building passion that she feared would blow her apart if ever they gave it expression, but he was patient and loving and unexpectedly gentle with her. She loved him with her eyes from where she sat, and he lowered the book and returned the look as if he'd sensed her very gaze. She dropped her head, smiling to herself, and asked if he'd seen the boys in the past few minutes, for they were suspiciously absent. He cut his eyes knowingly and replied that, believe it or not, they were playing quietly in their room. They shared another look that fairly sizzled the air between them, and even after Adam went back to his book, a sense of anticipation and well-being simmered within her.

This happy feeling had started to grow the day they went into the city shopping. She remembered and held dear his every word and gesture from that day, especially those that had come at the end. *Just remember that I'd buy anything, do anything, say anything, to keep you with me.* She shivered anew with delight at the memory of the words, but it was more than mere words that swelled her heart and fired her imagination. The things he had done! The way he had kissed her, touched her, indulged her, spoke volumes, especially when she had carried her hard-earned money to him and insisted on knowing the cost of the outfit he had bought her for the reception.

He hadn't liked it, but he had held true to his word. She had nearly choked when she learned the total cost of all he'd purchased, for it was twice what she'd managed to save and then some, but when she reiterated how important it was to her, he had proposed a compromise. She would pay for the dress, the stockings and the shoes, but the coat, the jewelry and the frilly underclothes would be his gift to her. The very idea of those underclothes being a gift from him was somehow especially thrilling, but she hadn't dared tell him that. She concentrated instead on the cost of the dress, the shoes, and the stockings. Even that was beyond her, but he had taken what money she had and promised to withhold the rest from her pay in small increments. Then he had done the sweetest thing. He had beckoned her into the room, his room, and he had shown her a secret compartment in his desk. The money would be kept there, he had told her, and if ever she should have need of it, for any reason, she was simply to come and take it, no questions asked.

He had taken her pride money, but he hadn't taken her freedom to care for her personal needs, to act in an emergency. He hadn't made her beholden to him for every dime and nickel, and though he had said that he would buy or say or do anything to keep her with him, he had made it possible for her to go, proving that her feelings counted more than his own desires.

Oh, yes, life was good, very, very good.

Her eyes were shining with moisture when Wendy got up from the floor and skipped over to lean against her father's leg. "This is for you, Daddy."

Adam put down his book and studied with genuine interest the simple picture she had colored, complimenting its every aspect. Wendy beamed and visibly softened. She leaned across his lap and pointed to a certain spot on the paper, saying, "I got out of the lines some there."

Adam turned his head, as if seeking a different angle. "Um, yes, you did, but do you know something? It worked out rather well. I think it needed this wisp of extra color here." The *wisp* was more like a rat's nest of scribbled lines, but Wendy was patently thrilled. She crawled up in his lap and wound her arms around his neck.

"I love you, Daddy!"

"I love you, too, honey. Listen, I have a good idea!" With a glance in Laura's direction, he cupped a hand and whispered in Wendy's ear.

Wendy crawled down off his lap and plopped onto her belly, throwing open her book again and glancing eagerly in Laura's direction. Laura had little doubt that she was soon to be the recipient of a painstakingly colored picture, especially when Wendy popped up again a moment later.

"Hey, I got a good idea, too! How about when I'm done with this one, I color a picture for Aunt Rocky and Uncle Luke?"

Adam nodded in enthusiastic agreement. "I think that's a wonderful idea, Wendy. Aunt Rocky will be very pleased."

"Maybe we could even get a little frame for it," Laura suggested helpfully.

"Like a real picture on the wall!" Wendy exclaimed excitedly.

"We'll do that," Adam declared. "Then we'll wrap it up in pretty paper, and you can give it to Aunt Rocky at the reception."

A thrilled Wendy got to work. Not a minute later, a muted crash, coupled with a terrified scream, shattered the companionable silence. Laura and Adam both jumped up and ran for the boys' room. Adam got there just a heartbeat ahead of her and threw open the door as she skidded to a stop. Laura gasped at the sight of the little body folded up unnaturally on the floor at the foot of the bed, surrounded by shards of milky glass.

"Robbie!" Adam pushed past her, falling to his knees beside his son, heedless of the glass. Just as he reached toward the boy with trembling hands, Robbie unfolded and lurched up onto his elbows, wailing loudly. Adam heaved a sigh of relief, and then relief flared into anger. "What on earth were you doing? Were you trying to kill yourself?"

Laura peered over his shoulder, realizing suddenly that she'd forgotten to breathe for a long moment. Adam ran careful hands over his son's small body before setting him firmly on his feet. Laura feared for an instant that he might shake the boy before gaining firm control of his own emotions, and she dropped a restraining hand on his shoulder. She needn't have worried, though, for Adam merely smoothed a hand over the boy's head. "You've got a knot the size of a golf ball back there! For heaven's sake, Rob! What were you doing?"

Suddenly he pulled the crying boy to him for a rough hug. It was at that point that Ryan peeked warily over the edge of the bed, his eyes huge with trepidation. Laura moved carefully to the side of the bed and crooked a finger at him. He scrambled up onto the rumpled covers and into her arms. She lifted him carefully free of the glass and carried him into the hall. Adam got up and followed with Robbie sobbing on his shoulder, saying, "I've got an ice pack in my room."

Laura sat Ryan on his feet, but kept his hand in hers. Together they trailed Adam to the master suite, where he placed Robbie on the side of the bed. He pointed a finger at Ryan, then pointed to the spot next to Robbie. Ryan obediently crawled up to sit next to his brother, while Adam went to get the ice pack, which he delivered to Laura with the request that she fill it while he talked to the boys. By the time she got back from the kitchen, Adam had pieced together the story.

It seemed that the boys had tired of playing quietly and had taken to throwing wooden blocks at one another. Robbie had come up with the bright idea of presenting his brother with a moving target, namely himself. He had climbed up onto his bed and started to jump up and down while Ryan chucked blocks at him. One block had hit and shattered the light fixture overhead, scaring Robbie so much that he'd slipped and fallen from the bed. Adam gave them both a good scolding, forbade them the sanctuary of their bedroom for play for a full week and confiscated the whole set of blocks for the same period of time. Then he sat down on the bed beside Robbie and tenderly applied the ice pack to the bump on the back of his head.

Predictably, Robbie soon wiggled his way onto his father's lap. Not wanting Ryan to feel left out, Laura snuggled him close and whispered that everything would soon be fine, that he would learn to play safely and not take chances with his and his brother's safety. Soon Adam was lying on his side across his bed, Robbie tucked into the curve of his body. Without even realizing that she was doing so, Laura sank down, facing him, Ryan snuggled against her. Tears and reticence gradually gave way to tentative giggles and relief and finally to fully restored spirits. As the knot on his head and the pain it engendered faded, Robbie asked to be let down. Adam lifted his arm and allowed the boy to slide free, telling him that he could go to the den. Ryan quickly followed.

As soon as they were gone, Adam lay back and groaned. "I think I lost ten years off my life. When I opened that door and saw him lying there..."

Laura wedged a forearm between her head and the mattress, her weight balanced on her elbow. "I should have been watching them more closely. I'm sorry."

He came up and twisted to the side, leaning over her. "The FBI couldn't watch those boys better than you do. Besides, you asked me what they were up to, and I dismissed the possibility of trouble because I'd checked on them not five minutes earlier."

"Five minutes can be a long time for a kid," Laura said.

Adam gave his head a wry nod. "Obviously."

She started to sit up, saying, "I'd better get that glass cleaned up."

His eyes caught hers, and he gave his head a little shake, his arm coming around her smoothly, snug against the small of her back. Her breath caught as he lifted her against him. Then his mouth covered hers, and he pressed her down onto the bed, levering his weight atop her. His free hand slid over her hip and down her thigh to the bend of her knee, which he tugged upward, opening her legs to him. With only a slight shift of his weight, he was cradled in the apex of her thighs. He slid his tongue into her mouth and, with a moan low in his throat, began to rock against her.

Laura lifted her arms and draped them around his neck, melting beneath him. Her head was swimming, and every time he rocked against her, it spun a little faster. In no time at all, she was frantic. She forgot to worry that the children might walk in. She forgot to worry about whether she was being fair to him, whether she was placing him in danger, whether this was right, whether she was going to get her heart broken. She forgot everything and everyone but the man in her arms, the strength of him, the power leashed by gentleness, the desire that poured from him, the heat that melted her into putty. She sought instinctively to please him, to make herself a part of him. Simply put, she gave herself up wholly, for the first time, to loving Adam Fortune, and she was good at it. Everything said so, every sound he made, every movement, the pounding of his heart against her breast, the quick jerkiness of his breath, the slant of his lips and the sweep of his tongue. He told her in every way possible how very good she was at loving him. When she dug her heels into the mattress and tilted her pelvis, he ground himself against her, and then, with a groan, he pulled back, breaking the kiss and burying his face in the curve of her neck and shoulder.

"My God!" he gasped, sliding his mouth up her throat. "I've dreamed of having you in this bed." He lifted himself onto his elbows, his hands smoothing the hair back from her face. "I want to make love to you," he said, "when it's right, when it can be perfect. I just don't know how much longer I can wait."

"I know." She sighed. "My nights have been . . ."

He grinned down at her, golden eyes framed by short, thick rusty-brown lashes. "What?"

But good sense was returning, and with it came embarrassment. Her cheeks turned pink. He laughed in delight.

"You are precious! I can't tell you how much I—"

"Daaaddy!"

"Oh, heavens! The children!" Laura began to squirm beneath him, wanting up, but her heart was pounding. What would he have said? Had he been about to tell her that he loved her?

Adam hissed something sharp under his breath and rolled off her, folding up into a sitting position on the edge of the bed, his hands ruffling his hair. It had grown longer on the top, its thick mahogany locks displaying a tendency to wave. Laura managed to get her legs folded beneath her before the twins came pounding into the bedroom.

"Daddy! Wendy won't let us color in her book!"

"Yeah, Wendy won't wet us color in her book!"

Adam leaned forward uncomfortably. "Well, um, Wendy's working on a special project."

"But we want to color!"

"Yeah, we wanna color!"

Laura slid off the bed, holding out her hands to the boys. "Maybe we can find something else for you to color. Let's go look, okay?"

"Laura?" Adam sprang up and reached out a hand to her, but then he glanced at the boys and dropped it again, saying sheepishly, "I'll, um, clean up that glass."

"Yes. All right." For a long moment, she couldn't look away, but then Ryan tugged at her hand and she realized that the boys were waiting, watching. She turned away reluctantly, pasting a smile on her face for the boys. "Maybe we could make some tracings from one of your favorite books, and you could color those," she suggested.

Robbie began to jump up and down, tugging at her arm. "Yeah! Yeah!"

Before they were out the door, they were arguing over which book to choose. Laura tossed one final look over her shoulder before allowing them to tug her out into the hall.

He was standing there all tense with frustration, one hand clamped to the back of his neck, but what thrilled her, what filled her heart to overflowing, was the poignancy of his smile, the tenderness in his eyes. The love. She couldn't believe that it was anything else.

"Who's hungry?"

"Me!"

"Me!"

"Me!"

Adam left one hand on the steering wheel and glanced at Laura, one eyebrow cocked. "What do you think? Want to stop in at the diner?"

Laura looked around her. He wondered what she was thinking as she recognized the little restaurant where he'd found her that day weeks and weeks ago. Wendy recognized it, too.

"Look!" She stuck an arm straight out, pointing. "That's where we got Laura!"

"That's where we *met* Laura," Adam corrected. His gaze intercepted hers. "What do you think, hon? Want to stop for a bite?" He didn't add that he'd very much like to tweak some noses.

Laura bit her lip, then shrugged. "It's all right with me."

Adam smiled to himself. Maybe it was wicked of him, but he couldn't help wanting to show her off a little. He wanted them to see that she was happy and loved, not to mention that she'd worked miracles with this family. He figured that he was entitled, since he'd let Laura talk him out of reporting the manager to the owner. He swung the car into an empty space in front of the nondescript little place and killed the engine. He hooked an elbow over the back of the seat and twisted in place, looking at the kids.

"Now listen to me. If you're not on your best behavior in this place, Laura's going to be embarrassed, and I'm going to be angry. Understand?"

The mulish expression on Wendy's face told him that she understood perfectly. "Is that nasty old man there?" she asked. "The one that got mad at Laura?"

"I don't know, honey, but if he is, we'll make him be nice."

She nodded emphatically, obviously remembering all that had transpired that day. The boys, however, were just as obviously adrift. Adam took pains to explain, reminding them that Laura used to work here and adding only that her old boss hadn't been very happy when she decided to come to work for them. "So look, guys," he said, engaging their attention pointedly, "I expect you to sit quietly, eat neatly and keep your voices down while we're in there. Understand me?" Both boys nodded enthusiastically. "I hope so, because if you misbehave in there today, everyone's going to look at Laura and think it's her fault. Know why?"

Wendy piped up. "'Cause last time we were here, we were so bad that Laura had to come home with us and take care of us or else you'd of just . . . just . . ."

Adam's mouth curved. "That's right, but Laura straightened us out, didn't she?" Wendy nodded. "That's why we owe it to her not to embarrass her," he said to the boys. "Okay?"

Both nodded again, and Ryan leaned forward to connect his gaze with Laura's. "We be weal good," he promised.

Laura smiled. "I'm sure you will be, sweetie."

Adam managed a sedate unloading of the boys, while Laura helped Wendy out of the car, then led the way to the entrance. He stepped up and swung it open, keeping the boys close to his legs while Laura and Wendy slipped into the small glassed-in foyer. They followed the same procedure with the inside door, and then they were looking over the late lunch crowd for a place to sit. One of the waitresses recognized Laura immediately. There was an elbow in the ribs of a companion, and a whisper in the ear alerted another, and she hurried away, apparently to spread the news. Laura glanced at Adam uncertainly. He lifted a hand to the slope of her shoulder and left it there. "How about a booth? We could pull a chair up to the end of the table for Ryan."

"That's fine."

They shepherded the kids across the narrow room and began the process of divesting them of their heavy coats. Laura tucked everything into the corners of the booth while Adam borrowed a chair from another table and fetched booster seats. Soon they were all seated. Out of necessity, Laura sat close to Adam's side, their coats and Ryan's tucked into the space next to her. The waitress appeared, her gaze sweeping over Laura curiously.

"What can I get you?"

Adam draped an arm casually across Laura's shoulders. "What do you want, hon? I think I'll start with coffee."

"Coffee will be fine. Kids, would you like some cocoa?"

Ryan and Wendy went for the hot cocoa immediately, but Robbie wanted a soft drink. Adam insisted that it was too cold for colas, then negotiated a compromise in the form of a glass of milk.

"Don't make the cocoa too hot," Laura warned the waitress. "Pour a little cold milk into it before you bring it out, please."

The woman gave her a disgruntled look, but the cocoa came back at a very drinkable, safe temperature. By that time, they had menus spread out before them. "We're ready to order," Adam instructed without looking up. Laura's hand drifted over his knee and squeezed warningly. He looked up to find the manager hovering over him. He pulled Laura a little closer to his side and smiled up at the man. "Well, hello there," he said, gushing with friendliness. "Remember me? Name's Fortune, Adam Fortune. You must still be a waitress or two short, if you're waiting tables yourself."

The man's smile strained. "Ah, actually, I just wanted to be certain that you have adequate service."

"Well, how nice!" Adam went on blithely. "Must be lowering, though, waiting on tables—but you've still got your job, after all." Laura's hand tightened convulsively at the subtle dig. They all knew that Adam could have gotten him fired. A simple phone call from a member of the Fortune family voicing a complaint would have been enough to see it done. Adam was just letting him know that it was still a possibility if he should get out of line again. He turned his attention to Laura. "What would you like to eat, darling?"

Her lips quirked at his use of the endearment, but she studied the menu with determined calm. "Um, what's the soup of the day?"

"Split pea."

"Sounds fine. I'll have that with an order of garlic toast, please—oh, and, a large plate of french fries for us all to share."

"I'll have the soup, as well," Adam said, "and a sandwich, I think." He took his time deciding which one, then sat back and smiled pointedly at the harried manager while Laura negotiated with the children.

Robbie got tired of the process and began swinging his feet, his heels thumping against the booth. Adam interrupted the proceedings with a cleared throat and said, "Rob, your feet, please."

The drumming immediately stopped, and Adam rewarded the boy with a proud wink.

The order was completed, and the nervous manager began to turn away, but Adam stopped him with a negligent lift of his hand. "Aren't you going to greet a former employee?"

The man's doughy face flamed beet red, but he inclined his head at Laura. "Lau—, uh, ma'am. D-doing well, I take it?"

Laura smiled innocently. "Very well, thank you."

Adam smoothed back a silky lock of her hair. "An understatement if ever I heard one," he said. "She's worked wonders with this family. Hasn't she, kids?"

Wendy looked up at the man, her eyes narrowing dangerously. Adam almost laughed, thinking, not for the first time, that she was going to be every bit as formidable as Kate one of these days. "We love Laura," she said, almost belligerently.

"Indeed we do," Adam added softly, for Laura's ear alone.

"And she loves us!" Ryan announced loudly.

Laura smiled and lifted a shushing finger to her lips. Ryan subsided at once. Laura raised a conciliatory gaze to her former employer of one day. "It's worked out for the best," she said, and to his credit, he seemed almost pleased.

"Glad to hear it. I've, uh, regretted the way...everything happened that day."

"I haven't," Laura said lightly, her gaze traveling to Adam's face. It was all he could do not to kiss her, driving his tongue into her mouth with all the possession humanly possible. Instead, he turned a placid look up at the man who had once insulted her.

"We'll have those fries right away, please."

The man's smile took on that strained look again. "Fine."

"Oh, and send someone over with a fresh pot of coffee, would you? I think Laura could use a refill."


Forty minutes later, they spilled out onto the sidewalk. Laura felt stuffed and warm, inside and out. Dessert had come "on the house," and she had enjoyed it immensely. So, too, she thought, had Adam. The kids would be lucky if they didn't have bellyaches, but she was almost too pleased to worry about it. They were at the car when Wendy clapped a hand over her mouth, giggling.

"What's so funny?" Adam asked.

"That mean old man," Wendy said. "He sure was nice this time."

"He's smarter than he looks," Adam muttered, opening a door for Robbie. Before the boy climbed inside, however, Adam passed a pleased look from face to face, around the car. "You all made me very proud in there. Thank you."

"I'm the one who should be saying thanks," Laura said softly over the top of the car.

Adam shook his head, grinning unrepentantly. "You'll never know how much I enjoyed that. Now let's go home." With that, he helped the kids into the car and began settling them.

*Home,* Laura thought. That word never failed to warm her, and yet unease shivered down her spine. Instinctively she turned her gaze back to the glass front of the diner. The same waitress who had hurried away at her appearance before was standing with arms folded, staring out at her. Laura hadn't really known her, couldn't even remember her name, and yet her interest seemed pointed. Why? But then Laura thought of the man belting his children into the car at her side and shook her head. Perhaps the woman was merely envious. After all, Adam was a remarkably handsome man, and a Fortune to boot, a fact which would weigh heavier with some women than anything else. Yes, of course, that was it. A man like Adam was bound to intrigue any woman, name or no. Feeling a certain kinship with the nameless woman, Laura pushed away the niggling prickle of alarm and got into the car, telling herself yet again how very lucky she was. In fact, she told herself as Adam flashed a warm smile at her before starting the car, *lucky* didn't begin to cover it.

Laura pulled the brush through Wendy's soft red hair a final time, then bent and dropped a kiss on the top of her head.

"It's growing, isn't it?" Wendy said with undisguised pleasure, studying herself in the mirror above the sink.

Laura fluffed Wendy's freshly dried hair with her hands. "Certainly it is, and see how prettily it shines?"

Wendy nodded, the corners of her mouth tucked up into the apples of her cheeks. "I want it to look just like yours," she said, her golden eyes twinkling. For the first time, Laura glimpsed the lovely young woman she would become and felt an overwhelming compulsion to be here to see it as it happened.

*Please, God. I need to be here. She needs me to be here. This is where I belong. Home.*

She folded the towel that she had used to dry Wendy's hair and draped it over the towel bar, then rinsed Wendy's toothbrush again and dropped it into the holder. When she was done, to her surprise, Wendy raised her arms in a silent request to be held. Stooping, Laura took her into her arms and stood, Wendy wrapped around her like a vine of ivy.

She was heavy, but Laura welcomed her weight as she carried her into her room and lowered them both to the side of her bed.

"Laura?" Wendy said mistily. "You're not like a real nanny, are you?"

Laura blanched, uncertain what she was getting at. "Well, I didn't have the formal training that some nannies have, but you know I grew up in a kind of orphanage, and I learned there how to... manage and entertain children. If there's something that you wish I would do that I'm not, though, just tell me."

Wendy shook her head without lifting it from Laura's shoulder. "I like you better than all those others," she confessed, adding in a whispery voice, "They didn't love us."

Laura closed her eyes, hugging her tight. "Well, then, that must be the difference," she said. "I love you all."

Wendy put her head back at that. "Daddy, too?"

Laura felt as if Wendy had reached into her chest and squeezed her heart with her little hand. "Daddy, too," she confirmed softly.

Wendy smiled. "Then are you going to be our new mommy?"

Laura's heart flipped over and swooned. "Would you like that, sweetie?"

Wendy tightened her arms around Laura's neck. "My old mommy went to heaven a long time ago," she said.

Laura felt tears start in her eyes. "I know."

"She won't never come back," Wendy went on solemnly.

Laura blinked against the tears, her smile a thing of comfort. "She can't come back, Wendy, but she left her love for you in your heart. That's what Sister Agnes used to tell me about my mom and dad. And you know, it's true that sometimes, if you're very still and very quiet and you remember very hard, you feel her love here inside you." She laid a hand over Wendy's chest, but Wendy continued to stare up at her with wide golden eyes.

"Do you think she would mind if you were my new mommy?"

Laura bit her lip. "I think she would want you to be happy, Wendy, and for you to remember how much she loves you, and—"

"I think she would like you to be my new mommy," Wendy said. "I think you'd be the best mommy ever since her."

The tears spilled over without warning. Laura hugged Wendy to her. "Thank you, sweetheart. Thank you so much." She bit back the words to tell Wendy how much she would like to be her new mother. Those were words better left unsaid, for even if Adam should someday want to marry her, she didn't know whether she could do it. Oh, she loved him, more than she had thought possible, and she loved this little girl snuggled in her lap and those two mischievous little peanuts in the room next door. But she could never completely forget that danger hovered somewhere in the background. Perhaps he would never find her, perhaps he no longer even wanted to, but how could she be sure? How could she take the chance? And yet, how could she go unless she knew that she must?

For the first time, Laura saw how very much the children had at stake emotionally in this relationship. They needed her. She couldn't just abandon them, but neither could she place them in danger. Oh, if only it were as simple as wanting to be Adam's wife and the children's mother! Her dilemma would be solved if what she wanted was the only criteria, for if it was left to her, she would never go. Even if Adam never spoke a word about marriage to her, even if he never said that he loved her, she would stay. She would always stay.

Laura murmured soothing words to Wendy, saying something about no one knowing for certain what the future would hold but the present being all that really mattered, for love was an ever-present thing. Wendy seemed to accept whatever Laura told her, or perhaps she was just too sleepy to realize that Laura had never really answered her question. Without looking into the room and revealing himself, Adam couldn't be certain, and he didn't want to do that. He didn't want to risk embarrassing Laura or making her uncomfortable in any way. But he was pleased that he had stopped by Wendy's room to say good-night, pleased that his young daughter was thinking along the same lines as her father. He was pleased, too, to hear the longing in Laura's carefully worded replies to Wendy's questions. He knew that she loved him. He could feel it in her every glance, her kisses, her touch, in the peace that enveloped them whenever she was at his side, but most of all he felt it in the fierce sexual attraction that pulled them together even when they were apart. It was unlike anything else he had ever felt, and he didn't mean to lose it. No matter what she'd said in the beginning, he didn't mean ever to let her go. Whether or not she eventually agreed to marry him, she was his, and he meant to keep her, one way or another.

# Thirteen

Laura stared at herself in the bureau mirror. She looked—and felt—like another person, from the sleek roll of her upswept hair to the dyed fabric of her shoes. So this was what it was like to be a Fortune. She didn't think she could stand this day in and day out, but it could be fun once in a while, and tonight she intended to enjoy herself. Tonight, she was Cinderella at the ball. She considered her image once more. Yes, put a long, full skirt on this dress and she'd feel right at home in a coach and four. But there wasn't time to act the seamstress; Prince Charming waited in the hall. Laura took a deep breath and strode from the room.

Prince Charming had stuffed the little princes into their coats and was now down on one knee, trying to get them to stand still long enough for him to zip them up. It was Wendy who called a halt to the proceedings. The instant she saw Laura, she gasped and flung herself down the hall to stop at Laura's side.

"Laura! Oh, you look so beautiful!"

Adam stopped what he was doing and stood. He turned, and Laura watched him take her in, his jaw dropping a little. She felt a surge of pride and then pure love as he strode toward her, arms outstretched.

"My God!" He took her hands in his and held them wide. "You look like a queen. My queen." He made a gallant bow from the waist.

Laura laughed. "I don't know too many queens who walk around in skirts this short." She grimaced, an old worry surfacing. "It's too short, isn't it?"

Adam's gaze seemed to linger on her legs a very long time, but since he was shaking his head slowly side to side, she took heart. "Incredible," he breathed finally.

Laura laughed again and tilted her head coyly. "You don't look too bad yourself." *That* was an understatement if ever she'd made one. "In fact, you're stunning."

He grinned, smoothing a hand down one shiny lapel, then tweaking his bow tie. Suddenly Ryan flung himself around Adam and collided with Laura's knees. Bouncing off, he flung wide the sides of his coat.

"Wook at me, Waura! Wook at me!" His speech impediment was always more pronounced when he was excited.

Laura gasped, as if in delight. "My goodness! How handsome you are!"

"Me too! Me too!" Robbie cried, jumping up and down in place.

She made the same gasp and very nearly the same exclamation, then turned her gaze on Wendy. She had seen Wendy before, of course, having helped her bathe, curl her hair and dress between her own shower and dressing. She had made all the appropriate noises then, but she felt that Wendy deserved reinforcement, since everyone else was getting compliments. She addressed herself to Adam. "Doesn't Wendy look lovely in her new clothes?"

"She's a perfect beauty," Adam said, bending and curving a finger beneath his daughter's chin to lift her face for his kiss. "In fact," he went on, lifting an eyebrow at Laura, "if you're the queen of this night, she must be the princess." He smiled down at Wendy. "I'll have the two prettiest females in the place on my arms."

Wendy giggled and clasped Laura's hand, blossoming beneath the glow of her father's pride. "Oh, Daddy."

He thumped her nose, then smiled at Laura. "Let me get our coats."

"I'll do up the boys."

Laura stooped and wrestled Robbie's zipper up. To her surprise and pleasure, Wendy took a hand with Ryan. She shook her finger bossily in Ryan's face as he squirmed, admonishing him in a very adult tone to behave himself and be still. She couldn't get the zipper locked into place, however, so Laura had to help her. Nevertheless, she hugged Wendy close. "Thanks for your help, sweetie."

Wendy beamed at her, then turned her attention to her brothers. "You two better be good. Daddy wants everyone to be proud of us for Laura."

Laura smiled and dished out kisses, leaving behind lipstick prints, which she hastily wiped off, saying, "I'm always proud of you three, and I know you'll be very good tonight."

The boys gave confirming nods, while Wendy stood regally confident. Adam walked up behind them with Laura's expensive new wrap, having already donned his own tan cashmere dress coat. Laura stood and allowed him to assist her, noting that he wore around his neck the white scarf she had given him. She belted her knee-length coat in place as she ushered the children toward the foyer. Laura herself moved unseeingly toward the garage door, but as she put out her hand to open it, Adam stopped her.

"This way. Tonight we travel in style. Mother insisted."

He opened the front door and allowed the children to run down the walk toward the limo waiting in the drive. Laura gaped as the driver scrambled out of the car and opened a door for the children, bowing deferentially. It was obviously something they had done or seen done before, because they ignored him and merely climbed into the car. Adam smiled apologetically as he eased her out of the house and locked up. "Mother's only thinking of the safety of her family. It is a party, you know, and I'm quite sure she means to float us all in champagne."

Laura nodded, feeling woefully out of her depth, but Adam gripped her hand and squeezed it reassuringly as they moved down the walk, side by side. As he helped her into the car, he bent low and whispered in her ear, "Relax, love. You're going to fit in just fine."

The drive was short, but the boys made the most of it, taking every advantage of their freedom from their car seats. They climbed over everything and pushed every button they could find, opening and closing the sunroof, lowering the glass partition that separated them from the driver, then raising it again, locking and unlocking the doors, thrusting their hands into cavities meant to store drinks and other luxuries. Adam indulged them for a bit, then put each in his place firmly enough to let them know he meant it. "Settle down now. It's perfectly permissible to have fun, but you're to mind your manners, too. Don't forget."

"They won't forget," Wendy promised, splitting a determined look between them. It was clear that she had taken over the herding of her brothers for the evening. Laura felt certain that she knew why. Wendy wanted her to make a good impression on the family at large. It was reasonable to conclude that, as nanny and potential stepmother, she would be judged on the basis of the children's behavior.

Laura smiled at the thought, despite a sense of unease. It wasn't that she didn't want to be their stepmother—and Adam's wife, of course. It was just that she couldn't quite believe she'd ever get the chance. Too much stood in the way. No matter what Adam said about her fitting in with the Fortune family, Laura had her doubts. She was just an orphan raised on Catholic charity, after all, the ex-girlfriend of a dangerous drug dealer. All dressed up like this she might look as if she belonged with the wealthy Fortune clan, but anyone who cared to look beneath the surface would quickly discern otherwise. Still, she could not deny that she loved Adam and his children, or that they needed her—for now, at least.

She could have brooded on that thought all evening, but her first sight of the Fortune mansion knocked every other thought right out of her head. It was magnificent, absolutely palatial, and gleaming softly with the glow of countless floodlights, its broad steps sweeping upward gracefully to a colonaded palisade that sheltered double doors of brass and heavy lead-paned windows shaped like clusters of diamonds. Erica had insisted on using the family home—which was held in a trust administered by an attorney named Sterling for all the family's use—for the reception, saying that she wanted the family surrounded by Kate's memory, if not her presence. Laura could see her point as the limo pulled

up to the steps and the driver hopped out to hurry around
to her door. The woman who had built this house had undoubtedly put a great deal of herself into it. Laura could
almost feel a presence here, a will as strong as the walls that
rose before her.

Laura shivered, not with the cold but with the odd certainty that someone was watching. Doyal? Had he found her
after all? Her thoughts flitted back to the waitress at the
diner. Had she alerted Doyal? But that was absurd. Wasn't
it? As Adam helped the children from the car and retrieved
Wendy's present from the driver's seat, Laura let her gaze
travel slowly over the facade of the great house. At a dor-
mer tucked below the eave of the upper story, she saw the
movement of curtain against light, and the knot of fear in
her chest began to unravel. A servant, someone who merely
wanted to see the Fortunes arrive in all their style, must have
been watching. When Adam slid his arm about her waist
and ushered her forward, she turned a genuine smile on him,
eager once more for this night of magic.

They moved up the steps. The wide portal at their crest
opened silently as they neared. Adam's hand at her waist
gave her a little nudge as he urged her ahead of him. She
stepped into the black-and-white marble foyer. A brass
chandelier gleamed overhead and brass fittings shone from
every corner and niche. More brass shined from hooks on
an enormous antique hall tree, a planter here and there,
knobs and handles and the fittings of the sweeping ebony
balustrades that flanked a broad, curving staircase.

Erica emerged from a wide, open pocket door on the left.
"We're here, darlings, in the large salon." She stopped and
spread her arms wide, mouth slightly ajar as she took them
in. "You're magnificent, all of you." She hurried forward
to accept Adam's kiss on her cheek. "I've never seen you so
handsome!" She cupped his cheek with her hand, then
turned to Laura. "My dear, you're beautiful at your worst,
but this!" She turned back to Adam. "She could model for
Fortune—"

"Oh, no!" Adam curved an arm around Laura's waist
and pulled her against his side, laughing. "Get that right out

of your head. The only Fortune she's going to model for is me!"

Laura stifled a gasp. He might as well have proclaimed them lovers! But his mother seemed merely amused.

"I should have guessed you'd say that." She wrinkled her nose at Laura. "Laura darling, if you have some secret ambition to model, we'll work right around him, I promise."

"Oh, no! No, I couldn't. That is, I'd never want to be a model. It's so..." She'd been about to say that it was intimidating, for the very thought of posing before strangers made her want to run and hide, but the admission of such a weakness suddenly seemed immature. "It's just not me," she finished lamely.

"That's my girl," Adam said, and then, to her mortification, he kissed her gently on the mouth. Erica had turned her attention to the children, but Laura didn't really have much hope that she hadn't noticed! And yet she batted not an eyelash at the sight of her only son blatantly kissing his children's nanny.

Adam ushered her to the room his mother had identified as the large salon. It was there, on the threshold, that he slipped out of his own coat and finally handed it to a waiting servant. And then his hands moved to Laura's shoulders. She unbelted the slinky wrap and waited. Suddenly it was as if every eye in the room were on them, and only then did Adam sweep the coat off her shoulders and down her arms. Laura knew that the resultant buzz of comment was exactly what he had intended, but she could only wonder why, turning a puzzled glance over her shoulder.

He covered her bare arms with his hands and leaned close to whisper, "When his woman's as beautiful as you, a man can't resist showing her off." The light in his eyes, like a banked and slowly burning fire, swept over Laura, making her catch her breath and warming her from the inside out. Her breasts swelled against the tightly fitting bodice of her dress. She felt promise in that gaze, promise and desire and more.

"I love you." The words fell out of her mouth in a whispered rush. She hadn't even felt them on her tongue before they slid out.

Adam's arms came around her from the back, and he craned his head forward slightly, kissing her again fully on the mouth. The glow in his golden eyes was now a flame.

Erica slipped by them, the children in tow, Ryan perched on the hip of her elegantly beaded pale blue gown. "Rachel," she called, tugging the children forward, "Wendy has a gift for you."

Adam urged Laura to follow, his palm warm against the small of her back. Laura ignored the burn of color in her cheeks and followed the trail laid by Erica and the children. They were not to catch up with them, however, for no sooner had they stepped fully into the room than they were surrounded by Fortunes.

"Hello, Adam."

"Michael, good to see you. Julia. Ah, Caroline. Nick! How are you?" He shook hands, then curved his own arms protectively around Laura. "All right, all right, everybody. Here she is. Allow me to introduce my lady, Laura Beaumont. Laura, this is my family, most of them."

He began pointing out sisters, cousins and spouses, but Laura simply couldn't take them in. She hadn't heard a word after "Allow me to introduce my lady..." Not "the nanny" or "my friend" or simply "Laura," but "my lady."

"I believe we're being paged," Adam murmured at some point, nodding toward a tall, slender, achingly graceful woman pushing their way, one hand held out in entreaty. Her smile was kind, and her eyes were sharp with intelligence as they skimmed over Laura. Her dark brown hair had been caught at the nape and allowed to wave with artful casualness around a face utterly devoid of artifice. "Lindsay," Adam said as she drew near enough to press her cheek to his. "Darling, I'd like you to meet my aunt. Dr. Lindsay Fortune Todd, Laura Beaumont."

"How do you do? Dr. Todd."

"Oh, no. It's Lindsay."

"Then you must call me Laura."

"Of course. The children look wonderful, Laura. I don't think I've ever seen Wendy sparkle so. But you're missing the big moment." She widened her gaze to take in Adam, too.

He craned his neck over those around him, saying, "Looks as if the presentation is taking place." He smiled at Lindsay as he urged Laura forward. They made their way to Erica and the children. The gift had already been unwrapped, and a tall, dark, ruggedly handsome man wearing gray slacks and a darker jacket had gone down on one knee before a thoroughly entranced Wendy.

"Did you do this all on your own?" he was saying. Wendy gave her head an emphatic nod. "My, my, what talent. I'd like to hang this in my office." He looked up at the tall redhead next to him. She was obviously pregnant, despite her sleekness, her chin-length wine-colored hair waving around her lean face, with its large, dark brown eyes. She was wearing a trim pair of black slacks and a big royal blue sweater that slid off one shoulder and sparkled with widely spaced beads.

Rachel Fortune Greywolf laid her hand on her husband's shoulder and said, "I know just the place for it, above the bookcase in the waiting room."

"Just so," Luke said, turning his smile back to Wendy. "We'll have a little brass plaque made with your name on it. It'll say Wendy Fortune, Artist."

Wendy looked for a moment as if she would burst, and then she threw herself at Luke Greywolf. Everyone laughed. Adam leaned forward to kiss Rocky on the cheek, while Lindsay took advantage of the lull in conversation to say to Laura, "Luke is a doctor, too."

Luke patted Wendy on the back and stood to acknowledge Adam and Laura. Adam shook his hand heartily.

"You look surprisingly fit," Adam told him, grinning. "Marriage to my baby sister must be decidedly less dangerous than courtship."

Rocky punched him in the arm. "Don't be a tease, big brother." She shoved her hair out of her face and turned her large, dark eyes on Laura. She smiled. "You must be the miracle worker."

Laura made a small sound of dismay. Adam instantly bristled. "Rocky! Mind your manners."

"I wasn't being ugly," she said lightly, her gaze remaining on Laura. "It's just that I've been hearing all about how you've mellowed my brother." She grinned as Adam's arm snaked around Laura's waist. "Domesticated him, too, I see."

"Daddy loves Laura," Wendy announced flatly, as if daring him to deny it.

Laura's mouth fell open, but Adam merely patted his daughter on the head. Then Ryan shouted, "He kisses her!"

Laura hoped the floor would open up and swallow her before her face burned to a crisp, but Adam merely instructed the boy to lower his voice. It was Wendy who whirled and clapped a hand over Ryan's mouth when he opened it again, saying, "You better be good and quit making Laura red!"

There were chuckles and sputters and murmurs all around them, but it was Jake Fortune's voice that sounded above it all. "I suspect congratulations will be in order here soon."

Laura felt him at her side and turned quickly in that direction, reeling from yet another shock. She realized vaguely that she was waiting for Adam to deny that the implied marriage was being considered. Jake Fortune smiled kindly at her and slipped a hand into the curve of her arm. Leaning close, he said softly, "Thank you, Laura. You will allow me to call you Laura, won't you? Considering how happy you've made my son, it seems silly to call you anything else."

"I, er... Please."

Before she could gather her thoughts to say anything more, Adam pulled her back against him and laid his cheek against hers, looking at his father over her shoulder. "Trying to make time with my girl, Dad?"

It was said in jest, and received in like manner. Jake Fortune chuckled. "Hardly. I know when I'm out-classed."

With a slap on Adam's back, he moved past them. Suddenly they were alone in the midst of all these people. Adam turned her to face him, his hands sliding over her back. She knew her eyes were filled with a confused wonder as she gazed up at him.

"Adam?"

"Yes."

"Adam, all these people... Your family seems to think we're going to..."

She couldn't quite say it, but she didn't have to. He smiled down at her, his hands restless on her back. "A natural assumption, I'd say, perfectly reasonable, very right."

Her whole body was tingling in a way she'd never felt before. It was as if a physical realization were skimming over her nerve endings. He meant to marry her. That was what tonight was all about for them. He was showing her that he meant to marry her and that his family was perfectly accepting of the idea. Her eyes filled with tears, and her hands gripped his upper arms through the fabric of his tux and shirt.

"Oh, Adam."

He laid his forehead against hers. "If you're going to break my heart, for heaven's sake, don't do it now."

She didn't know what she was going to do, only what she felt. She let her arms slide about his torso and allowed herself the shelter of his wide chest. "I love you," she whispered against his shirtfront.

"I'm counting on that," he murmured, and then he seemed to catch sight of something of interest just beyond her. "Ah," he said, reaching out to snag a pair of champagne flutes from the tray floating past on the hand of a white-coated waiter. "Just what this festive moment calls for." He delivered one delicate crystal stem into her hand, then clinked the edge of his flute against hers. "To us," he whispered, and his eyes promised the world and more as he sipped the sparkling liquid.

He stayed at her side throughout the evening, ignoring the talk about Monica Malone that surrounded them and whispering suggestively about showing her the rest of the house,

"So many bedrooms," or leaving early. "Mother will keep the children."

That comment seemed prophetic, as first Ryan and then Robbie and finally even Wendy wilted, yawned and snuggled onto a lap or into a corner of one of the several divans scattered about the luxurious room. "Let us put them to bed here," Erica urged, signaling a maid and Jake. "They can sleep in their underthings and be delivered home the first thing in the morning."

Adam grinned, ignoring Laura's whispered suggestion that perhaps they ought to just go. "Thank you, Mother." He kissed the sleeping Ryan, who snuggled into Erica's arms, patted Robbie's bottom where it jutted out over the maid's supporting arm and hugged Wendy after she was lifted into her grandfather's strong embrace. Wendy did not subside without a hug from Laura, too, however. Erica, Jake, and the maid left the room with the children, and it was then that Caroline slid close and tapped her brother on the shoulder, whispering into his ear. Adam made a face, but nodded.

Caroline started toward a certain corner of the room, from which Nathaniel Fortune had been pontificating for some time. Adam caught Laura's hand and tugged her along after his sister, muttering something about moral support. Laura noticed that Caroline was gathering other support, as well. Allie was there, Rocky's twin, and her scarred handsome husband, Rafe. Their sister Natalie joined them, as did Jake's sister Rebecca and, surprisingly, Jane. It was Caroline who bearded the lion in his den, with Nick standing at her back. She took up a stance in front of her uncle that was all business, her arms folded, her glance stern and strong.

"Nate, we want a word with you while Father's out of the room."

Nate showed clear surprise, but a moment was all that was required to discern the purpose of this confrontation. "You surprise me, Caroline," he said bitterly. "You above all should know how precarious a position he's put us in!"

"That's your interpretation," she returned smoothly. "We're here to let you know that we aren't about to stand aside while you push Dad out of the company!"

Nathaniel cast a disparaging glance over them. "Adam," he said, "Natalie, you can't know enough about Fortune business to even make a judgment, and you, Jane—"

Adam stepped up to cut him off. "I know my father," he said flatly, "and I know his dedication to this family and the business."

"As for me," Jane said gently, pushing forward, "I merely want to say that I think this is a time for the family to stand together."

Nathaniel made a face. "You cannot see that the business is at risk because of—"

It was an outside source that curbed Nathaniel's speech this time, voices raised in loud confrontation in the foyer. As if on cue, everyone turned in that direction. Suddenly that confrontation spilled over into the salon, in the person of a very tall, somewhat awkwardly thin man with blond hair plastered flat against his long, almost cadaverous head. He pulled a woman into the room with him, fending off the grasping hands of the butler, who was loudly proclaiming that the family was not receiving visitors.

"Here now! What's going on?" Leaving Erica standing in the doorway, Jake shoved past the distraught servant to glare at the intruders. "What do you think you're doing?"

"Jake?" The woman's drawling, tremulous voice pierced the confusion. "It is you, isn't it?"

Jake glowered at her. "Do I know you?"

The woman reached out a hand. "You should."

"A brother ought to know his own sister," said the tall, gangly man, sneering.

Jake's mouth fell open. A twitter of uneasy laughter circulated around the room. Erica suddenly appeared at Jake's side, seeming to bring him back into command. "Get out of here," he ordered, "before I call the police."

The woman, who was tall and slender, if slightly stooped, flung her dark brown hair off her shoulders, looking around the room anxiously. She was wearing a yellow peplum jacket over a short black skirt, and very high heels. Her eyes were shadowed with a rather heavy application of moss green, and her lips had been painted bright red. It seemed too young a look for a woman such as this, a woman in her later thirties or early forties.

"If you'll only let us explain," the blond man was saying, but suddenly the woman jabbed a pointing finger at someone else.

"There!" she cried, and an instant later rushed to Lindsay. Lindsay understandably recoiled, pushing the intruder away. "Don't you see?" the woman said loudly, her voice flavored with the lazy rhythm of the old South. She turned to Jake, stepping again close to Lindsay, and gathered her hair into her fist at the back of her neck. "Can't you see it?"

Erica was the one who gasped. "My God, they could be twins!"

"But we *are* twins!" the woman exclaimed, throwing her arms around the astonished woman she claimed as sister.


"I cannot believe it," Laura said, shaking her head as she descended the steps. Adam, at her side, nodded, wrapping his scarf around his throat.

"Nothing like the sudden appearance of a long-lost twin to break up a party."

"Poor Lindsay," Laura sighed. "What was that man's name? Potts?"

"Wayne Potts," Adam confirmed, "and the woman— God, can that really be my aunt?—calls herself Tracey Ducet."

"New Orleans," Laura murmured.

"Tracey Ducet of N'Awlins," he confirmed, mimicking the woman's drawl. He handed Laura into the limo, followed her inside, and nodded at the driver, who closed the door. Adam draped his arm around Laura's shoulder and pulled her against his side, sighing. "Never let it be said that a Fortune family gathering is without interest."

"That's putting it mildly," Laura said. "A lost twin! Oh, and lest we forget, there was that confrontation with dear Uncle Nathaniel."

Adam bared his teeth. "Can't say I'm disappointed to have had *that* put on the back burner."

"But a missing twin!" Laura exclaimed, laying her head back against his arm. She'd had enough champagne to make her feel rather fuzzy and warm inside.

Adam nuzzled her ear, saying, "I don't want to think about it, any of it."

"But, Adam, your whole family's in an uproar."

He pulled back to look her in the eye, his free hand resting against her hipbone. "Uproar is the Fortune family motto." She giggled. He kissed her nose. "I almost envy Jane her move to Maine."

"Oh, Adam, no. Your family's important to you."

He curved his arms around her. "Listen, Laura, I can't do anything about Tracey Ducet or Monica Malone, or much else, for that matter. It'll all sort out one way or another, but I'm not going anywhere in the meantime. All I'm saying is that what I want to concentrate on is a little closer to home—right here, in fact, if you take my meaning."

She smiled up into his handsome face. Such a dear face. She traced it with her fingertips. "I take your meaning."

He bent his head and kissed her. It was a long, lazy, thorough claiming that seemed to begin and begin and begin again, but never quite ended until the limo came to a halt and the driver tapped on the glass. Adam groaned, pulling back at last, and Laura knew that she ought to feel embarrassment, but her body was preoccupied with other emotions, emotions that made a blush seem a cool, colorless response.

He slipped from the car and helped her out, gathering her against him with one arm. She laid her head on his shoulder, and they walked together to the front door. He had his key out and the door open in a moment, and was already shrugging out of his coat before it was closed again. He draped the coat carelessly over the knob of the coat closet and steered her into the hallway, tugging at his tie. She turned slightly at her door, loosening the belt to her coat, but he stopped her, both arms about her shoulders, and guided her gently toward his own room.

"Not tonight," he whispered. "Tonight you're mine, all mine."

She had neither the heart nor the inclination to argue the matter. She opened her coat, and he pushed it off her shoulders, leaving it puddled upon the floor as he tugged her into his room. He shut the door at her back and pressed her against it, his mouth skimming her ear and temple as his hands lifted to her hair. Deftly he plucked the pins and combed his fingers through the shiny tresses, pulling them down to frame her face, which he kissed with gentle reverence. "Wait," he whispered. "I want to build up the fire."

She nodded, moving farther into the room as he hurried across it, tossing off his coat and stripping away his tie and cummerbund as he went. He knelt before the fireplace, opened the screen and stirred up the embers with a poker before tossing on a handful of kindling and several logs. The flames caught and danced merrily. He carefully closed the screen and rose, hands moving to the buttons on his shirt. Laura smiled to herself, slipped a hand beneath one arm and quickly unzipped her dress. When he turned, she let the dress fall to the floor.

He caught his breath, his eyes shining, and moved toward her. He released his cuff links and let them drop away, then peeled back the shirt. Laura lifted a hand to skim it across the firm contours of his chest. A light dusting of hair tickled her palm. He watched her—waiting, it seemed. Laura swallowed a lump in her throat, moved her hands behind her and released the catch of her lacy strapless bra. It fell away. He sucked in his breath and reached for her, pulling her against his naked chest. He wrapped his arms around her, smoothed his hands over her bare back, sighing with the pleasure of flesh against flesh. His kiss was fervent, passion-frantic, drugging.

At last he pulled away, chest heaving, to slip his fingers beneath the waistband of her hose. He peeled them down, kneeling when they reached her thighs to slip off her shoes, one at a time, before coaxing the silky stockings down her legs and off her feet. He looked up, his face limned by the golden firelight, to hold her gaze as he slid his fingers beneath the tiny elastic band of her panties. He tugged them down, and one hand slid between her legs, even as the other whisked her panties away. She cried out and let her head fall back, her eyes shuttering closed as he explored the moist cleft that gave him access to her body. She knew that he watched what he did, and that knowledge somehow heightened the pleasure to a trembling intensity. He stood, rubbing his body against hers as his hand made magic inside her. He wrapped his free arm around her shoulders and took her mouth in a promising, seducing kiss of lips and teeth and tongue, thrusting and pulling and nipping in concert with his hand.

His touch was more potent than the finest champagne, his kiss more thrilling than words whispered with solemn meaning. Almost without warning, her knees buckled, but he was there, sweeping her up and carrying her to the bed. He laid her upon the covers and, without a word, stripped off his remaining clothes in quick, jerky movements that belied the steadiness of his hot gaze. Gloriously naked, he lay down beside her and skimmed a hand over her body from breast to thigh. His hand moved between her legs, parting them, and then he lifted onto an elbow and eased himself atop her. The feel of so much skin and hard muscle jolted her eyes closed once more. Then she felt his hand between them, positioning the sleek, hot length of him. *Any moment*, she told herself on an indrawn breath. *Any moment.* She felt her body opening for him, waiting, anticipating. But then his hands brushed into her hair at her temples, his upper-body weight levered onto his forearms.

"Look at me," he whispered. He moved his hips, and the sleek hardness breached the soft opening of her body, ever so slightly. Laura caught her breath, her head spinning. "Look at me, Laura," he commanded again, and only then did she realize that she had not done so. She opened her eyes, the lids feeling heavy and hot. His face was testimony etched in firelight above her. His thumbs caught the skin at her temples, holding her eyes open as he flexed his hips against her. A look of utter ecstasy flickered across the muscles of his face. "I love you," he said, filling her, making them one in heart and body.

She wrapped her arms and legs around him and wept as he proceeded to merge their very souls.

# Fourteen

Laura hummed as she stacked the dirty breakfast dishes in the sink. Adam bent over a book at the table, consumed by a volume of Shaker furniture and its attendant history. A tome on Norwegian, Swedish and Danish cabinetry styles waited at his elbow.

"How strange," he muttered, "to consider ornamentation of the wood frivolous and then paint the furniture in shades of red, orange and yellow. Puts the lie to that blue and green stuff we see in the catalogs, doesn't it? Of course, they're only reproductions."

Laura smiled at this discourse but made no reply, correctly divining that none was required. A glance at the clock told her that she'd better speak out on another matter, however. "Adam, it's a quarter of eight."

The book slammed shut on a paper-napkin bookmark. "In that case, I'm out of here." He stacked his books on the corner of the table, popped up and spun around to grab her about the waist.

"Oh!" A spoon clattered into the sink, accompanied by soft laughter. "I thought you were in a hurry," she said, looping her arms around his neck.

He nuzzled her ear, whispering, "I'm never in too much of a hurry for you."

"Mmm . . . that's not what you said last night."

He chuckled and put his forehead to hers. "I didn't think they'd ever go to sleep!"

"It was six-thirty, Adam."

He sighed. "You're right. I'm a terrible father."

"You're a wonderful father," she told him, and got kissed for it. Things were heating up considerably when a small voice tossed cold water on the fire.

"Daddy, when's Laura going to take me to school?"

They pulled apart, throats clearing. Laura managed a smile for Wendy. "Right now, sweetie. Run and get your coat."

The moment she disappeared through the door, Adam groaned and pulled Laura back into his arms for a quick kiss. "I may be late. We've got to go over the whole inventory, all the appraisals and the audit before tomorrow's closing."

"I'll put your dinner back."

"Forget dinner. Just be here when I get home."

She smiled at the feeling of her heart expanding in her chest. "Nothing short of death or the threat of it could keep me away."

He hugged her, whispering, "I'll miss you. Be home soon as I can." He backed away, turned and picked up his books, heading for the door.

"Drive carefully."

"You too." He paused in the doorway and turned back. "Laura, did you ever get your driver's license replaced?"

She felt the color drain from her face. "Oh. Uh..." She struggled for a normal tone and an unconcerned smile. "I completely forgot."

"Well, take care of it, will you? Before you get a ticket."

She kept her smile in place and managed a nod. He turned away, colliding with Wendy in the process.

"I'm ready to go, Daddy, but Ryan and Robbie won't put their coats on. Can I go with you?"

Adam's hand landed on the back of his neck. He turned a look over his shoulder. "Maybe I should. I don't like you driving without the license."

Laura glanced at the clock, feeling guilty about the inconvenience and the lie. She couldn't do anything about the lie, not now, anyway. "You don't have time. The school's too far out of your way. It'll be all right."

He shrugged. "Maybe you're right." He dropped an apologetic look on Wendy. "Sorry, Princess, but I've got Aunt Jane and a whole team of accountants waiting on me in the city. Laura will take care of you. Now give me a kiss." He bent and puckered up. She smacked her lips against his, and he went on his way with a final wink for Laura.

She tried not to think about the lie with which she had let him leave, but she knew that soon she would have to tell him something. Would he be disappointed in her if he knew what kind of man she'd been involved with before him? Would he choose to send her away for the safety of the children? She didn't want to think that she could be endangering them. She wanted to believe that Doyal had given up looking for her, that she could stay safely with Adam for the rest of her life.

Wendy stomped her foot impatiently. "Laura! Let's go!"

Laura pushed her worries away and hurried out of the kitchen. The boys proved more cooperative with her than they had been with Wendy, and she had them in the car in no time. She concentrated on her driving, all too aware that she could not chance another encounter with a traffic cop. She pulled up to the curb in front of Wendy's school with time to spare. Leaning over, she smoothed Wendy's hair and repositioned her barrette before kissing her cheek and tugging her hood up.

"Have a good morning, honey. I'll see you at noon."

Wendy shoved and kicked and wriggled her way out of the car, then ran up the sidewalk, her little backpack flapping against her spine. Laura couldn't help thinking how much happier Wendy seemed these days. Had she done that? Was it prideful of her to credit herself with a little of Wendy's newfound contentment?

She glanced at the boys, who were playing quietly, for once, with tiny cars they'd stashed in their coat pockets, driving them along the padded fronts of their seats and up each other's arms. She made a mental note of that as she eased the station wagon out into the traffic lane. Maybe she ought to keep a bag of small toys in the car. As she guided the station wagon to a full stop at the sign on the corner, she decided that she'd mention the toy idea to Adam, see what he thought about it. She was smiling to herself as she looked to the right, checking traffic. Then she turned her head left, and her dream world of love everlasting shattered. There, on the crosswalk, a down-filled jacket open over flannel shirt and jeans, was none other than Doyal Moody.

For a moment, she sat frozen, unable to believe what her eyes were seeing and her screaming heart was already telling her was true. It was stupid, devastatingly so, for in the next moment, Doyal's gaze zeroed in on the car that sat too long at the stop sign. He broke into a run, face contorting in a savage grin, and that seemed to galvanize her. She stomped the accelerator without so much as a glance at the traffic. Her tires squealed. Heads turned as she sped by. She wasn't certain, but she thought more than one car slammed on its brakes, narrowly avoiding her.

"Laura!"

"Woo!"

She wrenched the wheel and slid around a corner in the opposite direction to where she would normally go. But that wouldn't fool Doyal for very long. The Fortunes were this town's most visible citizens. He could find her in a matter of minutes if he just asked the right questions of the right people. At the most, she had a few hours. The boys. Somehow she had to protect the boys. Where could she take them? The house wouldn't be safe very much longer.

Panic took hold. She was driving much too fast through sleepy city streets, but that fact did not register. All she could think to do was flee, to put as much distance between herself and Doyal as humanly possible. When the police cruiser appeared coming toward her, her first thought was to throw herself in its path and tell everything she knew. But what about Adam and the kids? If Doyal knew about them, he would punish her through them, and yet, in that moment, the police represented safety. She practically stood on her brakes. The police car locked up and skidded to a halt beside her. She caught one glimpse of the face of Officer Raymond Cooper and burst into grateful tears. Then a wave of nausea hit her, and she knew what she had to do. She bailed out of the car and doubled over, vomiting her breakfast onto the pavement. He was at her side in a heartbeat.

"Laura! Honey, you sick?"

She squeezed her eyes shut and started talking fast. "Terribly, terribly sick! I—I was afraid I wouldn't make it home. It hit me all of a s-sudden. My stomach and—and my head. Oooh..."

"I'll call for an ambulance."

"No! I—I mean...I just need to lie down, a-and the boys... I-if you could just take us home. I'll call Adam's mother. Mrs. Fortune will know what to do, and—and she'll take the boys."

Cooper shook his head. "I don't know, Laura."

She resorted to shameless begging. "Please! Oh, please! I just want to go home!"

Her tears seemed to distress him. He patted her shoulder awkwardly. "Okay. Uh, just let me call in."

"Thank you. Oh, thank you."

He walked her over to the car. "Think you can pull it over to the side of the street?"

"Y-yes, but hurry. Please hurry!"

"All right. Won't be a second."

She nodded and bowed her head over the steering wheel as he went back to his own vehicle, but there wasn't time for relief. Doyal could come along at any moment and spot the car. She sat up and jerked the station wagon over to the curb, out of the traffic lane. The boys were babbling questions, but she ignored them until she had the car parked. Then she merely informed them that they were going for a ride in a police car. They cheered. Thankfully, the whole thing was one big adventure to them. Cooper came and helped her transfer the boys and their car seats to the back of his cruiser. She was careful to keep her gaze averted and an arm folded across her middle. Within moments, they were traveling back the way she had come. Laura huddled down in the seat, shivering from the effects of her shock.

"You're having chills," Cooper said. He reached beneath the seat and brought out a dull green blanket. "Wrap up in this."

Laura took the blanket gratefully and wrapped it around her head and shoulders like a shawl. If they encountered Doyal again, maybe he wouldn't recognize her.

They reached the house outside town without further incident. It had never looked so dear to Laura. Raymond Cooper helped her and the boys inside, then insisted on calling Adam's mother himself. Laura thanked him profusely and took herself off to the bathroom to pretend she was throwing up. After what seemed an eternity, Erica Fortune knocked on the door.

"Laura? Darling, come out here and let me look at you."

Laura had little doubt that her stricken face would support her tale of illness. She kept her arm around her middle and leaned against the wall in the hallway. "Thank God," she said, keeping her distance from Erica, as if afraid she'd communicate illness to the older woman. "Is Officer Cooper still here?"

"No, I sent that kind young man on his way."

She nodded, relieved, despite her regret at having used him so shamelessly. "Can you take the boys home with you?"

"Of course, but—"

"And pick up Wendy at noon."

Erica made an impatient sound. "Yes, dear, don't worry about the children. But what about you? You can't stay here alone like this."

Laura groaned. "Oh, Erica, please. I just want to go to bed and pull the covers up over my head. The worst of it's over, and now I just want to sleep. Besides, I can't expose the whole family to this nasty bug."

"I think I should call Adam."

"No! Not today, of all days. This day is too important to him. Besides, what could he do except watch me sleep?"

Erica seemed to consider, one perfectly manicured nail pressed against her chin. "Well, the cook will be in soon. If she would look in on you from time to time..."

"I'm sure Beverly won't mind," Laura told her, seizing on that notion. "She'll probably want to make me one of her hot toddies, too, and that's just what I need. Now you go on, and take the boys with you. Please."

Erica nodded and held out her mink-clad arms in a gesture of helplessness. "I'm sorry you're unwell."

"Thank you, just take care of my...the boys." It occurred to her suddenly that she would never see them again, and tears gathered in her red-rimmed eyes.

"You go straight to bed," Erica ordered, and Laura nodded miserably.

The twins went without a backward glance, delighted at this change in their routine. Laura crept up to the door and watched through the peephole until they were tucked safely into their grandmother's luxury auto. Then she laid her forehead against that door and wept for all she was losing.

Finally she pulled herself together and went to the phone. She first called Beverly, telling her not to come in under any circumstances and using her supposed illness as the reason. Next she called a little motel on the far side of Minneapolis and booked a room. Then she called a taxi and went to pack. It didn't take long to throw her belongings into her bag. She hadn't come with very much, and she didn't intend to leave with any more. In a fit of sentimentality, she laid her pink dress and coat out on the bed, placed the shoes beside them and laid the jewelry on the pillow. Only the underclothes did she keep. After she'd sprinkled the clothes on the bed with her tears, she carried her bag into the hall and squared her shoulders for the ordeal ahead.

The money was exactly where he'd put it only weeks ago. She pulled the folded bills from the hidden cubbyhole and tucked them into her pocket. Then she wrote a brief note, dropped it inside and closed the secret compartment. She took a last look around the room. Here on this bed, Adam had made love to her. The light and warmth from that fireplace had glowed upon her skin. Her clothing had lain here and there and there. Her head had rested upon that pillow. Her heart had known true joy in this very place. Tears rolling down her face, she turned and left it all behind. It was her final and greatest gift to those she loved. Safety. It was all she had left to give.

* * *

Adam let himself into the house through the garage, wondering why the car was gone at this time of night. It was nearly ten. The children couldn't be awake now, and yet Laura would not have left them alone. She must have had mechanical trouble of some sort, at which point she would have called someone for help. He felt a pang of regret that he had not been close at hand, but then he smiled wolfishly. He would make his apologies in ardent fashion.

He stashed his coat and briefcase in the foyer closet and moved swiftly down the hall toward the den. He knew before he got there that she wouldn't be waiting. The room was dark, the television off. A small light burned in the kitchen. He pushed through the swinging door. The light over the stove was on, but nothing else. The breakfast dishes were still stacked in the sink. What had happened to Beverly? What had happened to lunch and dinner? The hair rose on the back of his neck. He tore out of the room and flew down the hall.

Training overcame fear as he drew near Wendy's room. He stopped and pressed himself against the wall for a moment. This was crazy. Nothing could have happened to his family in the short space of one day. And yet... He steeled himself and tiptoed into his daughter's room, switching on the lamp beside the bed. The bed was unmade, but Wendy was not there. He strode from that room to the next. The boys' room was in identical condition, beds unmade but empty. Something was wrong.

He swung out into the hall and ran to her door, throwing it open. "Laura! Laura, answer me!"

He knew by the very feel of the darkness that she was not there, and yet he had to see. He fumbled with the overhead light switch. Brightness flooded the room. Laura's bed was neatly made. Her dress and coat and shoes had been arranged upon it. The closet door stood open, showing empty hangers.

"God, no! Laura, no!"

He yanked open dresser drawers. Empty. Empty. All empty. He slammed them shut again, one by one. Gone!

How dare she leave him now? She had to know how much he loved her, how much he needed her. What about his children? She had let them love her. She had let them need her. How could she leave them without warning? He couldn't believe this. For a moment, anger overwhelmed all other emotions. He lunged the two steps to the bed, grabbed the lamp on the table at its head and threw it savagely against the wall. The shade bounced away. The glass base shattered satisfyingly against the wall, but it didn't help. He reached down and yanked the spread from the bed, sending her clothes flying. The dress hit him across the chest and shoulder. He ripped it away, crushing it in his hands. The unique perfume of Laura wafted up to fill his head and then his heart.

He dropped down onto the edge of her bed, forcing away the pain that flooded in behind the anger. He had to think. He had to reason this out. But none of it made sense. Only this morning, she had promised to be here when he got home. Only this morning... And she wouldn't have taken the kids with her. She wouldn't have gone away and left him nothing. Where were his children? He got up and made himself go into his own bedroom, trailing the dress from his hand. For a moment, he couldn't think why he'd come, but then he turned and checked the answering machine on his desk. The red light was on, indicating that a message had been left. He rewound the tape with shaking hands and played it. His mother's voice greeted him.

"This is Erica. I was calling to check on Laura. I hope you're sleeping, dear, and that you're feeling better now. The children seem fine, no signs of illness. Give me a call to let me know that you're all right, darling. Bye."

The children. His mother had the children. No signs of illness... Was Laura ill? Would she have left him because of illness? It seemed preposterous. The tape beeped, indicating another message. His mother again.

"Laura, I'm really getting worried. Wendy says that some of the kids at school saw a man running after your car at the intersection. Please call me right away."

A man? A man at the school had chased her car? He shook his head. He would not believe that Laura had left him for another man. He could not believe that. Who, then, had chased her? And why?

The third message was from Beverly. "Laura, Mr. Fortune, I was just wondering if I should plan on coming in tomorrow. You didn't say anything about it when you called earlier today, Laura. I hope you're feeling better. Um, someone needs to call me, I guess. Thanks."

So Laura had called Beverly and told her not to come in today, supposedly because she, Laura, was ill. But if Laura was ill, where was she? Why would she have left and taken all of her clothes?

The final message made his blood run cold. "Adam," his father's voice said, "your mother is very concerned. She sent a man over to the house to check on Laura, but no one was there. She says Laura was ill earlier in the day, and she's called all the hospitals in the area and the police. Your station wagon is sitting abandoned on the street. Some police officer apparently took her home earlier, but now she's gone, disappeared. Anyway, it's a mess. You'd better call, son, or better yet, come over right away."

Adam tossed the dress on the desk and started for the door, but suddenly he stopped and turned back. If Laura had left and meant never to return, she would have needed money. He bent over the desk again, quickly popping open the secret compartment. Gone. The money was gone, and in its place lay a white slip of paper. He extracted it gingerly, his fingers shaking so badly that he had to try twice to unfold it.

I.O.U., more than I can ever repay. I'm sorry, my love. I tried to stay. I hoped to stay. But it wasn't meant to be. The past has caught up with me, and I must go, for all our sakes. Please don't try to find me. I know you'll do your best to make the children understand. Be safe and happy.

Laura.

*Happy?* he thought. Didn't she know that he couldn't be happy without her? But the telling word was *safe*. Why shouldn't he be safe? He reread a portion of the letter aloud. "The past has caught up with me, and I must go, for all our sakes." He ran a hand through his hair and wandered toward the bed, dropping down on its edge. What did it mean? Who was the man at the intersection? Why hadn't she trusted him enough to tell him what threatened her from the past? Suddenly he remembered exactly what she'd said that morning when he told her to forget putting back his dinner, that she was all he wanted, all he needed to find waiting for him when he got home.

*Nothing short of death or the threat of it could keep me away.*

Oh, God. She was in trouble, desperate trouble, trouble so desperate that she was trying to protect him and the children from it. No matter what she had written, he had to find her. He had to find her and bring her home. Before it was too late.

"Did you see the man at all, Rob?"

Robbie shrugged sleepily. "I dunno."

"Try to think about it, son. Did you see somebody in the street, maybe?"

"Oh, that man," Ryan said, sitting up a little straighter on the bed. "He pointed at our car."

"Laura went real fast!" Robbie reported eagerly. "We went woo-woo-eeeee!" He pantomimed skidding around a corner.

"When did Laura get sick?" Adam asked pointedly.

The boys looked at each other and shrugged. "When the policeman stopped us," Ryan began.

"She got out and puked!" Robbie finished.

"And that's when the policeman took you home?"

They both nodded vigorously. Adam looked at his mother, who stood behind his shoulder. "Did you get a name?"

"Uh, Crocker. No, Cooper."

Raymond Cooper. Yes, that made sense. If Laura could have convinced anyone to give her and the boys a ride home, it would have been Cooper. But what had made her speed through town like that? What had made her ill? Fear. Fear for her life. That had been it all along. Laura hadn't been saving her money to go to college. She'd been stashing cash in case she had to run. That was why she wouldn't promise to stay. It had nothing to do with ambition. It had to do with wanting to stay alive—and protect the family. She might have been sick with fear, but she'd had the presence of mind to ditch the car in which her pursuer had spotted her and find another way home. She'd sent the kids away to safety first thing, and then she'd made certain that Beverly wouldn't be in the house if *he* tracked her to it.

Adam stood and absently ruffled the heads of his twin boys, then quickly tucked them in and kissed them. "I'm going to tuck in your sister," he said, smiling, "then I'm going to get Laura and bring her home. You enjoy your stay with your grandmother, okay?"

Ryan nodded and rolled onto his side, folding his hands beneath his cheek, but Robbie looked up at his father with wide, worried eyes. "Where is Laura?"

Adam smoothed back his son's unruly hair. "I think she went off by herself to protect us, um, from what was making her sick," he said carefully. Robbie seemed satisfied with that. He turned his back to his brother and closed his eyes.

"I don't like that," he said sleepily. "Tell her not to do it again."

Adam smiled crookedly. He would tell her. Somehow, he would find her and he would tell her. He would make her understand that no matter what or whom she feared, she could not leave them again. She could never leave them.

Adam stood with arms akimbo before his father. "The police won't do anything until she's been missing twenty-four hours. They won't even take a report. Officer Cooper says that she was definitely ill, but I think she was frightened. I think she was frightened of that man who chased her through the intersection. I think she's been hiding from him, and when he tracked her down, she bolted to protect me and the kids. I think he's a danger to her. She wouldn't have gone for any other reason.''

Jake nodded thoughtfully. "I understand your reasoning, but are you sure you should go after her? If the danger's real, it's real for you and the children, too. If it's not what you think ... well ..."

Adam sighed. It was two o'clock in the morning, and he was utterly exhausted physically. Mentally, there was no way he could rest. He took a deep breath and sat down in the chair at his father's left. He leaned forward, elbows on knees. "She loves me, Dad. I know she loves me and my children. And I know she's in trouble. You can't expect me to just sit with my head in my hands worrying."

Jake shook his head. "No. No, of course not. What do you want to do?"

"Officer Cooper and I agree that if she's running from someone, she'd try to get lost in a crowd. I think she's gone to the city. Right now, at least, she'd have to be hiding in some out-of-the-way motel or something. I'm afraid that if we wait, she'll bolt again, or move into an apartment, where it would be infinitely more difficult to find her—or worse. We have to find her now."

Jake cocked his head. "It'll take an army to find her as it is."

"If the Fortunes can't raise an army, no one can," Adam pointed out. "If the Fortunes can't exert enough influence to get the police moving, then the police can't be moved."

Jake's smile was a touch ironic. "Is this my son asking to wield the Fortune power at last?"

Adam swallowed. Tears rose in his eyes. "I've never been so glad to be a Fortune in my life! I'll never deride this family again. This is what Kate and Grandpa Ben worked for. This is what you've given your life to. I see that now. I understand, finally, why the power is dear, why we need it. And Laura gave that understanding to me. Please, Dad, you've got to help me find her."

Jake got up and squared his shoulders. Strength emanated suddenly from his tired eyes and his rigid stance. He dropped a hand on Adam's shoulder. "We'll find her, son, and whoever that creep is who's after her, we'll crush him like a bug. There's just one thing."

"Yes?"

"Get her married after this, will you? She'll be easier to protect once we've brought her into the fold. She'll be part of us then, family, and what we have, she'll have. We owe her that. *I* owe her that." His hand tightened on Adam's shoulder. "Hell, I owe her more than I can say, and I won't ever forget that, on my word as a Fortune."

Adam got to his feet and clapped his arm around his father's broad shoulders. "I'll get her married. Don't worry about that. You find her for me, and I'll make her your daughter-in-law. My word as a Fortune."

Jake grinned and swung his arm around his son's back. They went out, side by side, Fortunes both of them, and for the first time, both understood just what that meant.

# Fifteen

It was a search as finely coordinated as the invasion of Normandy. A team of private investigators armed with descriptions and cold, hard cash fanned out across the area. Taxi services were called. Motels were searched. Adam himself accompanied the investigator who rousted Laura's former employer and co-workers from their beds. Meanwhile, a computer search began. Before noon the next day, they had begun piecing together a story and had in their hands a copy of Laura's Colorado driver's license, which was current, adding weight to Adam's fear that her trouble was serious. He could think of only one reason Laura would lie about having an expired license: She didn't want that license run through anyone's computer. She was hiding from someone, someone with the power to hurt her. A team of investigators were already en route to Denver in an effort to find out who that someone might be. And yet, Adam could not dispel the sense that time was running short. He slugged back coffee, paced, and pushed everyone who came within earshot for answers. He could only pray that it would be enough.

Laura had wet her pillow through with tears, and long before morning she had given up hope. What was the point? Without Adam and the kids, her life was meaningless, anyway. She didn't have the emotional energy to run anymore. If she had, she'd have thought better of taking a single taxi to this run-down motel. She'd have used some name besides Laura Fortune—as if that would fool anyone for very long. She'd have put herself on a plane headed for Tahiti or New York or Miami, anywhere but here, where the very cold

reminded her that she wouldn't have Adam to warm her
anymore. And yet she'd be damned if she'd just let Doyal
Moody snuff out her life and walk away without a price.

She got up from her shabby, tearstained bed and
scrounged up a yellowed envelope from the wobbly desk in
front of the window. She tore the blank pages from the front
and back of the aged Gideon Bible in the bedside table and
dug a pen from her purse. Thus armed, she sat down at the
desk and began to write with painstakingly small, readable
letters every incriminating bit of information she had gathered on Doyal Moody and his drug operation. Tears marked
the pages at places, but she set it all down doggedly, ending
with a message of love and gratitude to Adam and his children. His children. She felt she had the right to think of
them as hers. No mother could love them more. No mother
could do more for them. She put the folded pages into the
envelope and wrote Officer Raymond Cooper's name on the
front. Then she gathered her purse and coat and slipped out
of the room.

She bought a stamp from a machine at a convenience
store on the corner, then hurried to a pay phone across the
street. She dialed information for St. Cloud and waited. The
operator could give her no mailing address for the St. Cloud
police force, but she did give her a number for information. It seemed at first that the person who answered the
phone in St. Cloud wouldn't be of much more service, but
when Laura requested a specific business address for Raymond Cooper, she at last was given a post office box, then
was grilled about her identity and location. She hung up
without preamble, wrote the address on the envelope, then
took a long, nervous walk to a mailbox. When the letter
safely disappeared into the slot, she breathed a sigh of relief and walked through lonely predawn streets to her room.

She actually slept after that. The room smelled of stale
cigarette smoke and old mold. The bed was lumpy. The
walls were dingy and depressing. She suspected that the
sheets were not clean, but she lay down atop them in her
coat, closed her eyes and actually slept.

She jerked awake hours later. Light glared around the perimeter of the cheap plastic-backed draperies that shielded the one window in the small room. A movement on the periphery of her vision sent her gaze to the corner, and she looked into the smug, smiling face of Doyal Moody.

Adam clenched his fist as the investigator rattled on.

"The guy's name is Moody. Cops in Denver say he fits the profile of a drug dealer, but they don't have enough evidence to charge him. Seems that everyone who could tie him to the trade winds up dead in odd places."

Adam swallowed hard. "Go on."

"They dated a few months, then she moved in with him. Her friends all say that she expected him to marry her, but they apparently had their doubts. No one said anything. They didn't really seem all that close to her, but they all agree that she wasn't very experienced. Moody was her first serious relationship. She can be excused for being taken in. What doesn't figure is why she disappeared without a word to anyone who knew her. They all suspected foul play. Moody himself turned in the missing-persons report. The reporting officer says he seemed all broke up about it, but it didn't quite add up. According to Moody, they were deliriously happy. So why'd she run? Friends say she suspected him of cheating on her. Cops say a woman fitting her description was seen getting on a bus heading for New Mexico. She seemed nervous, but she was alone."

Alone. Adam rubbed a hand over his face and head. "When was that?"

The investigator checked his notes. "Some ten-plus months ago. Moody has checked in from time to time to see if the cops have any more information on her. They haven't, though they did flag her license in case she got stopped somewhere."

That was exactly what Adam had expected, and what she had expected, evidently. Adam nodded and buzzed his father's secretary, ordering her to give the investigator a cup of coffee and show him where the sandwiches were. When the man was gone, Adam leaned back in the desk chair and closed his eyes, then popped upright again and swiveled to plant his elbows on the desk blotter, staring down at the copy of Laura's driver's license. She looked like a grinning, ponytailed teenager in her photo. Hell, she had been a grinning, ponytailed teenager back then. And she had been alone. No family, no one to protect or guide her. Kate would have understood that. Kate would have admired her pluck.

Adam closed his eyes. "God, Laura, where are you?" It was just another unanswered question, one of many. Had she been disappointed in love? What did she know about Doyal Moody that had made her run? What did she know that had put her in danger? He was beginning to doubt that he could find her in time. Even the Fortunes had their limits. Tears gathered in his eyes.

Just then the door burst open and Jake strode into the room. "We've got her! I've ordered a car brought around, and I've sent an investigator and a lawyer to the local law enforcement. We should meet them on the way."

Adam got up and snatched his coat off the back of his chair. It was too soon for relief, but strength surged through him at the prospect. "Let's head for the street," he said. "And get me Raymond Cooper!"


"You're too late," Laura said, leaning up on her elbows.

Doyal shook his head, his long black hair clubbed at the nape. His bright blue eyes shone with an almost demonic gleam. His straight white teeth flashed in a smile. Laura wondered how anyone who looked so handsome could be so evil.

"I don't think so. You wouldn't be here if you'd ratted on me already."

"I wrote a letter," she said quietly, "and sent it to a friend."

Suddenly he lunged toward the bed. She put her hands up to fend him off, but he grabbed a handful of her hair and yanked her head around, bringing his face next to hers. "What friend? Tell me!" He clapped a hand under her chin. "Tell me or I'll break your pretty neck!"

She almost laughed. As if he weren't going to do that anyway. As if she'd been running all this time because he wanted to sit and talk to her. He must have seen the laughter in her eyes, for his hand loosened and slid down her throat. Her stomach churned.

"Tell me who it is, Laura," he said silkily. "Tell me who you sent the letter to, and we'll go get it. Then I'll take you home to Denver, and we'll pick up where we left off. All right? You'd like that, wouldn't you? Remember how it was with us, Laura? Remember this?" He slid his hand down to her breast and squeezed it.

Bile rose in her throat.

He slanted his head to kiss her, but she jerked her face away, ignoring the burn in her scalp where her hair pulled. He growled an obscenity and yanked her hair tighter. His hand tightened on her breast, so painfully that she gasped.

"Tell me who it is," he rumbled in her ear, "or I'll make you hurt so bad you'll beg to die."

The car slid to a stop. Adam jumped out before the dust had settled and glared at the flashing lights on the vehicles blocking the road.

"What is this? We're supposed to have an escort, not a roadblock!"

The investigator behind the steering wheel let down his window and craned a look up at Adam. "We're maybe six minutes away now. I've got a man on-site. I'd appreciate it if you'd see to it that the police don't mistake him for our bad guy."

Adam bent and pointed to Raymond Cooper, who immediately left the car and walked toward the nearest police vehicle. Adam paced, panic and anger barely leashed, as he watched Cooper operate. Flashing his shield, the big cop bent to speak into the driver's side window. After a few seconds, he stepped back and strode toward Adam's car, while the police car executed a three-point turn and started off in the other direction. It seemed to creep by the others, the driver clearly bent on taking the lead. Adam tamped down his impatience, denying the urge to snap at Cooper.

Raymond was a good man. He was as concerned for Laura as Adam was, not that he'd ever allow anything to come of it. Laura was his. Period. If he found her in time. He looked at the investigator's eyes in the rearview mirror as he swung down into the back seat of the car once again.

"Make it four minutes," he said flatly, and closed the door.

Laura attempted to draw air into her lungs, her head drawn back at an awkward angle as the pain in her breast spread throughout her chest. Doyal leaned his weight onto the forearm slashing across her sternum. She managed a satisfied smile. "His name is Raymond Cooper," she said breathlessly. "*Officer* Raymond Cooper, in care of the St. Cloud Police Department."

Enraged, Doyal took his hand from her breast and backhanded her. She fought him then. Hands balled into fists, she struck out wildly at his face and shoulders, forcing him to let go of her hair in order to defend himself. She felt a surge of elation, but then he threw a leg over her body and slid his weight onto her hips. She fought harder, but he finally managed to catch both her wrists in one strong hand. She turned her head and bit him. He yelped, yanked her hands over her head and slapped her.

"I ought to finish you now," he hissed, "but a quick killing's too good for a spying snitch like you. I trusted you, Laura. You were my lady, and now you've betrayed me. You owe me."

On the edge of panic now, she surged upward, hoping to buck him off, but he was much too heavy, and the movement only made him laugh.

"Now you've done it," he said huskily. "Now you've got me all hot." He smirked down at her. "Nothing's so sexy as a helpless woman."

Desperately she bucked and twisted and kicked, but he sat back on her legs and reached into his coat pocket, whipping out an oblong silver object that she knew to be a knife. He flicked a lever and a long, wicked blade snapped out. Laura froze, her eyes glued to that blade as it moved toward her and settled at her throat. She closed her eyes and began to pray.

Adam shrugged away the shiver that moved across his shoulders, then felt the hair lift on the back of his neck. He couldn't shake the feeling that Laura needed him now, right this minute. She was terrified. He didn't stop to question how he knew, he just accepted that he did. *Hold on, baby,* he told her silently. *I'm on my way.*

Hurry. Hurry.

He leaned forward and dropped a hand on the shoulder of the driver. With a nod of his head, he indicated the police car in front of them, its lights flashing. "Pass him," he said.

The driver shot a glance at Raymond Cooper, who occupied the front seat next to him. Cooper hesitated a split second, then dipped his head in agreement. The driver hit his flashers, whipped out into the oncoming lane and stomped on the accelerator.

Adam sat back, fear tightening his facial muscles, and silently prayed.

Doyal tilted the knife against her throat, sniggering when a thin thread of blood appeared, and slipped it beneath the neck of her sweater. He drove it down and up, slicing through the heavy knit. The blade came back to her throat, dipped again and cut the front of her nylon camisole. Laura trembled as cool air touched skin heated by exertion. Doyal grinned and leaned down, bringing his face close to hers, the knife lying against her belly, between them.

"Please me really good, beautiful Laura," he whispered, "and I'll kill you quick. I won't make you suffer like you deserve."

She laughed soundlessly. As if pleasing him would not be a fate much less attractive than any other he offered her.

He slid the knife blade beneath the waistband of her leggings, the point aimed, appropriately, at his own groin.

Resolve hardened in Laura. He liked helpless women, did he? Too bad. For him. A mental stillness filled her. She basked in it, gathering strength even as her muscles relaxed to buttery softness. He chuckled, believing he'd won, and lust glittered like shards of ice in his too-beautiful gaze. Laura spit right in his blue eye and surged upward with all her strength, arching her back and locking her legs, hips bucking hard. She felt the knife lift and heard his howl of rage and pain. Something warm and thick spilled onto her skin. She'd cut him. She hoped she'd cut him where it hurt most. She was still smiling, gloating, when the knife flashed upward. She knew that the instant it crested he would drive it down again. Straight into her heart. She thought of Adam, winging her thoughts of love to him, and her smile broadened.

*I'll always love you.*
The words ran through his mind with awful finality. He sat bolt upright on the edge of his seat. The car wrenched into a turn and skidded to a halt in a gravel parking lot. A man appeared at the window of the car, his arm lifted to point at a row of fifties-vintage motel rooms. He said a room number, but Adam didn't wait to hear it. He bailed out of the car, hitting the ground at a run.

"He's in there with her!" somebody called out.

Adam homed in on a door. He didn't question how he knew it was the right door. He just did. And he didn't bother to try the knob, just angled his shoulder at it and went at it at a run.

The door gave slightly at the impact, but it held. He backed up a step and hurled himself at it again. Suddenly Cooper was there, throwing his own body weight into it beside him, and the door burst open.

Adam froze in horror at the sight that greeted him. She was on the bed on her back, Moody sitting atop her, her arms pinned above her head, a knife poised in Moody's hand. Adam's heart dropped, and his gaze went straight to Laura's.

Laura saw him swaying there, horror on his face, love spilling out of his eyes, and thought, *Too late*. She knew then, with wordless certainty, that she should have trusted him with the whole truth long ago, and apology filled her expression. It was then that the other man—Cooper, she realized belatedly—dropped into a semi-crouch, hands whipping up and out. A gun was pointed at Doyal Moody, and suddenly it was all over. She was free, Doyal falling back and throwing up both hands. Free.

She reached for Adam, crying out as he sank into her arms. She heard Cooper telling Doyal that he was under arrest, the words seeming to come from a great distance as sobs built in her chest and spilled over onto Adam's shirtfront. His arm scooped beneath her, lifting her against him as his hand skimmed her hair.

"Are you all right? Did he hurt you?"

She shook her head, then nodded, confusing him. He laid her down and pulled back.

"You're bleeding!"

"No." Her hand drifted up to the stinging slash on her throat. "It's just a scratch."

His hands were running over her busily. They touched the sticky mess on her belly.

"His blood," she said quickly, adding with pride, "I made him cut himself."

Cooper loomed over Adam's shoulder. "She cut him, all right. Nicked the big artery in the bend of his left leg. A few minutes more and he'd have bled to death."

"A few seconds more," Adam began, his voice breaking, "and I'd have lost you!" He closed his eyes against the vision that summoned up, and Laura lifted herself up and against him, her arms wrapping around his neck.

"I'm so sorry, Adam," she whispered. "I should have told you."

"You were protecting us," he said in that same quaking voice.

"I put you all in danger."

"I know the whole story, everything but the evidence that will put that scum away."

"I wrote it all down and sent it to Officer Cooper in care of the St. Cloud police. I should have done it long ago, but I was scared."

"For good reason," Adam said, his hands splaying across her back. "You were trying to protect yourself, but you never meant to risk us in the process. I'm certain of that, because when it came down to it, you sacrificed your own safety for ours. I understand that. I even admire it. But if you ever do anything as dangerous again, I swear I'll—" He gulped. "You should have trusted me with the truth!"

"I wanted to," she said, blinking back tears, "but that would have made you a target, too. I just couldn't do that."

"And I nearly lost you because of it!"

"But you came for me," she pointed out tearfully. "I should have known you would!"

"You certainly should have," said a deep voice beyond them. Laura lifted her head from Adam's shoulder and looked around. Jake stood with a shoulder against the wall next to the head of the bed. He lifted a big hand and patted the top of her head, smiling. "Let this be a lesson to you, young lady. We Fortunes take care of our own. Period."

"That's all I was trying to do, sir," she told him firmly, shifting her gaze to Adam's face. "Take care of my own."

Adam tightened his arms around her. "Let's go home."

Laura laughed. It was a throaty, watery sound that adequately conveyed everything her heart contained. "Home," she said. "Oh, yes, let's go home."

The limo waited, motor humming, one of many flanking the curbs of the street in front of the tall, narrow redbrick church. The man and woman inside both exclaimed in satisfaction as the white double doors burst open and people spilled out onto the bare walkway. Tossed rice filled the air as the newly married couple ran out, hand in hand.

Laura's long blond hair had been coiled into a heavy knot at the back of her neck, leaving tendrils free to waft about her face and cling to the fine tulle of her veil. The veil billowed around her, caught on a breeze that smelled of spring and sunshine and new life. The breeze ruffled her bangs and pinked her cheeks as it lifted the veil heavenward from the wide band of pearls atop her head. Laura clutched her flowers in one hand and Adam's fingers in the other, laughing as she pattered down the gently sloping walkway toward the limo there. The driver got out and opened the back door, but Adam's arm snaked around her trim waist, halting her at the end of the walk.

Resplendent in gray tails and white tie, he took his wife in his arms, pressing against the full skirt of her embossed silk gown. One hand skimmed across her bare shoulders. Her silk-encased arms wound about him. He tilted her head back with the force and possession of his kiss. Rice showered down. The children jumped in place beneath the gently restraining hands of their grandparents. Adam lifted his head, blew his family a kiss, then turned his face to the sky, throwing a kiss heavenward from his fingertips before handing his bride into the car and following her.

"That one was for you," Sterling said in a gravelly voice.

Kate nodded and dabbed a handkerchief at the tears spilling from her eyes. "She's changed him. I knew it that day I saw him and his father at the restaurant." She sniffed and rubbed at her nose. "I couldn't hear what they were saying, but I could tell that my grandson's whole demeanor had changed. He had softened, opened. I watched him embrace his father." She smiled. "I never thought to see it."

Sterling nodded sagely. "I had my doubts," he said, "but you knew she was right for him even before you saw her."

Kate sighed. "I felt it, and none of the information you gathered for me blocked that feeling, but I had to see her. I know it was taking a risk, hiding in the upper floors and peeking out the window, but at least I was there when those two imposters showed up."

She turned to stare out the window at those gathered on the still-brown lawn of the old church. They waved in clumps of laughing family as Adam's and Laura's limo pulled away and moved down the street. She spied the pair in question at the back of the crowd, like thieves lurking in wait of an unguarded pocketbook, and shuddered. Sterling laid his hand over hers and sought to divert her.

"I shouldn't have doubted you," he said. "After all, no one needs to tell me what miracles a strong woman can work."

Kate laughed and put back her head. Gray streaks glinted softly in her thick auburn hair. Her smile was impish, knowing, as if she sensed the way his old heart lurched in his chest. Then she sobered, auburn brows arching as her quick mind moved on to other thoughts.

"Adam is settled now," she said briskly, turning her gaze back to the window. The family had begun to disperse, but knots of talking people still remained. Kate watched Tracey Ducet and Wayne Potts insinuate themselves into the nearest group. Tracey's smile was tentative, almost shy. Wayne's was ingratiating, oily. Kate's patrician face settled into bold, hard lines. "What are we going to do about them?"

Sterling cleared his throat. "I don't see, at the moment, what we can do."

Kate frowned. "Obviously I cannot step forward and unmask them. Even if the family did not think me dead, I'm uncertain that revealing Tracey Ducet as a fake would be the best course."

Sterling nodded and pursed his lips. "I wonder if someone else might accomplish that task for us."

Kate shook her head. "I can't imagine who it would be. Everyone who knew the truth is dead. Ben, the midwife..." She smiled cryptically. "Even me, at this point."

Sterling's hand closed around hers. "What of the kidnappers? They would know."

A spasm of pain flashed across Kate's face, leaving resolve in its place. "They wouldn't dare. It would mean exposing themselves."

"Ah, the lady is correct yet again."

Kate softened, smiling, and turned her hand, palm up, into his. "The lady once again has no choice but to watch and wait," she said sadly.

Sterling gazed at her, his eyes full of sympathy that would not find utterance, as she turned for a last, longing look at the remnants of her family.

"As if my son didn't have enough to deal with."

"Jake will be fine," Sterling assured her. He pursed his lips. "It might help, however, if he knew that you are alive. You've always been a source of strength for him, for the whole family."

Kate stared longingly another moment, then shook her head. "I can't risk it. If whoever came after me should learn they failed, the whole family could be in danger."

Sterling made a sound of reluctant assent. "Well, Jake can manage on his own a while longer. He's strong. You saw to that."

"I hope you're right."

"Of course I'm right. When have I ever been wrong?"

Kate cut him a sly look. "Any time you've disagreed with me."

Sterling chuckled. "I hope I'm smarter than that."

Kate glanced out the window again. "I hope we're both as smart as we think we are," she said, and then she sighed and pressed a button tucked into the armrest of her door.

The speaker hidden in the frame of the door crackled. "Ma'am?"

"Get us out of here."

She slid a worried glance in Sterling's direction. He kept his expression carefully impassive and lifted his shoulder in the barest of shrugs.

"One more identical limo in a long line," he said dismissively.

Kate let a smile tug at the corners of her mouth, the lines of worry easing out of her forehead. "You're a pretty smart cookie, after all."

"I'm a fast learner with a good teacher," Sterling said smugly.

Kate turned her narrowed eyes to the front and pretended not to notice that he still held her hand. Let the old smoothie fret a while longer. Kate Fortune was not the sort of woman to easily give up her heart—or anything else.

\*     \*     \*     \*     \*

**FORTUNE'S CHILDREN**
continues with
*A HUSBAND IN TIME*
by Maggie Shayne

Available in January

Here's an exciting preview....

# A HUSBAND IN TIME

Cody Fortune glanced up from the laptop computer his mom had given him for his tenth birthday, turning his head just in time to see the three shooting stars arching over their car as they headed toward the coast of Maine and their new home.

"Did you see that, Mom? Three shooting stars right in a row!"

Jane Fortune smiled at her son. "So why don't you make a wish?"

Cody was far too intelligent to believe in wishing on stars, but some touch of whimsy moved him to close his eyes and whisper the things that lately had been on his mind the most. "I wish I had a dad," he said softly. "And a little brother, 'cause it's boring to be an only child. And I wish..." He opened his eyes and stared up at the sky. His eyes watered a bit, but he blinked them dry again. "I wish for my mom to be happy. Really happy. 'Cause I know she isn't. And I can't remember when she was."

*A few weeks later*

Jane breathed a sigh of relief. They were all settled into their new home, and her antiques business was up and running. The only thing disturbing her was the incredibly handsome man in the portrait on her bedroom wall. Zachariah Bolton had owned this house one hundred years ago, until the death of his son had driven him crazy and he'd disappeared. No one ever knew what had happened to him.

She looked wistfully at the painting beside her bed. Zachariah Bolton. His soft sable hair fell across his forehead, his brown eyes gleamed. The narrow black tie hung in two thin ribbons, and his vest was unbuttoned. The top of a gold watch peeked up from a small pocket.

Next to him was a boy who greatly resembled her own son, which may have been why she liked the painting so much. The two sat very close to one another, at a wooden table with an oil lamp at either end. Each intent on his own work, but still, somehow, aware of the other. You could almost feel the love between them. He was a father whose work meant the world to him, she thought, but who had never once allowed that work to come before his son.

If only Cody could have a father like that.

Jane sighed, and relaxed deeper into her pillows. It was no use dreaming. She'd never find a man like that in the nineties. Not even in this nostalgic town. And she wouldn't settle for less. She didn't want another man whose career meant more than his own child. And she didn't want an ambitionless bum, or an immature, overgrown kid, either.

She wanted . . .

Her gaze wandered back to the man in the painting. The passion in his eyes was for his work. But it was intense enough to make her wonder if it had ever been there for a woman. His wife, the boy's mother, perhaps?

Oh, but all this speculation was silly. The man was no longer living. And that probably wasn't passion at all in his eyes, but perhaps the beginning of insanity. Once a man considered to be a genius, and far ahead of his time, Bolton had, the books claimed, crossed that fine line between brilliance and insanity. Two accounts said that Bolton had claimed he'd discovered a way to travel through time. He'd been ridiculed for that claim, and, soon after, he refused to discuss it. Some said it was the ridicule, as much as the death of his son, that had sent him into seclusion. Whatever the reason, he'd dropped out of sight in 1880-something, never to be heard from again.

A shame. A crying shame.

"Mom! Mom, hurry!"

The alarm in Cody's voice pierced straight through every thought to her very soul. Something was wrong. She ran to his room, exploded through his bedroom door and froze in place.

A rumpled, tousled man knelt on the floor, holding her son in his arms so tightly she wondered if Cody could breathe. The man's back was toward Jane, and his shoulders shuddered and convulsed as if he were sobbing. Cody stared at her as the man rocked him back and forth.

"My son," he kept whispering, his voice raw. "My boy, my son. Thank God..."

"Listen, mister. I don't know how you got in here, but stay away from my son!" Jane picked up a baseball bat and advanced threateningly.

The man slowly straightened, staring at Cody more closely. "But you...you're not my son!" The surprise in his voice seemed genuine. "And this isn't my room...." He let go of Cody, looking around the room, turning to face Jane fully, right beneath the overhead light.

She saw his face and her jaw fell. She caught her breath, forced her shock into submission. But then she noticed the clothes he wore, and her heart flip-flopped all over again.

My God, he was the image of the man in the painting!

# THE FORTUNE'S CHILDREN WHEEL OF FORTUNE SWEEPSTAKES
## OFFICIAL RULES—NO PURCHASE NECESSARY

To enter, complete an Official Entry Form (and return it in reply envelope, if provided), or 3" x 5" card by hand printing your name and address thereon and mailing it in the U.S. to: The Fortune's Children Wheel of Fortune Sweepstakes, P.O. Box 9076, Buffalo, NY 14269-9076, or in Canada, The Fortune's Children Wheel of Fortune Sweepstakes, P.O. Box 637, Fort Erie, Ontario L2A 5X3. Limit: One entry per outer mailing envelope. Entries must be received no later than 2/28/97. No liability is assumed for lost, late, damaged, nondelivered or misdirected mail. Entries are void if they are in whole or in part illegible, incomplete or damaged.

One winner will be selected in a random drawing to be conducted no later than 3/31/97 from among all eligible entries received. Prize consists of an audition to be on "Wheel of Fortune," including round-trip air transportation for two from winner's home to Los Angeles, California, two nights hotel accommodations (one room, double occupancy), free use of a rental car while in Los Angeles and $500 spending money (approx. value: $3,500 U.S.). Travelers must provide their own transportation to and from the commercial airport nearest winner's home and be responsible for taxes, tips and incidentals; must execute and return a Release of Liability prior to travel; and must agree to depart and return on the dates specified (with a minimum of 30 days' notice given) by Harlequin Enterprises, Ltd. In the event winner is selected to be a contestant on "Wheel of Fortune," he/she may be responsible for his/her travel and accommodations to attend the taping.

Sweepstakes offer is open only to residents of the U.S. (except Puerto Rico) and Canada who are 18 years of age or older, except employees and immediate family members of Harlequin Enterprises, Ltd., and Sony Pictures Entertainment Inc. ("Sony"), their respective affiliates, subsidiaries, and all agencies, entities and persons connected with the use, marketing or conduct of this sweepstakes. All federal, state, provincial, municipal and local laws apply. Offer void wherever prohibited by law. Taxes and/or duties are the sole responsibility of the winner. Any litigation within the province of Quebec respecting the conduct and awarding of prize may be submitted to the Regie des alcools des courses et des jeux. Prize is guaranteed to be awarded; winner will be notified by mail. No substitution for prize is permitted. Odds of winning are dependent upon the number of eligible entries received.

By participating, participants agree to release, discharge and hold harmless Harlequin Enterprises, Ltd., Califon Products, Inc. and Sony, their affiliates, subsidiaries, advertising and promotion agencies and their respective officers, directors, employees and agents from damages arising out of the acceptance, use, misuse or possession of any prize received in this sweepstakes.

Potential winner must sign and return an Affidavit of Eligibility within 30 days of notification. In the event of noncompliance within this time period, prize may be awarded to an alternate winner. If prize or prize notification is returned as undelivered, prize may be awarded to an alternate winner. By acceptance of his/her prize, winner consents to use of his/her name, photograph or likeness for the purpose of advertising, trade and promotion on behalf of Harlequin Enterprises, Ltd., without further compensation unless prohibited by law. In order to win a prize, a resident of Canada will be required to correctly answer a time-limited arithmetical skill-testing question by mail.

For the name of the winner (available after 3/31/97), send a separate stamped self-addressed envelope to: The Fortune's Children Wheel of Fortune Sweepstakes 4677 Winner, P.O. Box 4200, Blair, NE 68009-4200 USA. WHEEL OF FORTUNE is a registered trademark of Califon Productions, Inc.© 1996 Califon Productions, Inc. All Rights Reserved.

# You could
# Win Your Own
# Fortune with

**F**ORTUNE'S *Children*™ & **WHEEL of FORTUNE**®

If you are one of the truly fortunate, you can win a trip to Los Angeles to audition for Wheel of Fortune®. Enter now, and you could win your own fortune!

And don't miss a new Fortune's Children title each month!

*The Fortunes—a family whose legacy is greater than riches. Because where there's a will…there's a wedding!*

See Official Sweepstakes Rules for more details.

To enter, complete an Official Entry Form or a 3" x 5" card by hand printing "The Fortune's Children Wheel of Fortune Sweepstakes," your name and address, and mail to: In the U.S.: P.O. Box 9076, Buffalo, NY 14269-9076. Or in Canada: P.O. Box 637, Fort Erie, Ontario, L2A 5X3. Limit one entry per envelope. Entries must be sent via first-class mail and be received no later than 2/28/97. No liability is assumed for lost, late or misdirected mail.

---

## OFFICIAL ENTRY FORM
## FORTUNE'S CHILDREN SWEEPSTAKES

Name: _____

Address: _____

City: _____

State/Province:_____ Zip/Postal Code: _____

KDD

---

WHEEL OF FORTUNE is a registered trademark of Califon Productions, Inc.©
1996 Califon Productions, Inc. All Rights Reserved.

Look us up on-line at: http://www.romance.net

FC-ENTRY

He's able to change a diaper in three seconds flat.
And melt an unsuspecting heart even quicker.
But changing his mind about marriage might take some doing!
He's more than a man...
### He's a FABULOUS FATHER!

**\*\*\*\***

Cuddle up this winter with these handsome hunks:

October:

**INTRODUCING DADDY by Alaina Hawthorne (RS#1180)**
He just discovered his soon-to-be ex-wife "forgot" to
tell him he's a daddy!

November:

**DESPERATELY SEEKING DADDY by Arlene James (RS#1186)**
Three little kids advertise for a father—and a husband for
their beautiful single mom....

December:

**MERRY CHRISTMAS, DADDY by Susan Meier (RS#1192)**
A bachelor fumbles with rattles and baby pins—and his love for
a woman—all in time for Christmas!

January:

**MAD FOR THE DAD by Terry Essig (RS#1198)**
Overwhelmed by his new daddy responsibilities, he needs a
little help from his pretty neighbor....

**\*\*\***

Celebrate fatherhood—and love!—every month.
FABULOUS FATHERS...only in ▼ Silhouette ROMANCE™

## FAST CASH 4031 DRAW RULES
## NO PURCHASE OR OBLIGATION NECESSARY

Fifty prizes of $50 each will be awarded in random drawings to be conducted no later than 3/28/97 from amongst all eligible responses to this prize offer received as of 2/14/97. To enter, follow directions, affix 1st-class postage and mail OR write Fast Cash 4031 on a 3" x 5" card along with your name and address and mail that card to: Harlequin's Fast Cash 4031 Draw, P.O. Box 1395, Buffalo, NY 14240-1395 OR P.O. Box 618, Fort Erie, Ontario L2A 5X3. (Limit: one entry per outer envelope; all entries must be sent via 1st-class mail.) Limit: one prize per household. Odds of winning are determined by the number of eligible responses received. Offer is open only to residents of the U.S. (except Puerto Rico) and Canada and is void wherever prohibited by law. All applicable laws and regulations apply. Any litigation within the province of Quebec respecting the conduct and awarding of a prize in this sweepstakes maybe submitted to the Régie des alcools, des courses et des jeux. In order for a Canadian resident to win a prize, that person will be required to correctly answer a time-limited arithmetical skill-testing question to be administered by mail. Names of winners available after 4/28/97 by sending a self-addressed, stamped envelope to: Fast Cash 4031 Draw Winners, P.O. Box 4200, Blair, NE 68009-4200.

## OFFICIAL RULES
## MILLION DOLLAR SWEEPSTAKES
## NO PURCHASE NECESSARY TO ENTER

1. To enter, follow the directions published. Method of entry may vary. For eligibility, entries must be received no later than March 31, 1998. No liability is assumed for printing errors, lost, late, non-delivered or misdirected entries.
   To determine winners, the sweepstakes numbers assigned to submitted entries will be compared against a list of randomly pre-selected prize winning numbers. In the event all prizes are not claimed via the return of prize winning numbers, random drawings will be held from among all other entries received to award unclaimed prizes.

2. Prize winners will be determined no later than June 30, 1998. Selection of winning numbers and random drawings are under the supervision of D. L. Blair, Inc., an independent judging organization whose decisions are final. Limit: one prize to a family or organization. No substitution will be made for any prize, except as offered. Taxes and duties on all prizes are the sole responsibility of winners. Winners will be notified by mail. Odds of winning are determined by the number of eligible entries distributed and received.

3. Sweepstakes open to residents of the U.S. (except Puerto Rico), Canada and Europe who are 18 years of age or older, except employees and immediate family members of Torstar Corp., D. L. Blair, Inc., their affiliates, subsidiaries, all other agencies, entities, and persons connected with the use, marketing or conduct of this sweepstakes. All applicable laws and regulations apply. Sweepstakes offer void wherever prohibited by law. Any litigation within the province of Quebec respecting the conduct and awarding of a prize in this sweepstakes must be submitted to the Régie des alcools, des courses et des jeux. In order to win a prize, residents of Canada will be required to correctly answer a time-limited arithmetical skill-testing question to be administered by mail.

4. Winners of major prizes (Grand through Fourth) will be obligated to sign and return an Affidavit of Eligibility and Release of Liability within 30 days of notification. In the event of non-compliance within this time period or if a prize is returned as undeliverable, D. L. Blair, Inc. may at its sole discretion award that prize to an alternate winner. By acceptance of their prize, winners consent to use of their names, photographs or other likeness for purposes of advertising, trade and promotion on behalf of Torstar Corp., its affiliates and subsidiaries, without further compensation unless prohibited by law. Torstar Corp. and D. L. Blair, Inc., their affiliates and subsidiaries are not responsible for errors in printing of sweepstakes and prizewinning numbers. In the event a duplication of a prizewinning number occurs, a random drawing will be held from among all entries received with that prizewinning number to award that prize.

5. This sweepstakes is presented by Torstar Corp., its subsidiaries and affiliates in conjunction with book, merchandise and/or product offerings. The number of prizes to be awarded and their value are as follows: Grand Prize — $1,000,000 (payable at $33,333.33 a year for 30 years); First Prize — $50,000; Second Prize — $10,000; Third Prize — $5,000; 3 Fourth Prizes — $1,000 each; 10 Fifth Prizes — $250 each; 1,000 Sixth Prizes — $10 each. Values of all prizes are in U.S. currency. Prizes in each level will be presented in different creative executions, including various currencies, vehicles, merchandise and travel. Any presentation of a prize level in a currency other than U.S. currency represents an approximate equivalent to the U.S. currency prize for that level, at that time. Prize winners will have the opportunity of selecting any prize offered for that level; however, the actual non U.S. currency equivalent prize, if offered and selected, shall be awarded at the exchange rate existing at 3:00 P.M. New York time on March 31, 1998. A travel prize option, if offered and selected by winner, must be completed within 12 months of selection and is subject to: traveling companion(s) completing and returning a Release of Liability prior to travel; and hotel and flight accommodations availability. For a current list of all prize options offered within prize levels, send a self-addressed, stamped envelope (WA residents need not affix postage) to: MILLION DOLLAR SWEEPSTAKES Prize Options, P.O. Box 4456, Blair, NE 68009-4456, USA.

6. For a list of prize winners (available after July 31, 1998) send a separate, stamped, self-addressed envelope to: MILLION DOLLAR SWEEPSTAKES Winners, P.O. Box 4459, Blair, NE 68009-4459, USA.

### EXTRA BONUS PRIZE DRAWING
### NO PURCHASE OR OBLIGATION NECESSARY TO ENTER

7. The Extra Bonus Prize will be awarded in a random drawing to be conducted no later than 5/30/98 from among all entries received. To qualify, entries must be received by 3/31/98 and comply with published directions. Prize ($50,000) is valued in U.S. currency. Prize will be presented in different creative expressions, including various currencies, vehicles, merchandise and travel. Any presentation in a currency other than U.S. currency represents an approximate equivalent to the U.S. currency value at that time. Prize winner will have the opportunity of selecting any prize offered in any presentation of the Extra Bonus Prize Drawing; however, the actual non U.S. currency equivalent prize, if offered and selected by winner, shall be awarded at the exchange rate existing at 3:00 P.M. New York time on March 31, 1998. For a current list of prize options offered, send a self-addressed, stamped envelope (WA residents need not affix postage) to: Extra Bonus Prize Options, P.O. Box 4462, Blair, NE 68009-4462, USA. All eligibility requirements and restrictions of the MILLION DOLLAR SWEEPSTAKES apply. Odds of winning are dependent upon number of eligible entries received. No substitution for prize except as offered. For the name of winner (available after 7/31/98), send a self-addressed, stamped envelope to: Extra Bonus Prize Winner, P.O. Box 4463, Blair, NE 68009-4463, USA.

SWP-S12ZD2

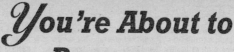

# You're About to Become a *Privileged Woman*

Reap the rewards of fabulous free gifts and benefits with proofs-of-purchase from Silhouette and Harlequin books

# Pages & Privileges™

It's our way of thanking you for buying our books at your favorite retail stores.

**PROOF OF PURCHASE**

FC-PP20

Offer expires March 31, 1997

Pages & Privileges ™

## Harlequin and Silhouette—
### the most privileged readers in the world!

For more information about Harlequin and Silhouette's PAGES & PRIVILEGES program call the Pages & Privileges Benefits Desk: 1-503-794-2499

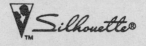

*Silhouette*®

FC-PP20